A Kind of Tragic

Gem Burman

Copyright © 2021 Gem Burman

All rights reserved. No part of this book may be reproduced, scanned, or transmitted in any forms, digital, audio or printed, without the express written consent of the author.

This is a work of fiction. Names, characters or businesses, places, events and incidents are either the products of the author's imagination or used in a fictitious manner. Any resemblance to actual persons, living or dead, or actual events is purely coincidental.

For Dale, my non-fiction 'Mr Wonderful'.

Contents

Title Page	1
Copyright	2
Dedication	3
Prologue	7
Chapter 1:	9
Chapter 2:	36
Chapter 3:	59
Chapter 4:	74
Chapter 5:	92
Chapter 6:	109
Chapter 7:	131
Chapter 8:	153
Chapter 9:	173
Chapter 10:	205
Chapter 11:	219
Chapter 12:	241

Chapter 13:	258
Chapter 14:	279
Chapter 15:	298
Chapter 16:	323
About The Author	343
Books In This Series	345

Prologue

Do you know what it feels like to love somebody who's totally and utterly out of your league? We're not talking a little crush; we're talking the mad kind of love that possesses you. The kind that makes you do silly things like writing your first name alongside his surname just to see if it gels well, before going on to write the imaginary address of your imaginary suburban marital home, along with the names of your imaginary children. Merrily, you advance to signing off imaginary Christmas cards from all the family and when you finally come to your senses, you realise you've been writing on your personal development plan the whole time - the one your supervisor needs you to sign, date and hand back first thing in the morning.

Of all the possible pain-inducing scenarios in life, nothing hurts like one-sided love. You invest every fibre of your being into the person and receive absolutely zilch in return. It's like walking into the bakery a salivating mess, eagerly ordering and paying for a box of iced buns with your last fiver – guilty – before going home without the buns *or* your change. You feel so out of pocket – a feeling I have somehow lived with for the past year. A feeling that crushes your insides like one of those waist trainers you spent a good fifteen minutes forcing on, only to yank off furiously ten minutes later having quickly established you cannot bend, sit down, eat or do any more than stand bolt upright. It cuts deep like the straps of that ill-fitting bra you still wear because it makes your tits look a bit perky. It chafes away at your heart like the too-tight thong buried in your knicker drawer that you only wear when you've not kept on top of the laundry and are forced to choose between that or going commando. And even though you know in your heart of hearts that it's hopeless, the tiniest part of you still dares to dream that, one day, Mr Wonderful will notice you.

I can't go on like this. He's on my mind 24/7. He's all I ever talk about. My best mate is pig-sick of hearing his name. My affection-starved cat has started pissing indoors to get my attention! Something simply *must* give! Possibly the elastic in my knickers. Let's see, shall we?

Chapter 1:

He's so Lovely!

Having arrived at work by the seat of my pants, as per, I dump my massive, fake Louis Vuitton tote onto my desk and switch on my computer. My heart quickens as I clock him sat at his desk with that lovely back of his facing me. He would have been here a while. He probably would've run to work, changed, and had his protein shake before I'd even dragged my arse out of bed. Dan Elliott. Dan the Man. Danny Boy. The object of my unrequited affections and hijacker of my every thought.

Studs like Dan Elliott don't give people like me the time of day ... and that's just the problem. I've spent the past year lusting after this man and I am by no means the only one. You don't want to know the countless times I've imagined us in the disabled toilet together when I'm supposed to be clinching sales. Nor would you care to know how many times I've mentally undressed him from my desk as he visits the water dispenser ... and neither would he, I'm sure. I start and end each day thinking about Dan Elliott. In fact, it wouldn't be an exaggeration to say that pretty much all 86,400 seconds of every single day are spent thinking about him. I know I've more chance witnessing a rocking horse taking a dump than dating him, but it doesn't stop me dreaming … hoping …wishing.

My eyes are still boring into his back as we leave our desks at 8.50am like clockwork to join the morning huddle of Trip Hut holiday sales staff, all of us unenthusiastically awaiting our sales manager, ~~Pissface~~ Sue, to kickstart the day with her needless micromanaging. Now I'm not an aggressive person by any stretch, but there's something about the shrill of Sue's voice first thing in the morning that makes me want to punch her in the throat!

There's an enormous whiteboard in full view upon which our daily sales targets and last week's sales data is emblazoned in Sue-scrawl, but for some reason she still insists on summoning us for these ridiculous morning huddles to repeat everything that's already written. She calls it "driving the message home". I call it bollocks and, consequently, it's not long before I find myself daydreaming, or Dan-dreaming I should say. I notice his shoes: stylish, trendy. His feet are pretty big, which somehow escaped my notice up to now. You know what they say about men with big feet, don't you? Christ! Could this man be any more perfect? He ticks every bleeding box! His arms are folded out in front of him and I can't help but notice the guns. I *always* notice the guns. I *never fail* to notice the guns ... Shit, he's looking at me looking at the guns!

'Nice s-shirt,' I stutter, observing two seconds too late that it's just a plain, white one. 'My, er... Dad has one just like it.' Of course, he does, along with just about every other man in the world. Doh!

Dan does a sort of half-smile and looks away immediately.

After Sue has driven the message home that we must "sell, sell, sell" and when we've done that, "sell some more", I skulk back to my desk. A person like me shouldn't be in sales. Why *am* I in sales? I sell people what they can afford which, I guess, makes me both a nice person and a shit salesperson. I'm not sure how I've held the job down this long. It's a bloody wonder I haven't been sacked by now. Each working day is a continuous loop of willing the phone not to ring, staring at the back of Dan's head, losing myself in the disabled toilet fantasy ... and thinking about food. When the last hour hits, I'll panic and blag just enough sales to stop me getting my P45 before trundling home to my pokey East London flat where I'll spend the rest of the evening alone – well, with my cat, Smudge – eating myself stupid and thinking about Dan, before I wake up to do it all over again the next day ... and the next ... and the next. How did it get to *this*? Surely this isn't the extent of God's so-called plan for me? If it is, he's taking the piss! Ugh – you can see why they call it "crushing" because that's exactly what it bloody well is to be so head-over-heels for someone who barely knows you exist. The way I see it I have two options: take the plunge and ask him out (*never!*) or forget him (*never!*). Okay, so I have two non-options.

Heart-throbs like Dan Elliott have a type, and the reason they have a type is because they can afford to be choosy. So where does this leave not-so-little old me, Lizzie Bradshaw, who has never been anyone's type – other than the cat's, who sadly doesn't count – throughout her entire twenty-nine years of life? I ponder what Dan's type is as I continue to stare at the back of his head, chewing the top of my pen until the lid comes off in my mouth causing me to turn heads with the series of loud, barking coughs that follow. I'm 99.9% certain he's not into the scatty, unmotivated, overweight sloth type. Being the fitness freak he is, I'd wager an obvious guess that such Adonises are attracted to the sophisticated lean and lithe type. But you never know, he could be a man who likes something he can grab hold of, in which case he'd have a field day with me!

Does he go for blondes? Brunettes? Redheads?

Who knows?! All I know is whatever Dan Elliot's type happens to be, I must become it – and fast!

Owing to excessive daily grimacing at my own reflection in the mirror of the staff toilets, most of my tube journeys home are spent staring into space while plotting a weeknight evening image overhaul to include the following- painting nails a high-fashion matte chocolate or similar. Mastering the Instabrow. Doing full body self-tan. Sleeping in curlers overnight so will wake to mermaid hair avoiding need for time consuming tonging, multiple hand burns and risk of setting flat on fire. Ensuring early bed time so can wake super-early to apply flawless base complete with heavy contour. Meticulous sculpting of eyes with dramatic crease-cut shadow to give 3x magnified doe-eye illusion. Over-lining of pout using three different shades of lip liner, colour and gloss. Can then saunter into work looking like sex goddess. Dan will notice me. Will ask me out. We'll fall in love. Get married. Have babies. The End. *However*, the significance of the aforementioned is long forgotten by the time my key hits the lock of the front door and is subsequently abandoned in favour of some – all – of the following. Scoffing. Half-watching soaps. Facebook scrolling. Instagram envy. Adding items to basket of various online retailers which I have no intention of purchasing and duly abandon in favour of 'What's in my bag?', 'Get ready with me', 'What I eat in a day' videos on YouTube. Logging into online banking and doing double-take at low funds, convinced have been victim of bank fraud thus angrily trawl statement in search of suspicious transactions and gutted when find all tally and have overspent again. Order late night cheesy chips via fast food app and stare into space whilst hastily devouring. Immediately appalled at gluttony once last chip swallowed and polystyrene lid closed. Vow will never do again and set about writing shopping list to include grains and pulses, exotic fruits and such which will only sit around going off until eventually binned. Graphic visualisation of being stuck in lift at work with Dan, where rescue unlikely for hours resulting in urgent standing sex. Having imaginary conversations with Dan. Marrying Dan. Yada. Yada. Before I know it, it's 12:05am and too late to even brush my teeth, let alone action a single step of said War and Peace-like weeknight evening image overhaul masterplan. I am then confined to endless tossing and turning before the dreaded alarm on my phone sounds and, having exhausted all reasonable snoozes, am forced to drag my arse out of bed and do what I can with my appearance in the time I have. Daily struggle!

∞ ∞ ∞

As well as my own reflection, the one thing I don't want to see first thing on a weekday morning before work is a spider in the bathroom. The very bathroom in which all my make-up and toiletries are ensconced, without access to which I am, to put it bluntly, rather fucked. It's a bloody big spider too. Gigantic in fact. Just what I need when I'm running late. Well, one thing's for sure, I cannot possibly be in the same room as *that* monstrosity! I've had a phobia of spiders since I was five and it's only gotten worse over the years. It's moments like these that I really feel singledom. But in the absence of my very own arachnid-ejecting Adonis, I'm screwed. What'll I do?

The clock's ticking and I look like shit. I can't go into work looking like this, not when someone as beautiful as Dan Elliott works there. Holy flaps! I'd rather *die* than face Dan looking like a teeny-eyed walrus. I begin to feel sick at the mere thought of it – ah, yes! Sick! I'll just call in sick. Gleefully I reach for my phone before suddenly recalling the verbal warning Sue gave me last week about my attendance and think better of it. Bugger.

Peeping around the bathroom door, a sudden rage kicks in. How dare it?! How dare it enter *my* dominion? How dare it put itself between me, someone who needs all the help she can get in the looks department, and my make-up bag!? It's like depriving a baby of milk, god damn it!

Nanny Bradshaw once told me if you name spiders, they're a lot less scary. Right now, I'll give anything a try. I settle on Harold. It looks a like a Harold. Taking a deep breath, I brace myself.

'Now Harold, do not trifle with me!' I warn, inching forward with one eye on him and one on my make-up bag.

Harold moves suddenly, running like the clappers straight towards me. I scream – the blood-curdling type one might emit when encountering an axe-wielding maniac – and slam the door shut in terror. Shit, now what?! Well, I guess Harold has proven Nanny Bradshaw's theory to be wrong, since he very much remains scary as fuck!

I grab my tote off the kitchen table in search of a stray lipstick, tipping out its contents onto the floor with no recollection of having dumped a half-eaten sausage roll from the bakery in there. It slides straight out of its greasy paper bag and lands heavily on the floor, peppering the carpet with flaky pastry. Everything in my bag now smells off, like stale baked goods. Oh God, *why* did you have to make the shop next to my flat a pissing bakery?! Why not some place I'm guaranteed never to go, like a sports shop? I've battled with my weight since childhood. I only have to look at a custard slice and I'll put on half a stone. Mother begs to differ, obviously. She says it's all about willpower and, in my case, a significant lack of; a typically ignorant statement from someone who has never struggled with their weight. Just because food isn't a class-A drug, doesn't make it any less addictive. It's no different to an alcoholic living above an off-licence: temptation at every sodding turn.

I hurriedly sift through the contents of my bag, hoping to locate a peachy-pink lippy which might double up as a blush – just the ticket in these circumstances. Result! Only, ugh, it's less peachy-pink, more dominatrix-red. As much as I am an eternal make-doer and optimist, even I wouldn't rock up to a call centre before 9am wearing such a shade! Mumbling obscenities, I toss everything back in my bag, sling it over my shoulder, dart out of the flat and down the staircase, misjudging my footing and slipping down the last five steps. By the time I reach the bottom of the street, I'm already a sweaty, out-of-breath mound of pulsating, wobbly jelly. Dan would be appalled at my lack of stamina but I thank the heavens he's not around to witness it.

I tear down the steps to the underground and through the ticket terminal, hesitating at the top of the escalators. I'm fine going up them, but a nightmare going down. I seem to lose all sense of balance as soon as I stand on the top step, although it would probably help if this fuck-off great tote bag didn't add width and weight to me that I really don't need. The tuts and sighs of the impatient commuters behind only serve to panic me more. I dump my bag on the step out in front of me and watch, rooted to the spot, as it descends the escalator and moves further and further away from me. Great. Now what?

'Are you goin' down love or what?' comes the angry voice of the man behind me.

'I'm g-going. Just give me a second,' I insist, closing my eyes and bracing myself.

'Hurry up yer daft cow!' comes another, as people begin pushing past.

I let out a little squeal as I step forward onto the escalator and begin my scary descent. Oh, heck. My bag has arrived at the bottom and it's about to cause a pile-up! Chaos ensues as people trip over it before some dastardly lout sends it flying with a swift kick, causing the contents to spill out across the floor. I begin scooping up and returning the items to the bag for the second bloody time this morning as I feel a tap on my shoulder. I turn to see a smartly dressed middle-aged bloke holding up my latest read: *The Art of Self-love, a Singleton's Guide to Solo Pleasure.*

'This yours, love?' he asks with a smirk.

My face burns as I take it from him, shove it in my bag and hurry toward the platform just in time to see the train leave.

Three minutes later I battle my way onto the next one. I make it on board just as the doors close, thankfully my head still intact. An old bloke with a pervy glint in his eye hasn't stopped looking me up and down since we boarded. While I gratefully appreciate any form of male attention – as starved of it as I am – being leered at by an old git on the tube is no triumph. Even my sternest look isn't enough to deter him, leading to my fantasising about coolly kicking him in the balls before breezing out the doors at my stop to the applause of onlooking commuters like one of Charlie's Angels. In reality I keep my head down with a face like a smacked arse for the rest of the journey, emitting the odd displeased tut and sigh here and there.

Above ground, I catch sight of my shocking appearance in a shop window and do a double take. Shit! is that *me* or Jabba the Hut?! A rapidly increasing sense of panic ensues. There's nothing for it, I'm going to have to take a de-tour to the drugstore and hit the make-up testers. Sheesh! I thought I left those days behind in the murky haze of my high school youth but now here I am, aged nearly thirty and back in old habits ... all because of a sodding spider! I half-run into the nearest drugstore and do what I can in all of two minutes flat, spritzing myself liberally with the first perfume I pass on the way out.

In my hurry to get into work, I plough straight through a spider's web at the entrance doors and stop in my tracks, clawing at my face and hair in disgust! What is it with bloody spiders today? *I don't know*, you sail through winter not seeing a single one, then the minute we edge toward spring the fuckers suddenly pop up everywhere! Satisfied that it's all gone, I walk stealthily into work, my eyes doing a frantic Sue-scan as I enter in through the call centre. Hmmm, it's looking promising! I can't see her anywhere. Hopefully she's not about, then I can—

'GAHHHHHH!' I roar in fright, having felt tickly movement in my hair. 'IT'S ON ME, IT'S ON ME!' I freeze, flapping about in a mad panic as the whole room turns to look in my direction. 'GET IT OFF, SOMEONE GET IT OFF ME!' I wail, doing a mad sort of tap dance. I proceed to lunge toward the adjacent row of occupied desks with my head lowered, poised to wipe it off onto someone else, prompting them all to rise in tandem and vacate their desks in horror. With nobody rushing to my aid, I rapidly lose my shit and proceed to have a full-scale meltdown, my screams and squeals more akin to somebody on fire than someone with a spider in their hair. Eventually, a male colleague gets up from his desk, walks over and gingerly starts brushing me down. Well, *he* took his time; bastard! It's as though he's worried touching me might harm his credibility in some way, even with the cartoon frog-patterned tie he's wearing.

Moments later, a brown speckly garden spider tumbles out onto the chequered blue carpet before us. I sigh in relief, detecting an air of smugness as he scoops it up with a holiday brochure and takes it over to the open window for dispatch, cool as you like. Patronising git!

Suddenly, the managing director bursts out from his office. 'What's all the bloody noise out here, I'm in the middle of a sodding conference call!' he booms, red-faced and twitching.

'S-sorry ... s-spider,' I reply in a mousey little voice, feeling a tit of the highest order. He gives a look of astoundment, says nothing and turns on his heel, slamming the office door behind him. Well, the plan was to slip in quietly but er, yeah...

Oi-oi! There he is, Dishy Dan looking as sexy as ever with his lovely back ... and shoulders ... and neck ... and hair and ... ugh! He's *so* gorgeous. I stand rooted to the spot for a few moments just staring at the back of him before it dawns on me that not only will he have just witnessed all that, but my tongue appears to be ever-so-slightly hanging out and, thus, I shall appear even more off my trolley to anyone who may be watching right now. Coming to, I rapidly compose myself and switch on my computer.

Three minutes later, I find myself losing the will to live in a call with some old timer who doesn't know his arse from his elbow – join the club, mate. He has no idea what sort of holiday he's looking for but seems to think that I do. Good God, we'll be here all day!

'Well Mr Hodgson, tell me, where've you holidayed before,' I ask, feeling a sense of immediate regret as he recalls every single trip he and his wife Joy have taken since 1952. I mentally switch off less than twenty seconds in and find myself looking in Dan's direction, as ever. Hold up! He's stood up out of his seat, laughing and joking with Sue and what appears to be some Brazilian supermodel with legs up to her arse! My expression now resembles that of an angry dog who has just clocked a cat in its territory.

'Who the fuck is that?' I muse out loud.

'I beg your pardon!' exclaims a shocked Mr Hodgson, whom I'd quite forgotten about.

I wince and slam the phone down. There'll be a complaint coming my way no doubt, but this is bigger than Mr Hodgson. This is bigger than Trip Hut. This is my very worst nightmare! Who *is* she? And why is she flicking her hair in such a manner? She touched his arm! The bitch just touched his arm! Ugh! They're coming over—

'Lizzie, I'd like you to meet your new team member Rachel De Souza. Rachel, this is Lizzie Bradshaw,' Sue announces, making my surname seem so unglamorous and irrelevant in comparison. 'Rachel's starting with us on Monday, but I thought it would be a good idea to get her in today to introduce her to the team,' Sue continues.

'Hi!' Rachel chirps with a grin, highlighting cheekbones that could slice through steak.

I mumble back some vague English pleasantries while noticing how perfect she is. Perfect glossy dark hair, perfect eyes, perfect teeth, perfect figure: perfect bloody everything! I'll bet even her shits are perfect.

'Ooh, what are you wearing?' she enquires, leaning in to get a better whiff. 'That's a really familiar scent. Reminds me of' – she hesitates, appearing thoughtful – 'my grandad,' she adds, unapologetically. Wide-eyed I sniff myself suspiciously and note that, strangely, I do indeed smell like an old man. I must've picked up a bloke's tester at the drugstore earlier. And not even a trendy bloke's tester, a fucking ancient one! She studies my face curiously for a moment, gazing at me almost in pity.

'See you on Monday!' she says, her pearly whites gleaming as she sashays off.

I look over toward Dan who strangely, and for

the first time this year, appears to be looking my way. Oh God! Is this it? Is he *finally* noticing me? I twist in my seat to check behind. No, he's just checking out Rachel's arse. Obviously. Well then, I guess I've just discovered Dan Elliott's type. A type which, unless I were to die on the spot before immediately re-incarnating as East London's answer to Margot Robbie, I can never hope to compete with. There's only one thing to do now; try not to cry for the next eight hours, then go home and do just that.

I've spent the majority of the evening on the phone to the only person who can help me now. Levi Hilton: it-boy – or girl, whichever he feels like at the time –fashionista, life coach, confidante and the best bloody friend a girl could wish for.

'Listen, dahling,' he barks, 'now, I want you to repeat after me: I am *me*. I am *beautiful*. I am *enough*.'

'I am *me*. I am *beautiful*. I am *enough* … although I'm *not,* clearly!' I whinge, picturing Rachel as she catwalked through the office today. 'She's tall, I'm short. She's got to be a size eight, I'm practically tourniqueted in a twenty-two!'

'Dahling, if your weight troubles you that

much, then why don't you do something about it? All you have to do is eat less and do more.'

'But I don't *want* to eat less, and I don't *want* to do more!' I moan.

'Fine. Then you've got to accept your size,' Levi states matter-of-factly.

'But I don't *want* to accept my size!'

'Jesus! Am I talking to a nearly thirty-year-old or a toddler?' he asks exasperatedly.

We continue going around in circles for the next fifteen minutes until Levi announces in a panicked and even higher-pitched tone than usual that he must go. His brow tint has long surpassed its development time and he looks like Dracula.

I strip naked and stand in front of the mirror, shaking my head in disbelief not only that it's a Friday night and I'm stood here doing *this,* but also at the sheer sight of me. Levi can sugar coat it all he likes but me? Beautiful? He hasn't seen my bare, flat arse that somehow seems to reach up to my back with little crack or definition. Don't even get me started on my thighs and as for my belly? Let's just say, I haven't been able to look down and see my Mary – another Nanny Bradshaw-ism – since I was about ten. I step onto the scales for the first time this year and immediately wish I hadn't. Bugger me! I'm sixteen and a half stone! For someone of my height, that's big and definitely *not* clever. How did it get to this? Perhaps I've got an underactive thyroid. Maybe I should get tested. Or maybe I've got one of those yeast over-growth conditions which causes weight gain. Oh, it could be constipation … although it'd have to be a bloody bad case, mind. Or perhaps I've simply been lumbered with the fat gene. Ugh! I'm in denial. Like those people who pretend they don't use Facebook anymore but are always "active now". I know *exactly* how it got to this: sheer effing greed, that's how! And Levi's right, I have to either do something about it or accept it, and the latter is simply not an option. Not now Rachel sodding De Souza's on the scene and it's only a matter of time before she gets her perfectly manicured claws into the man of my dreams.

I've joined every slimming club you can think of. I've tried the cabbage soup diet, the boiled egg diet, low-carb diets, meal-replacement diets. You name it, I've done it … for all of five minutes. All the experts say the same thing: "it has to become a way of life, not just a temporary thing". Well, that makes sense I suppose. It stands to reason that one can't expect to look like Kylie in those gold hot pants while doing nothing more than lounging on the couch eating Magnums and spectacularly failing to seductively emulate the iconic crack of the chocolate shell seen in the advert.

The science part of weight loss is all very simple, it's the consistency that I struggle with. Good day? Let's scoff! Bad day? Let's scoff! But one thing that does tend to motivate me is some stiff competition, and Rachel De Souza has given me that and *then* some!

Now back to the subject of constipation, where I make a mental note that I haven't taken a dump since Tuesday. I've always been irregular. 'Ruffage, dear. You need more ruffage,' Mother always tells me – what the fuck is ruffage, anyway? I've never actually taken the time to find out. If I'm going to be starting a new healthy eating regime I really ought to have a good clear-out first, and I'm not talking about the kitchen cupboards! There's bound to be two, maybe three pounds of stool hanging around in there adding to my disgraceful mass, so I figure ridding myself of that would be a good start in the race to lose five stone in a fortnight.

I inch open the bathroom door and peep my head around it.

'Harold? Harold, are you there?' I call out, as though he might answer.

I scour the entire perimeter of the lavvy for any sign of the eight-legged monstrosity. Nothing. The place appears to be entirely arachnid-free, which probably means the rest of the flat is not. I open the bathroom cupboard and take out a packet of laxatives – I can't remember exactly when I acquired them, but the dust on the box would suggest they're ancient. It says they take ten to twelve hours to work so I ought to feel the benefit first thing tomorrow morning. That's ok, it's the weekend and I don't have a life; the perfect opportunity to clear out my digestive tract! Hmm, "take one for mild cases of constipation and two for more significant cases" – is almost four days without a dump classed as "significant"? I'm not sure. They've probably lost their effectiveness by now anyway. I'll take two then.

In the midst of a glorious dream in which Dan and I are engaging in some seriously heavy petting in the Trip Hut canteen, I feel it. The worst bastarding stomach pain I've ever known, starting as a good three before surging straight to ten on the Stanford Pain Scale. I'm hot. Sweaty. Nauseated. An assemblage of substantial gut noises meets our fictious gasps of pleasure and somewhere between the murky haze of kinky dream and reality I'm aware that the laxatives have kicked in … a lot bloody sooner than expected! Though I'm especially eager to discover how this dream develops, there is the very real and looming threat that I might shit the bed. Eyes pinging open with mere seconds to spare, I throw back the bed covers and make it to the lavvy by the skin of my teeth just as an explosion akin to an atomic bomb begins! The noise! The *smell*! I've never experienced anything like it. Why the fuck did I take two? I can't think. I can't breathe. The only thing to do is sit and sway back and forth, panting like an overheated dog, wailing and willing it with every fibre of my being to pass quickly. The situation reaches fever pitch as I spy the lesser-spotted Harold on the bathroom floor in front of me. He freezes. I freeze.

'Gahhhhhhhh!' I screech as he lunges forward and scuttles out under the bathroom door.

Phew, he's gone. Thank Christ for that! Perhaps the stench was too much for him.

My eyes are like slits. I've had multiple bouts between the hours of 1.35am and 9am, this being the fourth. Never again! I don't care how stopped up I am. Surely this so-called medicine can't be legal? It should be banned if this is what it does to people. I shall write a letter of complaint to the manufacturer the minute I'm recovered! Wait … was that the buzzer? I crane my neck to listen. Yeah, it *was* the buzzer. Ugh, what to do? Can't … stop … shitting! It buzzes again. And again. Am I expecting someone? What, me? The most unpopular person in the world? Er, no! But even so, who would have the nerve to be sounding the hell out my buzzer at this time on a Saturday morning? Aside from Mother, of course, but it can't be her since she and Dad are away for the weekend. Well, whoever it is will have to sod off. I am, after all, incapacitated in the most serious of ways.

Finally, with a perfect imprint of the toilet seat on my arse and having been left with the worst case of ring-sting known to man, the *Attack of the Clones* appears to have ground to a halt. Bleary-eyed and zombie-like I venture downstairs to my pigeonhole to fetch the post. Among an abundance of bills and other such dross, which soon find themselves jammed into one of the kitchen drawers for future Lizzie to deal with, there's a card displaying the logo of the local constabulary upon which a telephone number and Police ID are scrawled, urging me to call at my earliest convenience. Oh fuck! Fuckety-fuck! What have I done? I rack my brains. I've probably done a lot in my time which the law would frown upon, so to be fair it could be anything. I spend the next fifteen minutes practising my best upstanding citizen voice.

'Oh, hello there, you stopped by my apartment and left a card earlier?'

'Good morning, I believe you left a card at my property?'

'Er, hang on, *actually*! Why aren't you out catching real criminals, instead of posting scary cards through the doors of innocents?'

Ugh! This is ridiculous. If I don't call now, I'll never know. Here goes then.

'Um, yeah, hi. You left a door through my card

this morning?' Ugh, brilliant – nothing like I had rehearsed.

'Sorry?' a male voice replies.

'I mean, you left a card through my door. Flat 7, Primrose Court?'

'Ah, yes. Looks like we called by this morning but there was no answer. We've received a series of noise complaints, madam, relating to the loud intercourse coming from your flat during the early hours of this morning.'

'You *what?* I wish!' I bark before remembering the whole upstanding citizen demeanour. 'Er … sorry, it's just that I live alone and I can categorically tell you that nobody wants to have loud intercourse with me, sadly,' I say, the words becoming even more depressing – and true – now they'd been told to a complete stranger.

'Ah … then might there be some other reason for the level of noise coming from your residence then, madam?'

'Oh yes, there's a perfectly innocent explanation,' I say, before realising that I would now have to explain exactly what those animal-like noises were. Well, best be truthful – he already knows no one wants to have sex with me.

'I made the mistake of taking not one but two of the strongest laxatives known to man before bed last night, which caused me to spend the small hours of the morning in agony emptying-out on the lavatory. Oh! *And* there's a fuck-off great spider in the flat,' I tell him, all matter-of-fact.

A lengthy silence follows.

'Hello? Are you still there, officer?'

'Er, yes madam. Well, er … thank you for clearing that up. Might we suggest that you consider your neighbours and keep the noise down in future please?'

'Oh, don't worry officer, after the night I've had, I'll not be touching *those* things again!'

'Very good, madam,' he murmurs before audibly slamming the phone down.

Well, that went well all things considered. In fact, I think I handled myself brilliantly given the unpleasantness. Now all I need to do is work out which of my neighbours reported me and punish them accordingly. And by punish, I mean no more neighbourly waves or small talk centred largely around the crap British weather. And absolutely no more taking in their parcels. Yeah! That'll teach them!

Having ventured all the way to the bottom of the stairs to let Smudge in for his breakfast, I collapse in a weary heap on the sofa. I can't stop thinking about that De Souza cow! Who is she? Is she even single? It suddenly dawns on me that I don't know the slightest thing about the woman. She could be a perfectly wonderful human being and married with three kids for all I know, which would make her totally off limits to Dan Elliott … Hey, that's a bloody good point actually! Hurriedly, I take the immediate course of action a situation like this requires – to look her up on Facebook, obviously.

With my detective head on, a rhythmic tap-tapping of the laptop keyboard and my tongue ever-so-slightly hanging out in eager anticipation, my search begins. I spot the cow immediately at the top of the search results and find myself pulling a face at her predictably perfect photo grinning back at me. She has a typically modelesque profile picture featuring her smiling in a red bikini surrounded by umpteen girlfriends. All my former optimism about her having a husband and kids immediately morphs to vitriol upon seeing her relationship status: single. But it gets worse. I scroll down her profile page to find that Dan Elliott is only on her effing friends list! Already? He's not even on mine and we've worked within a metre of each other for a year now. Well, *she* wasted no time getting herself acquainted with him, and him with her! Feeling cheated, but with no actual right to, I continue through her page, my stomach churning at the swathes of magazine-like, polished pictures that accost me. Shots of her sunbathing, drinking cocktails, doing artistic yoga poses, cuddling some mutt while wearing an expensive-looking cashmere jumper, skiing, horse riding. The woman is stunningly beautiful and boy, does she know it! The air of sophistication and confidence; every bloke's dream.

'Oh, piss off, Rachel!' I huff, slamming the laptop shut and emitting a loud and exasperated wail which trails off abruptly as I remember my earlier noise warning from the Old Bill.

In a sudden moment of determination, I spring up like a jack-in-the-box from my dead praying mantis position on the sofa.

'Alright bitch!' – she hasn't done anything? – 'So, it's a fight you want is it?' – who said anything about that?! – 'Well, bring it on!'

Annnnnnd in this corner, weighing in at 231 pounds and the undisputed world's fastest donut eater, it's Fatty McPhat! And in this corner, weighing in at a mere 120 pounds (jammy bitch) it's Rachellll De Souuuzaaaa!

Round one of this fictitious fight with my oblivious opponent commences with the purchase of a month's gym membership, a yoga mat, workout gear, running shoes and me signing up to Bazza's Brutally Bad Bootcamp every Monday evening at 6pm at the community centre. I'm not entirely sure who Bazza is, but he sounds like a psycho. Just what a lazy fatty like me needs.

Having spent the gas bill money on the above, the only real fight I've started is with the gas company, but nonetheless I'm feeling empowered and accomplished. I can do this. I *will* be thin! I *will* be Dan Elliott's girlfriend!

Chapter 2:

Charmed

Yaaaaaas you, beauty! I'm three whole pounds lighter on the scales this morning! I'm really rather shocked – especially after scoffing the entirety of that set meal for two from the Chinese takeaway last night. Yeah, yeah, I know, but it's an unwritten rule that one must have a last fling before starting any new healthy eating regime. Although, granted, a set meal for two – that definitely only feeds one – is more of a five-year full-on romance than a last fling. How the hell did I lose three pounds overnight? I must've been quite literally full of shit. Who knew?!

Whistling jovially, I whizz up and neck a glass of what looks like green nappy matter but is, in fact, a superfood smoothie containing kale and other such trendy ingredients. I have to say, aside from the retching, I feel rather chic knowing my breakfast is on par with all the celebs in Hollywood, but simultaneously gutted that heart-attack breakfast baps are now off-limits.

Do you know, I have this sudden and unexplained urge to go running and I've never run in my life. Usually, just the thought of running is enough to make my hips hurt. My workout gear isn't even due to arrive until tomorrow but that doesn't matter, all you need is a pair of leggings and some old trainers, right?

Christ! I see why people run in spandex now! I've only done half a lap around the park and the chub-rub is already verging on intolerable ... the struggle is real! Despite the chafe, I feel strangely liberated as I begin working up a tremendous sweat while trying to imagine I'm JLo running through the park in L.A – a feat which takes some imagination. And you know what, this isn't as bad as I thought it would be. In fact, I reckon I've got this! Looking around, there's tonnes of runners besides me, all here for the same reasons; united in our shared fitness goals. Perhaps I ought to acknowledge them with a knowing nod or some sort of salute as they pass? I am, after all, one of them now.

Up ahead, I notice a couple running together. Ah bless. I get closer to them, ready to lock eyes and give my knowing "running club" nod. Oh wait. Hang on a minute. No! Not bless! Definitely not bloody bless at all and moreover, what the fuck?! It's Dan Elliot and the Brazilian supermodel! This isn't happening. This has got to be a dream. I cannot believe what I'm seeing! She only set foot in our workplace a mere 48 hours ago. She doesn't even start until Monday and already she's out running with *my* man ... and they've spotted me ... and it's too late to turn around ... and—

'Oh, hi Dan! Hi Rachel!' I pant. God, I'm so two-faced.

They both half-smile in recognition on their approach, slowing down until we're a few awkward feet away from each other.

'Liz, isn't it?' Rachel asks, not even out of breath.

'Lizzie,' I correct her, my fake smile drooping somewhat. Liz? Bloody Liz? While it may indeed be a diminutive of my first name, I hate it. It sounds too much like it belongs to some middle-aged scrubber with a fag hanging out her gob.

Rachel looks me up and down as she and Dan continue jogging on the spot. Dan barely acknowledges me, as per, and uses the opportunity to have a long and disinterested swig of his sophisticated-looking isotonic sports drink. Well, this isn't awkward at all!

'Oh, erm ... I think you might have stood in something,' Rachel announces, pointing down to my tatty, unbranded trainers. I follow her finger and find my right shoe to be covered in dog shit.

Yellow dog shit, obviously, because the usual brown variety would have been too mundane for this situation. How wonderful. Would fate like to add to that? Does it wish to invite every seagull in the sky to crap on my head?

Dan raises his eyebrows, having too observed my dog shit covered foot, before announcing they'd "better push on" and breezing off ahead.

'See you tomorrow,' Rachel says before she grins and jogs off after my prince, leaving me aggressively wiping the shit off my shoe on the grass and wondering how I went from feeling like a liberated A-lister to a total knobhead in less than thirty seconds.

Later...

'Alexa! Why am I such a twat?!' I wail, collapsing onto the sofa.

Ding!

'I'm sorry, I don't know the answer to that,' comes her reply.

'You and me both, babe. You and me both!' I sigh, staring at the ceiling.

'That's it, I'm leaving!' I announce dramatically to nobody, leaping up from the sofa and taking myself off to the kitchen to rake through the cupboards in search of some stray confectionary. Well, how can I possibly continue working at Trip Hut after today's events? How can I face

Dan now after Shitgate? Besides, my inner thighs are now red raw and burning from the chub-rub, making it necessary to walk with my legs wide open. Hmph, I can't be expected to commute in such a fashion!

Having been unable to locate any stray confectionary, I resort to taking my chances with the jelly beans from the Bean Boozled game tucked away at the back of the shoe cupboard, copping a rotten egg one which I had hoped to be buttered popcorn. Retching violently, I rush to the kitchen sink.

In a panic, I fling open my laptop and desperately scour the job sites as though finding a job, being interviewed, hired, and starting by tomorrow morning is an actual possibility. Other than carer's jobs, there's sod-all available and while I greatly admire those who can wipe old arse without batting an eyelid, this is not and shall never be a career option for Lizzie Bradshaw. I mean Christ, I can barely care for myself let alone a home full of OAPs! Closing the job hunt tabs, I check my emails to see that my recent fitness splurge is due to arrive tomorrow between 10am–12pm. Given that the possibility of handing in my notice effective immediately hasn't grown legs in the last three minutes, it looks like I won't be here to sign for it. Ugh!

In terms of neighbours who *will* be at home to sign for my goods, I have a choice of Pervy

Bob or Mrs Birch. With neither the time nor energy to brush off Pervy Bob's advances, I find myself standing outside Mrs Birch's door even though I've barely said two words to her since she never seems to leave her flat. I raise my hand to knock but before I can, the door opens and I am immediately enveloped in a waft of the overpowering incense she's burning. I stare at her in surprise, slightly taken aback by her appearance. She's dressed all in black with a long and unkempt white-grey mane; totally rocking the witchy look.

'Come in,' she beckons in an aged, croaky voice, waggling an old, crooked finger at me.

What the hell? Inviting me straight in without a word? She doesn't even know me! Or *does* she? And how did she even know I was coming? Now she's *seriously* giving me witchy vibes. I wonder if I'm about to be locked in a cage and fattened up for eating as I spot her stern-looking black cat perched on the arm of the rocking chair and lots of little glass jars on the kitchen table containing herbs and flowers and shit. Well, if that's what she's planning it's a pointless exercise; I could already feed an entire coven.

'Sorry to trouble you, I'm Lizzie from number seven and I—'

'I know who you are,' she interrupts in a gravelly voice.

Wait, what? How?!

'Oh. Well, it's just that I have a very important parcel due to be delivered tomorrow morning, but I'll be at work, so I wondered if you'd be kind enough to take delivery of it for me?' I tell her, trying to appear not at all creeped-out in the slightest while struggling to breathe through the incense smog.

'Hmm. A very important parcel you say. I'm intrigued!' she fishes. Nosey cow.

'Oh, it's nothing much,' I say, resisting the urge to mention a twelve-inch dildo and some tingly lube. 'It's just fitness gear.'

She looks me up and down. 'You don't look the type,' she cackles. Cheeky bitch.

'Well, that's sort of the point. I'm trying to *be* the type,' I tell her.

'And you *will* be, I've no doubt dear,' she mumbles, leaving me trying to work out if she's taking the piss or just being nice.

'Who's the lucky chap?' she enquires, knowingly.

'Sorry?'

'The fella you're trying to snare,' she adds.

My eyes widen in horror. She's *definitely* a witch!

'Oh er, a work colleague, actually.'

'Hmm, yes ... and quite a dish too!' she mumbles trance-like, turning to look me up and down. 'You're going to need all the help you can get,' she adds unapologetically.

Bloody charming! Although she does have a point.

'It's not fitness gear you need, my dear. It's a love charm,' she adds, as if the two were easily confused.

'I'm ... not sure I follow,' I say. What the chuff did she just say? A love charm?! Maybe she's gone doolally from that stuff she burns.

Without a word, Mrs Birch shuffles over to the old oak sideboard that takes up half of her living space and takes a red candle from the drawer.

'You'll need some strands of Prince Charming's hair, which you entwine and wrap around this candle. Then, you bury the candle and romance will find you!' she explains, flourishing it toward me.

I stand speechless, rooted to the spot in disbelief.

'Oh ... and you've got to recite the incantation as well,' she adds seriously.

'The ... incantation?' I repeat.

She nods. 'I am for you, you are for me, deep in love so shall we be,' she chants.

I remain dazed and speechless.

'Did you catch any of that?' she enquires, rolling her eyes.

'Oh, er ... I am for you ... you are for me, deep in love ... so shall we be?' I recite back.

She nods, thrusting the candle at me.

'Cheers, I guess,' I say, unsure whether I may have just inadvertently summoned some kind of demon.

'Anytime,' she grins with a wink, ushering me out and slamming the door in my face.

Mesmerised by what has just occurred, I stand in the hallway outside Mrs Birch's flat stinking of incense and taking in deep breaths of fresh – but still communal hallway – air. Oh bugger. I didn't even get an answer to my all-important question, the only sodding reason I went over there in the first place. But I do now have a red candle - and a sinister feeling!

Back at my flat, I call Levi straight away. For all his flamboyancy, Levi is responsible, grounded and level-headed. If anyone can discourage me from even thinking about entertaining this bollocks, it's him.

'Fucking go for it, girlfriend!' he sings.

Or not. I cannot believe I'm hearing this.

'But Levi, wouldn't that make me rather silly

and gullible? Not to mention a member of the sodding occult?!' I counter.

'Oh, dahling, as long as you're getting yummy Dan-sex, who gives a fuck?'

'What, you think it'll actually work?' I ask.

'Pfft! Fuck no, dahling! But you've nothing to lose in trying.'

'But Levi … what if somebody finds out? Do you want to see me burned at the stake?'

'Oh calm your tits, dahling! Society has moved on quite a bit since then! There is just one thing I'd suggest you do, should this thing work.'

'Oh? What's that?' I ask.

'Get me Mrs Birch's number as a matter of urgency, dahling!'

The next morning, I spend the walk from the underground to work wondering how best to go about acquiring some of Dan's hair – yes I've decided against my better judgement to entertain this bollocks. I barely ever speak to the bloke, so to obtain a sample of his actual hair seems rather ambitious. Well, bloody ludicrous actually!

I bump into Fat Ann in the staff toilet. Disclaimer, the former is a well-established nickname which her fellow employees lovingly gave her long before I started here. Any usage of said nickname on my part is no reflection of my moral standards, which I'll have you know are extremely high.

Fat Ann is a notorious gossip with a degree in shit-stirring, but very handy for getting all the office dirt.

'Heard the latest?' she teases, a trouble-making twinkle in her eye. I look at her and shake my head. 'Dan Elliott's knobbing the new girl,' she fake whispers.

All the colour drains from my face. My gob falls open.

'Are you alright, hun? You look like you've seen a ghost!'

Hun. Affectionate pet name overused among false women who use it when being false.

'How do you know he's ... knobbing her?' I probe, rubbing salt in my own wound.

'Oh, everyone knows it. Shelley saw them out running together yesterday. Plus, they're going on a date this coming weekend,' she says, raising her eyebrows.

'Can I assume you have this on good authority from a credible source?' I challenge.

'Yep! Straight from the horse's mouth, Rachel herself told me!' Fat Ann positively delights in telling me. 'She's gorgeous though, ain't she? She knows it, mind, but, cor, yeah. Proper stunner! No wonder Dan got in there,' she chuckles, twisting the knife.

Rage building, I whack the soap dispenser with extra vigour.

'Lovely-looking couple they make though, gorgeous pair like them,' she prattles on. 'Cor! Imagine their babies!'

Is this woman deliberately fucking with my head? Everyone knows I'm head-over-heels for Dan Elliott – everyone except Dan Elliott that is – which means Fat Ann definitely knows I'm head-over-heels for Dan Elliott.

'I don't want to imagine their babies thank you very much, you fat shit!' I long to scream. What was that about moral standards Lizzie? But I remain silent as I shove my hands under the drier which acts as the perfect silencer for her cutting words.

Thanks to Fat Ann's deliverance of such an excruciating blow, I've been in a foul, stinking mood all morning, exacerbated significantly by the sight of Dan and Rachel's office flirting. It's proving to be notoriously hard to sell holidays when all I want to do is go home, cry profusely and play Toni Braxton's "Unbreak My Heart" on repeat. In my emotionally charged state, I begin to wonder if there's a conspiracy against me which Sue is in on. She has, after all, allocated Rachel a desk right in front of Dan's and seems to have turned a blind eye to their constant chat.

Even the usually momentous occasion of lunch fails to lift my mood, but the fact that I only have fruit and a flask of that green shit might have a lot to do with it. With a face like a wet weekend, I push open the canteen door and there they are, laughing and joking like silly teenagers over funny videos on their phones. Ugh! Slowly but surely the canteen empties out until there's nobody else in here other than the three of us – although I might as well not exist as far as they're concerned. They don't even know I'm sat here in the corner with my tub of grapes and flask of green superjuice. I'm so pissed off I don't actually know if I want to get a sample of Dan's hair anymore, even if it were a possibility. I don't know if I want the guns wrapped around me and I don't know if I want to stay up all night making mad, passionate love with him. I've decided he is fast becoming equally as annoying as her … wait, what's happening? I think a grape has gone down the wrong hole. Oh, fuck! I'm choking. I'm choking! I … can't … breathe!

The gasping noise I make grabs the attention of the lovebirds and Dan rushes over and begins to thump me forcefully on the back. Oh, he *does* know I exist then. He orders the Brazilian supermodel to go and get help. Yes, go on! Get to it, bitch! Even in the midst of a choking fit and though my body ought to be fully focused on survival right now, I find myself pondering the many times I've imagined Dan with his hands on me and now they are, for real. Even though he's pretty much punching the shit out of my back. On observation that the punches aren't working, Dan grabs me around the waist and hauls me up out of my seat which results in me loudly and involuntarily passing wind. I'll worry about that later, assuming I survive. He starts performing the Heimlich manoeuvre, grunting and panting as he does so. I'm amazed I still have the cognitive ability to be having the dirty thoughts I'm having right now, even at this swimmy stage as the canteen starts to blur around me. My sense of smell still also appears to be functioning too as I catch a subtle, sexy whiff of Dan's aftershave. I make a mental note that I *do* still want to get a sample of his hair, I definitely *do* still want the guns wrapped around me and I absolutely, positively definitely *do* still want to stay up all night making mad, passionate love with him!

The sound of Dan's voice is getting worryingly distant, but I am sure I just heard him say, 'Come on Lizzie!'. He said my name! He actually said my name!

Finally, the grape fires out from my mouth like a bullet from a gun. I take in a massive inhalation of breath and collapse in a weary heap at Dan's feet. He kneels down beside me and breathes a huge sigh of relief, leaving me utterly gobsmacked when, suddenly and without warning, he flings his arms around me and pulls me into a hug. *How*, exactly, in the space of a minute or so did I go from unacknowledged and irrelevant to in his actual arms? Bloody hell! All my Christmases have come at once, so what do I do? I bring this highly anticipated moment to an immediate and abrupt end by ripping his hair out from his scalp. Well, it was now or never.

'Ouch!' he gasps.

'Sorry, sorry. I'm just … traumatised. I don't know what I'm doing,' I blag.

He nods, rubbing his head and appearing somewhat miffed just as the door bursts open and help arrives thirty seconds too late. Good!

I'm surprised to have been sent home early, what with Trip Hut being a bunch of callous, money-hungry slave drivers. Still, never look a gift horse in the mouth … whatever that means.

Lumped on the sofa, with Smudge doing his very best to ignore me intruding on his space during his sleeping hours, I can't stop thinking about Dan's arms around my waist. That Heimlich manoeuvre was tantamount to dry-humping doggie-style I tell you! I begin to melt as I recall it in more depth and … I farted. Fuck! In front of Dan. Double fuck! On Dan, in actual fact. Infinity fuck! Did he hear it? He'd have to be stone-deaf not to have! Well, there's not a lot

I can do about it now. In fact, let's look at this as positively as possible, they do say "those who fart together, stay together". *He* didn't fart and we're not together, but yeah, I'm sure it's still relevant.

With an expression similar to that of a kid about to half-inch a fiver from his Mum's purse, I take out the small mound of bog roll from the pocket of my chequered pencil skirt, in which Dan's hair is safely wrapped. I give it a sniff, slightly disappointed to find it odourless, although I'm not entirely sure what I expected a mere three of his hairs to smell like.

I locate the red candle and position myself at the kitchen table. This is nuts. What am I doing? Am I seriously entertaining this silliness? Of course, I am! I'm not hurting anyone and it's not going to cost me anything, unless Mrs Birch does a Rumpelstiltskin and demands Dan and I's firstborn as payment later on, in which case I'm already forearmed with her first name having seen it on her post. Ha!

Tongue out, I slowly entwine Dan's hair around the candle. Bugger, it's too short to wrap fully around it. Perhaps I ought to stick it in place with some Sellotape? Candle in hand, I rise from my seat and rake through the kitchen drawers. I could've sworn I had some Sellotape somewhere. Oh, for fuck's sake where is it?! Having pulled out the entire contents of the drawers, all I can find is some huge gaffer tape; I'm not sure how or why it's in my possession, but I can assure you kidnapping Dan has never once crossed my mind. *Yet.* I cut a piece in half lengthways and stick Dan's hair to the candle. Now, at which point do I begin reciting the incantation? Hmm, Mrs Birch wasn't particularly clear on that. Mrs Birch wasn't particularly clear on anything, come to think of it. Oh well, I'll just have to keep on reciting it then.

'I am for you, you are for me, deep in love so shall we be. I am for you, you are for me, deep in love so shall we be.'

Continuously muttering the words as I go, I make my way downstairs and outside to the communal gardens where I choose an optimal, earthy patch under a rose bush as my burial site, which I quickly discover is also the optimal, earthy patch of choice of the local cats to bury their shit. I feel a combined sense of disgust at the cat shit, hope that this might work and disbelief that I've actually stooped this low as I pat down the earth in the final conclusion of the ritual. I've just done a bleeding love spell ... what kind of a psychopath am I? Oh, shit! Speaking of psychopaths, I've just remembered it's Bazza's Brutally Bad Bootcamp tonight! Fuck. I so can't be arsed. Shall I just not turn up? No. Don't be a dick! You spent the gas bill money on it, remember? You've got to go!

∞∞∞

'YOU WANT THIS?' the insane voice shouts.

'Er ... yeah.'

'HOW BAD DO YOU WANT THIS?'

'Badly?'

'SHOW ME HOW BAD YOU WANT THIS!'

I begin sprinting with my game face on at what I consider great speed on the treadmill.

'FASTER!'

My stamina rapidly depletes.

'FASTER, YOU GREAT DOLLOP!'

My legs begin to buckle.

'FUCKING FASTER!' the insane voice screams.

I collapse in a heap and slide off the back of the treadmill.

'PATHETIC!'

They say to be careful what you wish for, don't they? I wished for a psychopath to train me and that's exactly what I bloody well got! With his tattooed, bald head, burly physique, wife-beater vest and fiery temper, Bazza is indeed both a psychopath and as "brutally bad" as his class promised. It's a wonder he has any vocal chords left seeing as he doesn't appear to converse in a normal speaking tone, he just screams and shouts like a madman. The bastard's given me tinnitus, I swear!

After what was the worst hour of my life thus far, I puke in the flowerbeds outside the community centre. Bazza has, for want of a more polite term, fucked me up royally.

I wake in the morning with not a single muscle group exempt from pain. Everything hurts. It hurts just to bend to sit on the lavvy. God, I hate Bazza! I step on the scales – as I have so far been doing every time I go in the bathroom – and I've lost another pound. God, I love Bazza!

As I reluctantly enter the Trip Hut call centre, walking very much like John Wayne, Dan not only notices my arrival but leaves his desk and walks straight over to me.

'Lizzie, how are you? I can't stop thinking about yesterday.'

Nor can I Dan, nor can I!

'Um. Good! I'm good. Thank you,' I reply in surprise. 'And thank you, by the way, for doing that … thing to me.' What the hell is it called again? That manoeuvre he did? Shit, my mind's gone blank!

Fat Ann's head immediately shoots up from

her desk beside us, as it always does when she senses juice.

'You're welcome,' he smiles, 'Are you ok? You seem to be limping quite a bit. I didn't hurt you, did I?' he asks as he follows – yes, follows! – me to my desk.

Fat Ann's eyes widen until they are mere millimetres from popping out of her sockets.

'Oh no, it's just these shoes,' I lie, making a wise split-second decision not to tell him I've become Brutally Bad Bazza's latest recruit.

'Right. Well, I'm glad you're ok,' he says before heading back to his desk.

I freeze in my seat for several moments. Dan Elliott? Thinking about me? Asking me how I am? Bloody hell, the spell's worked! Christ, that was quick. Mrs Birch, you fucking star! Well, hang on a moment, let's not get too excited. He merely enquired about my welfare, he didn't bend me over the desk and give me one in front of the entire room, as much as I wish he had. Besides, why shouldn't he enquire about my wellbeing? He was involved first-hand in my traumatic choking incident yesterday; I suppose it would be pretty cold of him not to speak to me ever again after saving my life like that. Wait. Shit! I hadn't really thought of it in that sense until now. He, Dan Elliott, saved my life. Oh my God, we now share an eternal bond!

I glance over at Fat Ann who is staring at me in confusion. I raise my eyebrows smugly and begin sucking my pen in a rude and suggestive manner. Her mouth hangs open in disbelief. Ha! That should give the nosy cow something to wonder about.

Although Dan's acknowledgment of me is indeed progress, there is still the small fact he's allegedly going on a date with Rachel this weekend. Is it true or is Fat Ann shitting me? My soul simply cannot rest until I find out. Hmm, who do I know who's well connected?

Me: 'Hey Le, can u ask around your mates and try to find out for me if Dan E is going on a date with her from work this weekend? Xx

Levi: Fuck off! Xx

Me: Care to elaborate? Xx

Levi: Having coffee with Asian Sex God! Xx

Me: Soz! Xx

Well, that was a non-starter. Now what? Well, if the mountain won't come to Muhammed, then Muhammed must go to the mountain! The mountain in question being Rachel herself.

In contradiction of my morals and everything I stand for, I resort to being false. Seizing my moment, I watch her catwalk into the toilets, count to thirty, grab my bag and follow her.

'Oh, hi Rachel! I hear your first day went really

well. Go you!' I say as she ventures out of the loo. Go you? God I can be a dick sometimes.

She flashes her megawatt smile.

'Ah, that's so sweet. Yeah, I'm definitely finding my feet.'

'Great! That's really great. So, um, you and Dan seem to be really hitting it off?'

'Yeah! He's a really great guy,' she says, baring her perfect teeth into a cute smile.

'Yeah, he is.' Damn! Now what?

She takes out a Chanel lipstick from her bag and touches up her pout. I glance down at my own cheap, tatty lip gloss complete with hair wrapped around the wand and attempt to conceal it from view.

'Got any plans for the weekend?' I ask in a treacle voice. What am I? A bloody hairdresser?!

She smiles knowingly.

'Let's just say, I doubt I'm gonna get much sleep,' she hints before Sue bursts in, clocks me standing there and starts interrogating me about my last sale. After a quick and final check of her oh-so-perfect appearance, Rachel saunters out of the loos leaving me to make various attempts to reassure Sue that, yes, I did upgrade my last customer and, yes, I did successfully sell them the insurance, which is an effing miracle given my enormous lack of motivation where work is concerned right now ... and the fact I'm not completely sure what the insurance is for.

Okay, so I didn't get the definitive answer I was looking for, but Rachel more or less implied that she's going to be up all night this weekend shagging- shagging *my* prince! For once in her life, Fat Ann must be telling the truth.

I spend much of the evening immersed in a depressed heap in the bath, trying to come up with a plan to stop that damned date. In the lengthy struggle to come up with any such plan, my skin has surpassed wrinkly and is practically peeling off.

'Ugh! Why did God have to make someone as perfect as Rachel De Souza and plonk her straight in front of the man of my dreams? Why?!' I wail, my groans echoing melancholically throughout the bathroom. My odds of ever getting with such a fine specimen were already a million to one, now they're off the charts ... and not in a good way. It's simply not fair!

Oh God. Nooo! As a consequence of my absent-minded foot-fondling of the bath taps, my big toe is now wedged inside the bottom of the cold tap. I tense up and go hot as I picture the fire brigade arriving to free me.

Note to self: you really are a massive, massive twat!

Chapter 3:

The Straight and Narrow

I often liken my life to an old seaside roller-coaster, ageing and ropey with a series of twists and turns, more lows than highs and, fundamentally, lacking the thrill factor.

I sank to a new low at the beginning of the week doing a love spell, continued on at a low point from there with some help from Fat Ann and the conversation in the staff lavvies, plummeted to scary depths by breathing in a grape at lunch, rocketed to an all-time high being dry-humped by man of my dreams, experienced a sudden descent thanks to Bazza's Brutally Bad Bootcamp, progressed to a modestly pleasant high after being acknowledged by said man of my dreams, followed by a dramatic plunge in the form of the Brazilian supermodel confirming her upcoming shag-a-thon with man of my dreams and, as of Friday night, I've hit rock bottom with the onset of PMT.

Now I'm not sure if it's the PMT, common sense or Levi's influence, but I've decided to wash Dan Elliott out of my hair, let said hair down and go out on the town tomorrow night; a sudden and dramatic turnaround on my part, I know, but if the man of my dreams is on a promise with a Brazilian supermodel, then it's a situation akin to being the UK entry in the Eurovision Song Contest … fucking hopeless! After the swift consumption of the best part of a bottle of gin, the branding of Mrs Birch's love charm a load of old bollocks and a spell of howling like a husky with two fingers up to the neighbours, I admit defeat.

∞∞∞

How is it that messy buns look so pretty on everyone else but they make me look like Miss Trunchbull? Pulling a face at my own reflection, I yank it out in fury and revert to my usual half-arsed ponytail.

A letter from the gas company in this morning's post has done its job of reminding me that not only am I in debt, but I also have a so far unused month's gym membership. I make the swift decision to get my arse down there before it runs out.

As expected for a Saturday, the place is rammed with spandex-clad bodies. The men's egos are more pumped than their pecs, and my anxiety about them looking and laughing at me begins to diminish as I note their focus seems to be purely on what the other men around them are doing, obviously with the sole intent of ensuring they out-do them on reps. The only ones to look me up and down are the women, but their interest in me soon subsides once they've observed I'm three times their size and, thus, no threat to them.

I'm just getting into the swing of the cross trainer when I hear the unmistakably loud and annoying tone of Tasha Wilkes, ex-Trip Hut colleague and big-gobbed girl-about-town who knows absolutely everyone.

'Lizzie?! No way! As if you're here! Oh my god!'

And why *shouldn't* I be here? Ah yes, because I'm fat, doh! Could she have shouted that out any louder than she just did? Everyone is now looking over at me. Ugh!

'Yeah, hi Tasha,' I greet her with a discreet roll of my eyes as I continue on the cross trainer with my back to her. It's not that I'm being rude, it's just that Tasha's a massive pain the arse. She's one of these people you always end up worse off in some way for having bumped into. She immediately proves me right as she tells me she's started selling Ann Summers – I know exactly where this is heading.

'The area manager reckons I'm not selling enough of the sex toys, so I'm really pushing those at the moment, you know? Anyway, you'll buy some bits off me, won't you? I mean, you're single. You need sex toys in your life!' she practically shouts above the pulsating music.

Wait, what? She totally just assumed I'm single! I feel my already scarlet face begin to reach a whole new level of vibrancy.

'I've got loads of stock in the boot of my car. I'll wait for you after and you can have a browse, yeah?'

'Yeah, alright,' I pant, simply to get her to piss off.

'Coolio! I knew you'd be up for it! Catch you in a bit then!'

'Yeah, see you later,' I puff, knowing I most definitely *won't* because I plan to stealthily peg it out of here the minute my session's over.

Twenty minutes later, as a consequence of my lacking in stealth, I find myself stood at the boot of Tasha's car where I pick up the first sex toy I see, thrust a score in her hand and shove it in my tote, "it" being an extra girthy, realistic ten-inch dildo. Surprisingly, I then go on to leave Tasha having gotten something from her – albeit just a lift home.

I decide I'll spend the afternoon having a

proper pre-night out pamper session and finally do that algae body wrap I've had in the bathroom cupboard for an eternity. Just as I thought it might be, the algae body wrap is quite a clusterfuck but if it does what it says it does then I ought to lose a few inches before hitting the town tonight and, hey, every little helps!

Semi-wrapped and semi-naked, I hear my phone ringing. I hurry at speed to the kitchen, struggling to fish it out of my bag, grabbing it just in time before it goes to voicemail. It's Levi. He's called to warn me absolutely *not* to wear the jumpsuit that gives me camel toe. Duh! Knew that.

Just as I begin to retreat back to the bathroom, the buzzer goes. I'm not expecting anyone, as per, so who could it be? I reason aloud that it can't be anyone important and return to the bathroom to add more layers of algae and bandage. But the buzzer keeps on buzzing. Who *is* this cheeky twat?! I ignore it and keep on layering until hurrah! Finally, I'm fully bandaged other than for my face, which I decide to treat to a charcoal sheet mask. What the hell? The cheeky twat is now outside knocking the door to my flat. Who the heck is it? And, more worryingly, how did they access the stairs?

Storming through to the front room, quite forgetting my appearance, I pull the chain across the door before opening it partially to reveal the cheeky twat as my landlord. Fuck. He all but jumps out of his skin at the sight of me.

'Mr Harrison!' I gasp in surprise. 'Er ... hi ... what can I do for you?'

'Well, I'm here for the six month inspection we arranged last week,' he replies, looking a bit pissed off.

'Oh, shit ... I mean, yes, the inspection. Erm, could we possibly re-schedule? Now is really not a good time.'

'But I've just driven here from the other side of London!'

'But *I'm* dressed like a mummy!' I counter, shifting behind the door to hide most of the bandages.

'Look, I'm here to inspect the state of the flat, not *you*, Miss Bradshaw. So, if you could let me in we can get this over with. It should only take five minutes assuming everything's in order.'

'It is, yes. All in order, yes!' I bark, defensively.

'Wonderful, but I would rather like to see this for myself, so if you could just give me access ...'

'Can I just grab my dressing gown first?'

I sprint to the bedroom, grabbing as many strewn items as I can along the way. Oh, bollocks! How could I have forgotten the inspection? We only arranged it last week. It's been the week from hell, mind, but even so I've just made myself look a total gimp in front of my landlord ... literally! Oh, why must these things happen to me? Why?!

Opening the door, I observe that Mr Harrison is wearing white socks with brown, Jesus-style sandals and take some small comfort from knowing I'm not the only one who looks a dick. Things take a pretty sharp turn for the worse though when he goes to inspect the kitchen and spots the newly acquired extra girthy, ten-inch realistic dildo on the kitchen table. Fuck! It must've rolled out my bag in the kerfuffle to answer the phone earlier!

'That's not mine!' I blurt out.

'What you choose to do in your private life is none of my business,' he mumbles, proceeding to check the boiler.

'But it's not mine, honest! Well, it *is*, but I only bought it to be charitable.'

He shoots me a strange look.

I conclude I'd better quit while I'm possibly ahead. I spend the rest of the landlord's visit aimlessly walking from room to room, opening and closing drawers and cupboards in a lousy attempt to look busy and wondering what happens if you leave the algae on for more than the recommended amount of time.

∞∞∞

I smooth down my white, sleeveless shift dress in front of the wardrobe mirror and notice I'm definitely looking slimmer. In fact, I look pretty good for me! My eyes are done up smoky and I wear my long, mousy hair down in loose, tousled waves. After a final slick of lip gloss, I make my way to the drugstore to douse myself in the tester sprays, because when can a skint singleton justify spending £40 on a single bottle of perfume? I make a staunch mental note to make sure it's a women's fragrance this time.

Having met Levi and his entourage outside the tube station, we make our way from one trendy West End London bar to another, drinking copious amounts of cocktails and prosecco along the way. I notice I'm getting a few looks from guys. My first thought is to check my tampon hasn't leaked and I'm not sporting a fuck-off great stain on the arse of my dress, but it hadn't and there wasn't.

By 11pm I'm pissed as a fart and perfectly happy ignoring the little voice in my head telling me to stop the booze now and start on the mineral water. With the witching hour close at hand, we progress on to the nightclubs and strangely as the witching hour hits, I spot him over at the bar and looking fit as fuck. Dan Elliott! I squint my eyes. Perhaps he's just a mirage? I mean, of the alcohol-induced kind not the dehydration kind. No, he's definitely not a mirage. He's as real and as sexy as ever.

I crane my neck in search of Rachel, but can't see her anywhere. Perhaps he's already bonked and left her? It'll serve her right if he has, the devious temptress!

I realise I've been holding my wee in since forever in keenness not to trigger the "pissing every five minutes" phase of the night. I conclude that I've now reached the point that I really must go to the toilet unless I should wish to piss myself imminently. I glide to the little girls' room, but not before first gliding into a wall and falling backwards on my arse. I take a moment to focus my eyes on something to stop the room from spinning. A pair of trendy loafers have appeared in front of me, followed by a pair of legs in some smart chinos. My eyes slide up to past an ample-looking crotch to a crisp white designer shirt and … wait a minute, I know those guns!

'Lizzie, hi! Thought it was you!'

I close my eyes and re-open them. Yes, he's definitely not a mirage.

'Why are you sitting on the floor?' he asks, puzzled.

I go to reply, before stopping abruptly. I think a

little bit of wee just came out.

'Jussst chilling. Going with the flowww and that,' I slur.

'Oh, right. Do you need a hand up?'

I nod, putting my hands out in his direction like a helpless infant wishing to be picked up. If I wasn't so pissed, I'd be mortified!

He pulls me to my feet, which has the effect of bringing on another little leak. If I don't get to the toilet right now, I'm going to wet myself. But there's something about the look he's giving me and the way our faces are the closest they've been yet. Get to the fucking toilets Lizzie, now!

'Er, I need to get to the tucking foilets,' I slur, before hobbling at speed to the ladies. The stream starts the second I drop down onto the seat and I take a moment to appreciate the pleasant sense of relief. I then find myself engaging with an equally pissed-up stranger with whom I strike up an immediate drunken allegiance. After we put the world to rights about periods being shit and men being total bastards not having them – not to mention total bastards in general – I wander out of the loos and am surprised to see Dan, who has been waiting for me outside the door after all this time. What the actual fuck?!

'What are you doing hanging arrround the ladies loooos, Mr Elliott, you perv?!' I slur.

'Oh, there you are,' he says, leaning back against the wall. 'Just wanted to check you're alright.'

'Yesss, why wouldn't I be?'

'Well, it's just, given you were on the floor and that,' he says, gesturing to the spot I may have pissed on a few minutes beforehand.

'Well, I'm fine. I'm perfectly fiiine. Anyway, where's ya date?' I ask, alcohol providing me the necessary balls to start down this road.

'Sorry?'

'Oh, you know, her from worrrk!'

He looks confused.

'So, you *aren't* shagging her then?'

'Sorry? Shagging who? I'm here with my mates,' he says, gesturing behind him.

I look over his shoulder and spot his mates at the bar, yelling at him that it's his round.

'Anyway, glad you're ok. You look gorgeous by the way. Have a good night,' he says, before leaning down and kissing me on the cheek like the total gent he is, leaving me both breathless and speechless in his wake.

So, he's *not* on a date with Rachel! Fat Ann *was* bullshitting me!

Trance-like, I put my hand up to my face to retrieve the kiss before kissing my fingers and thereby kissing the kiss. I'm off my tits and should probably go home now for my own safety.

I wake the next morning with a massive headache and a massive grin when I recall what happened last night, even though I'm supposed to have washed Dan Elliott out of my hair. Perhaps I could shampoo him back in? I find myself having a think-off with my inner voice of reason:

'So, Dan wasn't on a date with Rachel after all!'

'No, but he flirts with her at every given opportunity and goes for runs in the park with her!'

'He kissed my cheek!'

'Which, to be fair, he probably does to many ladies.'

'Sorry, you can't have heard me; he kissed my bloody cheek!'

'I heard you alright. Question is, did you hear *me*?!'

I spend ages typing out a long and informative text to Levi filling him in, apologising for having gone AWOL last night and giving him Mrs Birch's telephone number. I really think the love charm is working! I'm met with an instant "message not delivered" alert and, upon further investigation, I note that my text and data allowances have run out already. Just another indicator of what a sad life I live, glued to my phone. I grab my laptop and log on to Facebook to send Levi a PM instead, when … hold up! What's this? A friend request! From Dan Elliott! Oh my God! I quickly hit accept, realising too late it may have been a little too quickly. He only added me twelve minutes ago. Should I have waited a while, so as not to look too keen? Nah! I've already waited a year for this man to notice me, that's more than sufficient. Oh my God, he's been thinking about me! For him to now add me on Facebook, totally out of the blue, he must have been thinking about me. I knew there was a connection last night. He felt it too, clearly. I can't get to his page quick enough where I sit trawling like Miss Marple, scanning his pictures and statuses and … oh shit! I just accidently "liked" a topless mirror selfie. Now I totally look desperate. I notice he has tonnes of women on his friends list and, yet, he's single. Why? Someone like Dan Elliott could have any woman he wants. Unless he's not into women?! Shit! No! God! It's all starting to make sense! *That's* why he's such a nice person! *That's* why he gets on so well with women and has so many female friends! *That's* why he hasn't made a move on me! How has it taken me this long to join the dots?! Just as my bottom lip starts going into spasm, Levi calls.

'Dahling, where the fuck were you? You missed all the action! Sorry I didn't ring, I was absolutely wankered, dahling. I just assumed you were off getting shagged somewhere.'

'Oh, bloody charming!'

'You weren't, then?' he says, disappointed.

'I bumped into Dan.'

'You *were*, then!'

'No, actually …' I start. 'We just talked, that's all. Then I went home. Alone, as per! But never mind all that now, Levi, I want your honest opinion.'

He sighs. 'Dahling, I've told you before, you on Love Island would be a fucking disaster!'

'No, not that! Do you reckon Dan might be gay?'

An immediate silence hits me.

'What, just because you can't get your hands on him?'

'No! Because he could have any woman he wants, but he's been single for the past year!'

'That doesn't make him gay, dahling,' Levi reasons.

'No, but it is pretty suss don't you think?'

'Not really. Perhaps he's a commitment-phobe?'

'I doubt that. He's a gent. Proper husband material.'

'Well, I don't know, do I? Just because I'm gay myself doesn't make me a bloody gay-voyant!'

'Well, surely you know the signs to look for?'

'No, dahling. The only sure-fire way to know a bloke is gay, I find, is if he was to shove his tongue down my throat. There's no mistaking that!'

Well, he's hit the nail on the head there. Can't argue with that logic. But it has given me an idea.

'Of course! I've got it! Why don't you try it on with him?' I say.

'Pardon me?'

'Oh, go on! Just send him a message or something. Register your interest. See what he says!' I wheedle.

After browbeating Levi until he loses the will to live, he agrees to comply before swiftly hanging up on me. He hates to lose an argument.

I've tried and failed countless times to forget Dan Elliott, but if he really is gay, then I have no choice; this time, I'll be finally forced to move on.

I spend the day anticipating a text I'm not sure I want to receive.

Chapter 4:

Friday Night at Eight

Well, that was quick! One minute I was lying on the couch eating a Crunchie to fend off my Sunday morning hangover, the next I'm staring into space at my desk at work on what is yet another bloody Monday morning. Ugh!

I haven't heard from Levi. I wonder if he's done it yet? Curiously, I analyse Dan's face during the morning huddle, looking for clues in his body language that he might've gotten the come-on from a bloke. Hmm, not that I can see. He just looks fit; so *very* fit!

Later, I bump into Shelley in the loos.

'Oh, hey. Good weekend?' she asks.

'Could've been better. You?'

'Yeah, super!' Shelley looks at me, puzzled. 'Why so glum, Lizzie? I would've thought you'd be pissing glitter right now!'

'Eh?' I ask.

'You know! You and Dan Elliott.'

'As far as I'm aware, there *is* no me and Dan Elliott.' Tragically true, but still heartbreaking to say out loud.

'Oh? That's not what I heard,' Shelley says with a shrug.

Ah, Fat Ann strikes again! Shelley quickly shoves her vape back in her bag as the toilet door squeaks open and Sue enters.

'Chop-chop ladies! Big target today. Back to the phones quick as you can, please.'

I slink out of the loos, wondering if there has ever been an occasion during my year-plus at Trip Hut when there hasn't been a big target to hit. Back at my desk I angle my bag on the floor in such a fashion that I can periodically peek down into it to check for text alerts, my go-to solution for when Sue's on one.

I've been on a sales call for a while giving Mrs Bennett the hard sell. She's been umming and ah-hing about going for the luxury five-berth over the standard four-berth for what feels like an eternity.

'You'd be mad not to, Mrs Bennett,' I tell her, just as I feel a ground-level buzz beside my foot. A text! I've got a text! I peer down into my bag while simultaneously reeling off the pluses of the luxury berth to Mrs Bennett.

'It's got a front-terrace, a hot-tub, you get your beds turned down every evening and ... he's *not* gay!'

'Sorry?'

'Er ... bay ... bay window! It's got stunning bay windows,' I stutter, a smile spreading across my face at my quick-thinking genius. Brilliant!

'Has it? Well, that sounds lovely. I'll take the luxury berth, then.'

Having received the joyous news that the man of my dreams is heterosexual and having bagged a jolly good sale, I sit buzzing like an old fridge as I go on to take Mrs Bennett's card payment.

'Now you have yourself a truly wonderful day, Mrs Bennett,' I purr, grinning from ear to ear.

'Excellent customer service, Lizzie! Excellent!' comes Sue's voice from behind me.

'Oh ... thank you,' I reply in a high-pitched, kiss-arse tone.

'Upgraded?'

'Yep!'

'Insurance?'

'Also yep!'

'You're a star! Well done.'

I smile and nod, lapping up the praise and refusing to let the slight issue that Mrs Bennett will be arriving to a distinct lack of stunning bay windows rain on my parade.

My run of luck continues throughout the rest of the day, resulting in my name being listed as Today's Star Seller on the whiteboard. It's hardly a reward having your name displayed in Sue's shit handwriting on a whiteboard that nobody looks at but it's still, nonetheless, a massive achievement for a shyster like me. An achievement which I'm well aware will only serve to increase Trip Hut's expectations of me from hereon in.

I leave work on a high, even though I'm headed to the community centre to get fucked up at Bazza's Brutally Bad Bootcamp.

'This girl is on fiyaaaaaaaaah!' I sing to myself as I exit the Trip Hut entrance doors, breezing around the corner straight into Dan.

'Alicia Keys fan?' he asks, laughing.

'Um ... she's alright,' I say, regretting trying to belt out that note.

'Yeah, I guess,' he agrees. 'Er ... Lizzie?'

Oh shit. He's not smiling now. He looks serious. What the hell has Levi told him?! What was I thinking, involving Levi? Oh God, what's he gone and said.

'Yeah?'

'Can I ... take you out at the weekend?'

I freeze. I can't have heard him correctly.

'You ... what?'

'It's fine if you don't want to.'

Don't want to?! My whole body is literally going into spasm, I'm that keen.

'Um, yeah, can do,' I mutter, playing it ice cool.

We agree to arrange something in the week, and I walk off appearing as unmoved as possible before doing an ecstatic bell kick the second I turn the corner. I've just crashed into some wheelie bins, but who gives a fuck? I have a date with Dan Elliott! Did you hear that universe? I have a date with Dan Elliott! Me, Lizzie Bradshaw, eternal no-hoper and underdog! It worked! The spell bloody worked! This calls for the biggest God-damned celebration ever! But first, on to the community centre.

If the sight of myself naked in the mirror wasn't enough motivation to slim the fuck down, the thought of sexual relations with Dan now being a very real possibility rather than pure fantasy proves to be the ultimate motivator. I've run, I've boxed, I've squatted, I've lifted, I've crunched, I've been cruelly taunted and roared at and now I'm ... being sick in the flowerbeds again. God damn you, lactic acid.

I smell the cuisine of the China Palace as I walk

past and for once in my life it doesn't arouse my greedy senses enough to go in and order. They can jolly well keep their spicy prawn balls. The only balls I'm interested in are those of Dan Elliott.

Back at the flat, like an excited kid at Christmas, I get straight on the phone to Levi.

'Can you believe it, Le? A date with the most eligible bachelor ever!'

'No dahling, *that's* me! *You* have a date with Dan Elliott!'

'I know! I know! It's amazing isn't it? So, how did you find out he's not gay then?'

'Er ... confession,' he squeaks.

I let the silence speak for me.

'Never messaged him. Couldn't be arsed dahling.'

'You Judas!' I accuse.

'Well, what does it matter? All that matters now, is what you're going to wear, Cinders!'

'God, yeah! Clothes. Well, I've not really got anything other than my old faithful.'

'The old faithful, being ...?'

'The white shift dress,' I confess. The same white shift dress that's currently on the floor near the laundry basket, covered in a little bit of my piss and whatever else was on the floor of that club.

'Sacre bleu! Are you out of your mind, dahling? Now you know me, I'm all for recycling a classic, but you simply can't wear the white shift twice in the same week, it would be fashion suicide! Do you want Dan to think you're a bloody pikey?'

'Shit, no! But payday's another three weeks away and I'm skint,' I admit.

'Skint already? Lizzie, you're a fucking nightmare with sterling!' he sighs. 'Well, you'll just have to be a bit savvy, dahling.'

'How?' I ask.

'Get on eBay and bid like a bitch!'

I'm awake until 3.10am doing exactly that. Though I have to say the things some people attempt to sell on there. I mean, there's "used" and then there's "visibly rinsed to death!" That Marc Jacobs LBD definitely falls into the latter category, but still the seller has it listed as "only worn a few times"; a few times clearly meaning *all* the fucking time! I don't know where Dan's taking me yet, but an LBD is usually a good going out-out choice, assuming he's not planning on taking me swimming or to the zoo. God, that's a point! He did merely say "take you out at the weekend" which doesn't necessarily mean in the evening or to The Ivy for dinner. Still, all avenues must be covered.

I stumble across a lovely little number that's new and only a tenner. It's unbranded, but with my fake Gucci belt it could totally pass for designer. I've not found anything else and it's coming up to 4am and ... oh sod it! Where's the "buy it now" tab?

I wake absolutely knackered from my nocturnal frock-hunt. My eyes are stinging and pretty much resemble a new-born hampster's – yes, fully aware it's "hamster", but personally I choose "hampster", as well as "skellington" and "pacifically".

There's no way I'm going to make the tube today, there's a storm raging outside and my ugly mug needs too much work. Plus, I don't think my precious will be at all happy to note he has a date with Gollum this weekend. There's only one thing for it: I'll have to take the car.

As well as sit-ups and Brazilian supermodels, I cannot stand driving in the city. My pride and joy in the form of my yellow Mini Cooper subsequently doesn't get much use other than for ferrying my parents to the airport and home from the pub when they require it – Dad didn't pay for it purely out the goodness of his heart, you know. I crank up the volume on the stereo and wheelspin in the rain out of the carpark belting out my old-school forever-jam N-Trance's "Set U Free". For once the lyrics are fitting, particularly with this bloody storm beating down.

I arrive at Trip Hut, skidding into the carpark with a feeling that life just got good, as well as a sudden, massive urge to fart probably brought on by the combination of those not-so-awful green juices and my vigorous seat dancing. I let rip, carefree, before grinding to a halt. The rain is really coming down now. Having gone to all that effort not to look like Gollum, I can't now get out in torrential rain. I'll sit for a bit and see if it tapers off.

A tap on the passenger-side window makes me jump. Oh, it's Dan! The smile on my face falls as I catch whiff of my fart – a slow-burner which has been gradually peaking. Christ, it's a rotter! I sit, rooted to the spot in horror as Dan gestures for me to open the passenger-side door. I can't. I simply can't. He'll smell it and the date will be off. No amount of magic is going to keep his interest in me once he's smelt this!

'Open the door then!' he urges, tapping the glass and giving me a funny look, clearly questioning my cruel hesitation as the rain soaks him.

'Can't,' I mouth back to him.

'What, why?'

'Cramp. Got cramp.'

He tries the door handle and, owing to the fact Dad wouldn't let me get the higher spec model with automatic central locking, it fucking opens!

Shit. Shit. Shit.

'God, it's mental out there!' he exclaims, getting in. It ain't much better in here, as he's about to find out.

'You alright then?' he asks, his expression quickly changing which tells me he's smelt it already.

'Fine,' I blurt out, turning away in shame.

'Are you sure? You're not … ill or anything?'

'No? Er … should we get out now? Sue will be on the warpath…'

'We're alright for five minutes. Lizzie, what's that smell?' he asks.

It's my arse Dan, and you'd better get used to it.

'That's just the catalytic converter. Always does that,' I blag, thankful to Dad for imparting that bit of knowledge to me.

'Ah, that's what it is! Thought you'd done a monster fart or something!' he says with a grin.

'Ha-ha! No!' I laugh, as though that would be totally unheard of and completely against my ladylike nature.

While waiting it out in my cesspit of a vehicle, secretly cringing in the knowledge my prince is unknowingly breathing in said monster fart, we arrange our date for Friday night at 8pm at Luigi's, a top-drawer Italian. We swap numbers before heading into a different sort of cesspit in the form of Trip Hut.

Fat Ann's nose is pressed up against the staff room window as we enter through the main entrance together. I yank up the collar on my coat and walk in like a boss.

Five minutes later, my phone pings with a text. Smiling, I fish it out of my bag wondering if it's a flirty message from Dan now that he has my number, but no. It's just Levi texting to warn I should schedule a fanny wax asap to ensure the old girl is ready for whoopie-making.

Me: It's a mere first date. Hardly think we're gonna be making whoopie! Xx

Me: Plus, I have morals! Xx

Levi: No u don't & if u attend with full-on growler, ur tempting fate & thus, guaranteeing u will be making whoopie! Xx

Knowing my track record with tempting fate, I make a mental note to hit the drugstore after work for a home waxing kit. Well, Levi might be happy to bare-all for a back, sack and crack, but I'd rather die than get my Mary out for some beautician whom, despite her claims to be a professional, definitely runs home to tell all about the state of the many undercarriages she sees. I know I would.

I'm not sure how I should act around Dan at

work. Should I be acting like his girlfriend? Nah, that's a bit premature. Then how does one act around somebody they're scheduled to be going on a date with? Do I give him a periodic knowing wink from across the room? Sit next to him at lunch? I go on to rule out the latter when I walk into the staff room on my lunch hour to find the Brazilian supermodel sitting with him, dressed in a short leather skirt with her legs crossed seductively, giggling like a child. I wonder: A. if Dan's a leg or breast man; B. if she's planning to do a Sharon Stone and C. if my date with Dan is a cruel prank they've devised together. Surely not? No, I *know* Dan from staring at the back of his head for nigh on a year. He's too nice a person to do something like that. Plus, aren't they a bit old for pranks? Deep in thought, I recall the time I left a tube of lube beside the Elf on the Shelf in the staff room at Christmas, which I'd positioned holding a photo of Fat Ann grinning delightedly on a work's night out. Okay, so maybe they're not too old for pranks.

I feel an enormous sense of déjà-vu as I skulk off to the corner to drink my flask of green gunge. For my own safety, I no longer eat grapes.

Although we aren't yet a couple and I definitely don't want to be the sort of insecure saddo who bans her boyfriend from having female friends, the Brazilian supermodel definitely needs to do one!

My first course of action on getting in from work – besides taking my bra off and liberating the puppies – is to check my emails for shipping updates on my bargain frock, which I've been doing excessively ever since my payment went through. Nope. Nothing. Just the usual "get rock-hard now" erection-enhancer tommyrot. Oh, and an email urging me to hurry and claim the $20 million bequeathed to me by some billionaire businessman with no other family. While I've always been the gullible type, to the point of thinking staff in fast food outlets are offering me a freebie when they ask, 'Is that a large?' and my own Mother having said for years that I'll be found under some psycho's patio after him having promised to make me a star, even I would not "click the link to claim now".

The week leading up to my Dan-date seems to pass in a blur. Though I'm generally a person known for their lackadaisicalness and insistence on doing everything at the eleventh hour, I'm not at all comfortable with the fact it's bloody Thursday and the dress still hasn't arrived! I spend much of the working day glued to my phone for shipping updates that never come and contemplating the unthinkable; phoning Mother to ask for thirty quid. I'm relieved to return home to find a card from the courier in my pigeonhole upon which "Left with flat no.5" is scribbled in barely readable courier-scrawl, at which point my relief gives way to dread upon realising Pervy Bob has my frock. I hope he hasn't tried it on! I spend some time plucking up the courage to go and knock on the door of the sex-pest standing between me and my date attire and, when I eventually do, am relieved to find that I am the only thing he is trying it on with.

Back at my flat, I tear open the packaging and take out a note which reads "Friend, we hope you loving garment. If garment you finding is bad, please contact us for replacement before leaving negative feedback". Oh shit. I can guess what's coming now. Sure enough, my little black dress all the way from China has been crafted to the proportions of an eight-year-old, probably *by* an eight-year-old! There's absolutely nothing to be done here, I'd be lucky to get a leg in the bastard! I let out a loud and lengthy panicked wail while mentally dropkicking myself for thinking I could acquire a perfectly good date dress for a tenner. I'm livid and I've gone all hot! In a rage, I log straight onto eBay and give Dressydress4lady_25 a piece of my mind in full capital letters and with no punctuation, but, frankly, I'm too mad to care. What the hell am I going to do now? I'm skint as a bint. But skint as I may be, hell will freeze over before I go cap-in-hand to Mother. Mother has never been comfortable with my independence and would thoroughly delight in my calling her to ask for a loan. It would mean I had failed in my quest to live independently. It would mean I still need her. My blagging a date with Dan Elliott is up there with winning the lottery. Cancelling is absolutely out of the question!

'Help me!' I plead at the cat, who stares back vacantly. I'm almost disappointed that he doesn't answer with the perfect solution.

In the absence of a magic lamp complete with genie, I consult the next best thing – Google! With the white shift dress in mind, I type in:

"How-to-revamp-an-old-dress" Enter!

"Shorten the hem." Can't bloody sew!

"Change the buttons." Can't bloody sew!

"Add a slit." Can't bloody sew!

"Dye it." Bingo!

My next step is to consult YouTube, where there's bound to be a tutorial on dyeing clothes at home. I mean, what *can't* you learn from YouTube? Yes! Here we go.

Having skipped along through the tutorial, I'm both surprised and delighted to learn that you can dye fabric orange with onion skins. That's it! It's the perfect solution. Goodbye old, white shift, hello new, trendy orange shift – all for the price of a bag of onions!

I peg it down to Sainsburys for said onions before setting up a re-colouration station in the kitchen. I scour the cupboards for a decent sized pan in which to boil the onion skins to extract the dye from them. A cauldron would be perfect for this sort of thing and I briefly entertain the idea of popping across to Mrs Birch to ask if she has one. No, traditionally neighbours ask their fellow neighbours for sugar not cauldrons, although I could bet my arse she has one.

I find a modestly sized pan and get to work boiling the onion skins. The process is quite a lengthy one and so, consequently, it's not long before the place is rife with condensation and reeking of onions, which I note smell much like B.O. Finally, sometime later, I have my orange dye. It's getting late and I need my beauty sleep more than most so I don't piss about. I plonk the white shift into the pan and leave it to do its magic overnight while I take myself off to wax my muff, just in case.

Who was I to think I could possibly sleep the night before my Dan-date? I wake early too, in part excitement of said date with actual Adonis and in part angst about the sort of colour my white shift dress might now be. Nervous, I skid into the kitchen. Wow! It's a classy sort of burnt orange, it's coloured evenly and to my utter surprise, it looks pretty awesome! My luck is definitely changing! I take it out the pan, rinse it well in the kitchen sink, wring it with everything I've got and fling it over the clothes airer to dry.

As is usually the case when one wills time to pass quickly at work, it does the bloody opposite and drags like a bitch. When close of play finally hits, I mouth, 'See you tonight' to Dan, who is still on the phone, before swaggering past Fat Ann's desk like Danny Zuko.

By the time I've arrived home, eager anticipation of the looming date has turned to nervous anticipation of the looming date. I scour the kitchen cupboards in search of some alcohol to have a livener or two to calm my nerves. I don't usually have alcohol in the house; this is not an intentional, sensible decision on my part but purely down to the fact that I can't let alcohol sit in a cupboard for very long. I locate an ancient, dust-ridden bottle of Pernod which Mother probably brought round and left three Christmases ago and pour myself a Pernod and Dr Pepper, the only appropriate mixer in the house other than skimmed milk.

I take my portable Bluetooth speaker into the bathroom where I indulge in a long disco-shower, making sure to exfoliate and shave every crevice. I treat my tresses to a deep conditioning treatment and dance like a twat while it works. Recalling the saying "if you can't tone it, tan it", I slap on some fake tan, pulling a muscle in my shoulder in the process. In remedy of the subsequent pain, I administer medication in the form of two more Pernods.

I make a last-minute executive decision to wear the girdle I bought from Mother's catalogue to wear under a dress at a family wedding back at the millennium. It's fully boned, a bastard to get on and, owing to its incredible streamlining effects, has been suitably nicknamed The Gutbuster 2000 by Levi and I. Bugger me, I thought I was a heifer back at the time of that wedding, but now? Sheesh! I can barely get it to meet around the middle! I lay on the bed which has the effect of drawing my gut in enough to eventually fasten the bloody thing.

I clamber to my feet, wiggle on my dress and check myself out in the mirror. My circulation is pretty much cut off from the tits down and my breathing is drastically compromised, but my waist is significantly reduced and my gut significantly flatter and, thus, The Gutbuster 2000 is staying on come what may!

Ok Lizzie, deep breath girl. This is it! This is the moment you've dreamed of.

I do my hair toss, check for boogers ... and have a quick practice snog with a Valencia orange. And now, I'm ready!

Chapter 5:

Burning Desire

I'm on the tube and I can't stop smiling, partly down to the fact I'm on my way to a date with a MILDOS (Man I've Long Dreamed of Shagging) and partly down to the ancient Pernod. I'm getting some funny looks; the tubby bloke wearing crocs sat by the door clearly thinks he's pulled and, to be fair, a crocs-clad ogre with a beer belly and B.O is the usual extent of my pulling-power. But not tonight pal, for I am dating an actual Adonis!

I'm relieved to note that The Gutbuster 2000 appears to be holding up remarkably well as I sit perched on the edge of my seat with my tits forced up to my chin, giving me one of those medieval buxom cleavages. No wonder Henry VIII had so many wives! Everything is tightly and securely contained, though my entire body is pulsating rhythmically as a result.

Back on higher ground, the palpitations increase as I totter toward Luigi's. I've had many dreams and desires in my time, none of them ever coming to fruition of course, until now. Oh my God. This is it! I've arrived, both for the date and in life.

'Good evening madam, do you have a reservation?' the host asks.

'I do, yes. Well, Dan does, he booked it,' I garble.

'Pardon me?'

'Er ... it's Elliott.'

'Ah, Mrs Elliott, is it?'

I hesitate before naughtily nodding in agreeance. I bloody love being called Mrs Elliott. It definitely beats writing it on my personal development plan.

'Your husband is waiting for you. He's over on table twenty-four.'

I go all tingly at the mere sound of those words: "your husband". Hmm, Lizzie Elliott does have a ring to it. Sort of like Missy Elliott, I muse as I walk as sultrily as possible through the bustling restaurant, trying to act like a seasoned upmarket restaurant goer. Who *me*? I date beautiful men in classy restaurants all the time. I do this all the time!

Eek! There he is. Mr Wonderful. Mr Absolutely Fucking Spectacular, I should say! Phwoaaaaar!

Looking genuinely pleased to see me, he rises from his seat and kisses me on the cheek as I arrive at the table.

'Hey, you!'

'Hey, you!' Jeez, what are you Lizzie, a parrot?

His gaze does a little dip downward, enough for me to notice that he's noticed the buxom medieval cleavage.

'Can I get you a drink? I ordered a red and a white. Didn't know what you prefer.'

Pernod and Dr Pepper as it goes!

'Oh, lovely, I'll have a glass of white please,' I reply, fighting against The Gutbuster to sit down like a normal person.

'Here's the menu,' he says, handing it to me. 'It's a lovely place. Great food. You been here before?'

Fuck, no. Never! The last bloke I had a meal out with was my Dad, at a supermarket cafe. But I may have drawn Dan in with my tits in this dress, so I can't lose him to thinking I am an unsophisticated swine.

'Oh actually, yeah, yeah. Not so long ago actually. I come here all the time,' I say.

'Oh, really? You never said. I could've booked somewhere new to try. God, sorry. Here's me telling you all about one of your regular haunts! I guess you won't be needing the menu then, you'll already know what you want,' he says, looking slightly dismayed.

Yeah, I want you right here in front of the entire restaurant! I smile back at him, gormlessly.

'Well?'

'Well, what?'

'What do you usually have when you come here? Got any recommendations?'

Yeah, not to fucking lie!

'Er ... well, the ... chicken...'

He looks at me expectantly as I trail off, racking my brains furiously. '... curry! The curry's really good here!' I manage.

He frowns.

'Curry? You know this is an Italian, right?'

'Um, yeah. But they do a really good curry. They do,' I insist, wide-eyed.

'Do they?' he remarks, opening and scanning the menu dubiously.

'Yes, well, anyway ... do *you* ... come here often?' I stammer in a panic. Jesus Lizzie, pull yourself together!

'Not that often, no,' he replies, still examining the menu for that fictitious curry.

Well, this has gotten off to a totally shit start.

I feel less like I'm on a date and more like I'm on trial. Oh, why did I lie?! I had one chance to make a good impression and I've already pissed it up the wall before we've even ordered.

'Nope, definitely no curry on the menu. That's weird!' Dan exclaims, as I squirm in my seat. I'm getting all hot and bothered and not in the way I'd intended.

Pretending not to have heard, I reach for the wine, getting a sudden whiff of body odour as I do so. What?! I put on enough roll-on deodorant tonight to stop me perspiring for an entire month. This cannot be happening!

'Just going to the little girls' room!' I announce in a loud panic, springing up from my seat and knocking the waiter's order pad and pen straight out of his hands as he arrives at the table to take our order.

'Oh. Alright. Shall I order for you? What do you like?' Dan replies in surprise, standing up too.

'Anything, I'll eat anything' I pant making a mad dash for the loos. Oh, Christ! The smell is following me, what the hell am I going to do? All I have on me is a lip gloss, some gum and my phone. This is tragic! Only this sort of shit happens to me.

I head into a cubicle and swipe my hand frantically under my pits. What the hell? My hand smells of nothing. My dress, on the other hand, does have an odour. An odour which smells much like the clever, forward-thinking, eco-friendly onion dye I used on it last night! How did I not smell it before? The stench must have been gradually warming up with my rising body heat. What am I going to do? It's not like I can take the dress off, at least not now, anyway. I drift out of the cubicle, staring into space. It's hopeless! I should've known this was all just way too good to be true. Fortune does not, and has never, favoured Lizzie Bradshaw and if it does there's always a clanger around the corner just waiting to happen.

My eyes come to rest on the air freshener unit mounted up on the wall above the sinks. There's a green light flashing on it. It's one of those automatic ones which releases a periodic, freshening spritz. I wait for the place to clear before I totter over to the sink unit, hook my knee onto the edge and clamber up onto it, using muscles Bazza would be proud of. Standing up straight, the air freshener unit is now level with my chest. I figure it probably has a sensor on it, so all I need do is wave my arms to trigger said sensor into releasing a freshening spritz onto me! I can then just repeat the process, changing my position until I've covered the length and breadth of the dress, then subsequently exit the toilet smelling much like a toilet air freshener but a lot less like onions and B.O. My date with the MILDOS can then proceed onward and hopefully conclude with us playing tonsil tennis, as a minimum, before we each go our separate ways. Sounds like a bloody plan!

I quickly wave an arm in front of the air freshener unit and stand back in anticipation. Nothing. I give a quick wave of both arms this time. Nothing. Why is nothing happening?! Perhaps it's cheaply manufactured. Maybe the sensor isn't as "sensey" as it ought to be. I wave my arms around erratically and stamp my heels on the sink unit, hoping the added vibration might be enough to trigger it, but praying the sink isn't as cheaply made as this air freshener and will hold my weight a bit longer. Just as I do so, the toilet door squeaks open. From there, it all happens so quickly. I instinctively turn my head toward the door and drop down in fright, at which point the sodding air freshener releases a freshening spritz straight into my right eye at point-blank range!

'FUCK! IT'S BURNING! IT'S BURNING!'

The toilet reverb carries my screams from the ladies out into the busy restaurant area, where I observe with my left eye several shocked diners alarmed to see me standing on the sink, yelling and clutching one eye as the door gradually closes.

'Could you mind your language?!' fumes the Gloria Hunniford lookalike who's just walked in and who I immediately silently blame for this shitshow.

'No, I fucking can't!' I yell back, my eye already a bloodshot, mascara-stained, streaming mess. She shoots me a disapproving look and tuts loudly before storming into a cubicle.

The toilet door squeaks open again and a staff member walks in having heard the commotion from outside.

'Is everything ok, madam?' she asks, though it's blindingly obvious – pun intended – that no, everything is not ok.

'No, it is not! I've just been sprayed in the eye at close range by that bloody thing!' I complain, gesturing up toward the air freshener unit on the wall. 'You really ought to consider the safety of your patrons more!' I add, tutting and shaking my head.

'Goodness! How on earth did you manage that with it being all the way up there?' she asks, genuinely baffled.

I say nothing.

'I'll get the First Aid kit and call for the manager, you wait here.'

As soon as she's gone, I peg it out of the toilets and head back to our table with the intention of telling Dan I've got to go because I have an allergy, a *very* bad allergy. On my approach, I note he's engaged in conversation with none other than Rachel shitting De Souza! Who, incidentally, appears to be wearing a smart, black LBD with a genuine Gucci belt nipping in her already svelte waist. Like an angry bull, I storm over.

'Now just *what* is going on here?!' I demand to know, looking enraged and clutching my streaming eye.

'Lizzie what's happened to you?!' Dan exclaims in shock, no doubt puzzled at the fact I left looking like me and returned looking like some sort of evil, irate Halloween doll.

'I've been ... I've had an allergic reaction actually,' I tell him, 'but never mind about that, what is she doing here?'

She raises a perfect brow but says nothing.

'She's here with friends. Look Lizzie, I really think you ought to calm down, people are staring,' he urges, gesturing to the diners who are surreptitiously looking in our direction.

'I couldn't give a rat's arse! I've had about enough of all this!' I shout.

Oh God, our first argument, already!

'Enough of all what?' he replies.

Rachel sits in feigned observational shock before looking back at Dan all doe-eyed and innocent, clearly loving the drama.

'Well let me think! The sitting with you at lunch, the giggly private jokes, the slinking about like Sharon Stone in slutty skirts, the running alongside you in the park like the perfect little wifey and, by pure coincidence, of all the restaurants in London she could choose to eat at, she shows up here, at our date!'

'Lizzie, I've already said, she's here with friends and I'm a personal trainer outside of work. A lot of people run alongside me in the park.'

Shit, I totally didn't know that about him.

I pause, looking around the room which has by now, fallen silent.

'So? Doesn't mean she doesn't want to have it off with you!' I yell. I hear tuts from various tables as my words echo around the room.

'Excuse me? Mrs Elliott? You're causing a disturbance. I'm afraid I'm going to have to ask you to leave,' says the restaurant host from behind me.

Out the corner of my eye I notice Dan's look of confusion at the name, before observing Rachel sniggering behind her hand as I'm led gently away and out into the foyer where I am told in no uncertain terms that I am banned for life from Luigi's.

'Fine! Pasta is laden with carbs, anyway!' I

manage as a lame attempt at a vengeful parting remark before skulking off into the night.

I will Dan to race after me up the street shouting that there's been a dreadful mistake before spinning me around and snogging my face off. He doesn't. Well, that's bloody champion, isn't it? My date with Mr Wonderful lasted all of 45 minutes! That's got to be a new world record for briefest date ever. My eyes begin to well up as I journey home, early and alone.

My vision of the date with Dan had been a remarkably different one which centred largely around me looking radiant in the subtle candlelight, some romantic conversation akin to a black and white movie, crackling sexual tension, top-class cuisine and a saucy French kiss on the street outside my flat, which may or may not have led to passionate lovemaking. At no time did I foresee myself being practically blinded in one eye and frog-marched out of the restaurant with a lifetime ban. I should've known it would end it disaster. Anything good in my life always ends in disaster. I *am* a disaster!

Once I've extracted myself from The Gutbuster, I wail and sob into Smudge's fur before heading into the kitchen to polish off that age-old, ancient Pernod. Now, where did I put that Toni Braxton album?

I wake the next morning spreadeagled on the

sofa with gritty eyes, a bad taste in my mouth and a sinking feeling. This is not how it was meant to be. The morning after the date-of-all-dates was meant to mirror either of the following scenarios: wake like a queen with pleasant recollection of the evening's events, still buzzing from Disney kiss on the street with Mr Wonderful, or wake like a queen with pleasant recollection of the evening's events, still throbbing from hot, rampant sex with Mr Wonderful. There was to be no waking like the Sea Witch from *The Little Mermaid* with a gammy eye, an unpleasant recollection of the evening's events, still smarting from my restaurant ban!

I feel a pang of hopeful excitement as my phone begins ringing on the floor beside me. However, said hopeful excitement is immediately diminished to nothing when I note the caller to be Mother, not the MILDOS.

'Yeah,' I answer.

'Well, you could sound a little more pleased to be hearing from your mother. You know, she who gave you life!'

'What life?' I counter.

'Well, *you* chose to move out, dear! Anyhow, I'm calling to see if you'd like to come with us to the supermarket. Do you need anything?'

Yeah, a vat of vodka, a big dirty pasty and a share-size bag of cheesy puffs!

Recalling that I have nothing else to do and, for want of a more polite term, fuck-all in, I casually agree to said supermarket outing, being careful not to appear too destitute – which I am, but am aware would be music to Mother's ears.

I open the door to my parent's car an independent but destitute woman but by the time my seat belt is fastened I have morphed into the hen-pecked seven-year-old whom I always revert to when in Mother's company.

'What's new then, Lilibeth?' Dad enquires from the driver's seat.

I do a brief mental assessment of the fortnight since I last saw them. Well, other than nearly choking to death on a grape, farting on a male work colleague, opening the door to my landlord naked under bandages sporting a gimp-style face mask and being ejected in disgrace from an Italian eatery, not much. You?

I return from my parentally supervised supermarket outing armed to the teeth with bags of crap. Rather than address and deal with the mountain of dirty dishes in the sink, I scoff instant chicken noodles from a Pyrex jug before devouring an entire tub of Ben and Jerry's with a dinner knife.

I log on to Facebook with an instant sigh on observing I've been tagged in the night out pictures from last weekend and it's not good; I look like a sort of jawless, cock-nosed butternut squash. I am overcome with immediate panic when I remember the MILDOS is on my friends list and rapidly set about removing all tags, although he was last active 15 minutes ago, has probably already seen them and is probably thanking his lucky stars for his escape last night as we speak.

I proceed to have a paranoid stalk of Rachel's open page and am enraged to see her last cryptic status of "Oh, what a night", followed by several suggestible winks and heart emojis. I drop both the c-bomb and the laptop before sinking back into the sofa and the depths of despair.

Just when I think things can't get any worse, I follow up a knock on my door to discover Pervy Bob through the spy hole, standing with his feet at quarter-to-three armed with an enormous bouquet of flowers. I blink and blink again, but the git's still there. No! Fuck no! This cannot be happening. I'm aware I'm a saddo of the highest order, but when I asked the universe to manifest my very own Edward Lewis, I didn't bank on him being the fat, middle-aged, bespectacled pervert from Flat 5! What do I do? Open the door and tell him to shit off? Pretend not to be in?

'I'm not in!' I call out without thinking. Good one, Lizzie.

I observe his even more gormless than usual

expression at hearing my voice, which only results in further loud knocking. Oh, God! Help! I'm being ambushed by a sex-pest!

'Open up, Lizzie,' he calls out in a sing-song voice which does nothing for my nerves.

'No, never! I don't care how desperate I am!' I call back.

'But I have a lovely bunch of flowers for you!' he badgers.

'Yes, and I have pepper spray and I'm not afraid to use it!'

'Cor, that's gratitude for you!' he scoffs.

'Listen Bob, as a sex-starved borderline nymphomaniac myself, I totally empathise, I really do. But you and me? It's never going to happen. You'll find someone who'll have you sooner or later,' I tell him through the safety of the door.

He pauses.

'I think you've got the wrong end of the stick, love. You weren't at home when these flowers were delivered so I took them in for you. Then I saw you'd arrived home, so I thought I'd better bring them over.'

'Oh … oh! So, you don't want to molest me?'

'What?! Good grief, no!'

'Why? What's wrong with me?' I ask, tearing open the door.

'Nothing. I mean, I wouldn't say no if you're offering, but I'm only here to give you your flowers,' he insists.

'Well, thank you. Thank you very much,' I tell him, feeling terrible and hoping my door was thick enough to mask some of the insults I had thrown at him.

'So?' he enquires.

'So, what?'

'You offering then?' he says with a wink.

'Absolutely not, goodbye!' I declare, taking the flowers and flinging the door closed on him.

'Wow! These are some flowers!' I muse aloud, placing them on the kitchen table. I never get flowers. That's no exaggeration, I mean I've *never* been given flowers before. I often joke I'll finally get flowers at my funeral, the only snag being I shall be very dead and thus not there to see them. Given this, you'd think I'd be as excited as a dog with two dicks right now to have received this fuck-off great bunch, but I'm actually pretty subdued as I slide out the little pink envelope and open it to reveal a message card:

Gutted it didn't work out last night. Re-schedule? D x

My eyes light up like Augustus Gloop's on entering Willy Wonka's chocolate factory and a Grinch-like grin creeps up my face. Romance isn't dead! Not yet, anyway.

Chapter 6:

Another Chance

Me: Thank you for the flowers. They're gorge!

Dan: Ur welcome. Wanna re-schedule?

Er, not half! Just name the time and place and I'll be there with my knickers down, baby!

Me: Yeah, sure x

Dan: My place, say 7.30? x

Me: Great! I'll be there x

Me: …what's your address? x

Armed with an address, I hurriedly begin the "tramp to vamp" transformation. After last night's fiasco, I've quite a bit of ground to make up so I figure a Brigitte Bardot half-up would be a good first step to redemption. This accompanied with a Brigitte-eye, cream eyelash-knit jumper and skinny jeans screams casual meets Hollywood glam. At least it will do once I pick myself up from that violent crash into the wardrobe … Jesus! There's got to be an easier way to get oneself into skinny jeans.

As Dan-o-clock draws closer, I make a mental note that, this time, I must not: A. lie like a rug, B. almost blind myself, or C. do anything else whatsoever to fuck things up.

I do a series of seductive, sultry looks in the mirror before doing my hair toss, checking for boogers and having *another* quick practice snog on a Valencia orange. One can never have too much practice.

In the absence of anything at all alcoholic in my flat, I am forced to journey to Dan's place stone cold sober. But on the plus side, it might just stop me chatting shit. I arrive outside the tidy Georgian townhouse in which Dan's manpad dwelleth. I push the button for Flat 3 on the intercom outside and wait. There comes a buzz and a click before the front door opens back. Showtime!

Arriving outside the door to his apartment, I give it a knock and stand back in anticipation. It opens back to reveal my prince.

'Oh, hey! Come in,' he says, flashing me one of his sexy smiles. 'You look gorgeous,' he adds, planting a kiss on my cheek and causing it to tingle instantly.

The place smells good, certainly not how I expected a bachelor pad to smell. How did I expect a bachelor pad to smell? Like a combination of oily man-scalp, washing that hasn't dried properly and a hint of Lynx Africa somewhere in the mix. I notice he's burning a Jo Malone candle, and, like the candle, I begin to melt a little.

'So, how are you? How's the eye?' he enquires awkwardly.

'Better. But God, I'm so embarrassed,' I reply, biting my lip.

'Look, let's just forget it. Start over with a clean slate, yeah?'

'Yeah,' I nod in agreement, noticing the plethora of cookbooks on the bookshelf. 'You like cookbooks,' I point out as a swift conversation changer, with all the intellect of a pre-schooler.

'Oh, yeah. I like to eat well. Proper, healthy food, you know?' I nod in agreement, recalling myself sat scoffing noodles out of a measuring jug earlier on, happy as a pig in shit.

'I'm doing coq au vin,' he tells me, 'followed by something a little bit naughty...' Mm Coq au Dan, I hope. '...gingerbread soufflé!' he announces, proudly. Maybe later then.

After fifteen minutes of careful small talk, I'm sat at the table enjoying Dan's cuisine, taking extra care not to eat as quickly as usual so as not to appear a gluttonous fiend.

'Any good?' he enquires, pouring the wine.

'Yeah. Yeah, lovely! The coq is very,' – he shoots me a funny look– 'juicy,' I add, in instant regret.

'Sorry, Sorry! Doesn't sound right, does it? What I meant was, it could've been dry, couldn't it? The coq? Not that you'd be serving up dry coq of course, but it's not dry coq it's … moist coq,' I add. And that's before I've had so much as a sip of wine!

'Well, that's good to know!' he laughs.

Despite that moment of verbal diarrhoea, it all appears to be going really rather well and, oh, look! Not a single Gucci-clad Brazilian supermodel in sight! I really cannot think for the life of me what could possibly go wrong this time.

'How's your souffle?' he asks as we get on to dessert. I glance at the caramel coloured souffle before me, instantly reminded of Shitgate.

'Good, really good,' I tell him, hoping he's forgotten about that awkward meeting in the park.

'So, Lizzie. Tell me about you,' he asks, swirling his spoon around the remnants of soufflé.

'About me?' I half-choke.

'Yeah! I want to get to know you better. I mean, what do you like to do in your spare time?'

I carefully consider my response, swiftly deciding not to mention that I occasionally eat ice cream with a knife, fall over a lot and sometimes wee in the shower – I mean, who doesn't?

'Um, I don't know really,' I say slowly.

'Films? Music?' he prompts.

'Well, my favourite film is *Pretty Woman* and I just *love* nineties Dance,' I tell him proudly.

'Cool,' he replies, in a careful-not-to-judge tone. 'Well, I'm a bit of a film buff. I love the theatre too.'

'Oh, yes. Me too,' I exaggerate, wildly.

'Really? What've you seen?'

'Saw Les Misérables once,' I tell him, pronouncing both s's.

'Oh, Les Mis, cool,' he replies.

I continue knocking back the wine and, as Dan clears away the dishes, I feel an impending sense of doom as I notice a poo is beginning to threaten. I've become a bit of a master at holding in poos over the years. If there's one thing I will not do it's poo out in public or, even worse, poo in other people's toilets. God, no! I much prefer to clench until it practically calcifies, although I do end up literally shitting a brick later on. Consequently, I've somehow trained my system to only kick into action when I'm at home. Only, tonight, it's unusually and unexpectedly chosen to kick into action in the middle of dinner with the man of my dreams! Probably the ongoing effects of those bloody laxatives. Bastard! It's as though even my own body is conspiring against me to bring about my downfall.

'You can pissing well wait, mate!' I order under my breath.

Dan joins me back at the table and I cleverly steer the conversation toward fitness, something I know he can talk about until the cows come home while I sit and nod, quaff more wine and mentally undress him. I cross my legs and squeeze my inner thighs together as I sit listening to him speak. Nothing kinky, just holding that damn poo in!

After a period of in-depth discussion about the core, I make the mistake of telling him I've never been able to do a press-up.

'Seriously? Well, it's all in the position. If you can master the position, you really should be able to do them. Look, I'll show you,' he says, getting up and demonstrating beautifully on the kitchen floor.

I check out both the guns and his arse as he does so. Shit, is that drool on the table? Phwoarrr! That's my man, that is!

'Your turn,' he announces, rising to his feet.

'Er … sorry?' I reply, nearly spitting out my wine.

'Well, I love a challenge and you've given me one now!' he says grinning and gesturing to the floor.

'Oh, no. I can't,' I reply, still clenching my

thighs together and trying to ignore the slow cramping of my stomach.

This could get messy for two crucial reasons:

1. I might fart, making it the third occasion in front of this man.

2. I'm touching cloth.

Dan continues to badger me as I frantically rack my brains for solutions to this situation. The mental pressure seems to have the effect of bringing on the poo even faster, thus I quickly determine that if I don't get to a toilet I will most likely shit myself and be forced to leave for the second night on the trot. It would appear there is no solution to this sudden dilemma, other than to get to the toilet and hope for a quick, clean deposit.

'Um, could I just nip to the loo first?' I ask, rising shakily from my seat as beads of sweat start to break out on my forehead.

'Yeah, sure,' he says, showing me the way.

'Thanks,' I reply, willing him to bugger off quickly to the farthest part of the flat and not move an inch until I've done my business.

I head inside and stand with my ear to the door listening for movement, trying to ascertain his whereabouts. I hear him wandering down the hallway and there's a few seconds of silence before strains of music I don't recognise start playing through his living room speakers. Deciding it's safe, I scurry over to the toilet. Thankfully, it's the quick, clean deposit I was looking for and I'm finished in less than a minute. All I need do now is flush it away before the smell has a chance to circulate and the job's a good'un! I turn to flush and gasp out loud at the enormous width and length of the specimen as I catch sight of it down the toilet, nestling under some paper but looking extra offensive against the shiny, brilliant-white porcelain bowl and ultra-bright bathroom lighting.

'Get gone!' I order it, giving the toilet a vigorous flush. I should've known it wouldn't. I should've known that this would be *far* too easy. Instead of flushing, it simply bobs about a bit, then sits there at the bottom smiling back at me. Taunting me. Oh God, no! I try flushing it again but the water hasn't yet returned to the cistern.

I glance casually in the mirrored door of the bathroom cabinet as I wait, frowning as I notice that I appear to be sporting visible facial hair above my top lip. Damn this perfect lighting. In a panic, I grab Dan's electric shaver off the side and begin shaving it.

Moments later, I notice the smell is beginning to circulate as I stand staring in horror down the toilet. All it needs is a little flag poking out of it that reads "Property of Lizzie Bradshaw!". I go all hot and shaky as I yank the handle again, giving it a second good, hard flush, before standing back in desperate, hopeful anticipation ... nope! It just sort of slides and bobs a little, before reverting back to its former position.

'Flush, you big bastard!' I demand through gritted teeth, 'Oh, please! Please!'

I conclude that putting some toilet roll down mid-flush might just help it along. Then, I can wash my hands and hotfoot it back to my prince where I'll keep him busy with fitness talk and push-up demos, allowing the stench to subside before he ventures anywhere near the vicinity and, God forbid, smells my shit!

I give the chain a third forceful yank, tossing some toilet roll down mid-flush. It's looking promising. The loo roll saturates, concealing the offending item. Water level rising ... creeping higher now ... and higher ... and higher. I grimace, watching in utter horror as it rises dangerously close to the top before spilling over onto the bathroom floor, splashing my feet and jeans in the process. In wide-eyed panic, I make a grab for the towel on the handrail, skid in the water and somehow manage to fall backwards into the bath in the process. I remain there with my legs in the air and a stunned expression for a few moments considering my options, or lack of, and thanking God that whatever music Dan is listening to is obviously loud enough to mask the racket in here.

But apart from that saving grace, things are looking decidedly bleak. We're a mere hour and twenty minutes into date 2.0 and I'm already considering a window escape and my immediate resignation. Still, looking at it from a positive perspective, we've surpassed the duration of initial date by thirty-five minutes, so we're improving!

I clamber out of the bath and drop to my knees in prayer position.

'Please, God. Please make this massive shit flush. I promise I'll do your good work if you just make it go away!'

I peep over the toilet bowl and am both shocked and amazed to see the water – gradually at first, then more and more rapidly – descending. A loud glugging sound follows and my monster shit disappears like magic, along with all of the toilet water!

'Bloody hell, it worked!' I muse aloud, making a mental note to attend church from now on.

I grab the hand towel, pat down my jeans and mop up the spillage before opening the teeny, tiny window to help dry the floor and disperse the stench.

'Are you ok?' comes Dan's voice from outside, causing me to jump, 'I should probably have warned you, the plumbing's not the best so go easy on the loo roll.'

Too bloody late, mate!

'It was a number one. I only did a number one, honest!' I call back in a defensive echo.

'It's fine, just thought I better mention it,' he says with a laugh.

'Thanks. Um, I'll be out in a sec. Just ... powdering my nose.'

I furiously scan the bathroom for a place to hide the saturated towel before throwing it out the window in mad panic in the absence of a hiding place. Oh, God. *Now* what?! What the fuck did I do *that* for?! That was a new kind of stupid, even for me.

I take a deep breath and a moment to compose myself. It's uncanny. During my short trip to the loo, I've had a shit and a shave. The only thing I didn't have was a shower, although I did end up in the bath.

'You're wet,' Dan announces as I arrive back at the table.

'Pardon?' I exclaim, instinctively looking down at my crotch.

'Your legs!' he points.

'Oh, yes...' Think, you twat, think! 'Splashback,' I mutter.

'Splashback?'

'Yes, from the ... taps. I ran the taps too quickly

when I washed my hands.'

He seems to buy it thank Christ and date 2.0 continues with me lying on the kitchen floor with the MILDOS. It sounds way better than it is: I'm in the plank position, clenching my arse for all I'm worth simply not to fart. I collapse onto the floor the second I begin to lower into a push-up.

'Use your core,' Dan instructs.

'I don't think I have one of those,' I tell him in a muffled voice, still face-down on the floor.

He bursts out laughing. 'Of course you have. Everybody has!'

'Well, mine doesn't work, then.'

After a further ten minutes of face-planting, Dan is left scratching his head and telling me he's, 'Never seen this before!'.

'Shit! I have the weakest core in the world,' I groan in shame, rolling onto my back.

'No. You're just a unique case,' he says, gazing at me, his face dangerously close to mine. He called me unique and … oh, my God! This is it! Here comes that kiss! I gaze back at him. It's best to close your eyes, isn't it? So, I close my eyes and pucker up in anticipation of the moment I've fantasised about for so long. I wonder what he kisses like and how he tastes as I wait for his lips to touch mine. Moments later, I hear the flip of a switch, running water and Dan's distant voice asking me if I want a coffee. What the fuck? Oh! *Oh!*

I clamber to my feet and politely decline, fully aware that coffee will only give me teacher breath and the last thing I want, assuming we do bloody kiss, is teacher breath. Besides, I haven't had nearly enough wine to confidently allow Dan anywhere near my special area yet.

Sometime later and having acquired the warm, sort of fuzziness that tells me I'm in Merryville, we withdraw to the sofa. I nod, raising my brows and smiling occasionally to look interested as he talks Bond films. There's one on the telly. When is there not? None of it's going in. I couldn't give a toss about Bond; all I care about is Elliott. Dan Elliott.

By 11:40pm we still haven't had that kiss and I'm contemplating forcing myself on him. What bloke invites a gal to his flat, wines her, dines her and doesn't even attempt to cop a feel? I'm seriously starting to wonder what Dan's intentions are.

'It's getting late, I should call a cab,' I announce as a call to action, my face immediately dropping as he replies: 'ok, yeah'. Totally not the response I was angling for. It's down to the toilet episode, I *know* it! The stench must've seeped out under the door and now he's put off at the thought of my potentially dirty undercarriage.

Five minutes later, I get a text telling me my cab is waiting.

'Well, thank you for tonight. It's been,' – disappointingly lacking in sexual activity – '…lovely,' I tell him.

'You're welcome, was nice having you,' he replies.

Wish he would've "had" me for real!

I remain in the doorway staring at him expectantly, like a Labrador waiting for scraps. He stares back. I stare back to him staring back, tipsy enough to believe I'm not fucking leaving until I've had that snog.

'Bye then,' I say.

'Bye.'

'Yes, bye,' I insist.

'Yes, goodnight.'

'Goodnight then.'

Just as I begin to feel like an unwanted charity door-canvasser, he leans in. Yes! Yes! Here it comes … wait? A kiss on the cheek? A poxy kiss on the cheek! Seriously?!

With a face like a kid who just unwrapped a shit Christmas present, I freeze in disappointment.

Just as I turn to leave, we have a bit of a Charles and Di moment as he leans in for another but misses and kisses my ear.

'Oh, sorry,' he mumbles.

I do a silly, fake laugh and turn back to face him. He looks embarrassed. Oh, for God's sake, I'm done! Taking the bull by the horns, I grab his face and snog him.

Whoah! This is amazing! His lips are so soft and I swear to God he tastes better than chocolate. He touches my face, moving his hand up to my hair, running his fingers through it … wait. He's tugging it. Is this some sort of revenge for me pulling out his hair in the canteen?

'Ouch, fuck!' I exclaim.

'Sorry, sorry! My hand's stuck in your hair.'

Good lord, the Bardot backcomb! There's no getting out of that – it's been cemented to within an inch of its life!

He wiggles his fingers, trying to free them but creating even more tension on my scalp.

'Jesus, ouch!'

'Oh, God. I'm so sorry. Come back in for a second. I need more light,' he says, guiding me back into his apartment by the hair. 'Christ, it's really knotty.'

I laugh awkwardly as he battles to free his fingers, before slapping him hard on the thigh in a knee-jerk reaction to a sudden, sharp yank.

'Shit, sorry. I didn't mean to do that,' I gasp, cringing.

He shoots me a strange look, rubbing his thigh.

My phone pings again with a reminder that my cab is waiting.

'Dan, my cab.'

'Yeah, yeah. I'm trying.'

Thanks heavens nobody else is around to witness this farce!

'There!' he announces, having finally untangled his fingers. 'I thought I was going to have to cut myself free at one point!'

I wonder how a doorstep snog could ever possibly turn into a haircut! Well, in my life, anything is possible. Thankfully, Dan doesn't seem too phased as he leans in for another kiss. I leave with the promise of a text, a Grinch-like grin and a spring in my step.

I feel my phone vibrate in my bag before I've even arrived home. Wow, he's keen!

Dan: Hey. Do u know where bathroom towel is? Seems to have vanished x

Yeah, it's outside somewhere

Me: No idea, sorry x

∞∞∞

I try to visit Nanny Bradshaw every other Sunday. Her health isn't the best and she gets lonely living by herself, so we all try to do our bit for her in the midst of our busy lives. Dad bought her a tablet and we'd tried to get her set up on Facebook as a means of keeping in touch more. Initially, the first hurdle was case sensitivity and remembering her password, resulting in her acquiring six different accounts, all of which are still currently active because nobody – least of all her – knows the bloody passwords to deactivate them! On the mere two occasions she did manage to access Facebook, she did little beyond posting 'dvddddddhhhr' as her first and only status, share someone else's status three times trying to read it and get herself hacked in record timing. Beyond this, she found an alternate use for the tablet by using it as a very expensive wedge for the kitchen door! Every now and then, a spam message from one of her six accounts will pop up in my inbox alluding to my being caught on camera doing something illicit and providing me with a link to see it.

Having spent most weekends during the prime of my life holed up in my flat with only a bag of Kettle crisps for company, I empathise more than most with Nanny. She's not getting any younger either – much like myself – such that she's always telling me in her typically crude tone to 'get those eggs of yours fertilised before they shrivel up', so I expect she'll be pleased to learn I am now one step closer in my journey to fertilisation!

Still high on Dan, I'm practically walking on air as I venture out to the car thinking how unusually great life is at the moment. Other than to be a size eight, I couldn't ask for more. I stop off along the way for sweets for the long, ten-mile journey and to replace that fudge I bought Nanny Bradshaw but scoffed myself. I bounce out of the corner shop armed to the teeth with confectionary and a bunch of true-life mags. There's nothing I like more than reading about other people's tumultuous love lives.

As I arrive at some traffic lights with a mouth full of Maltesers, the unmistakably deafening sound of ABBA's "Dancing Queen" draws closer and closer as a baby pink Fiat 500 pulls up alongside me. I instinctively turn to look and do a double-take as I spot the driver, sat swaying and singing their heart out at the wheel. Is that who I think it is? He turns to face me and seems to recognise me too as his face drops and he goes all stiff ... it's only bleeding brutally bad Bazza! My mouth falls open as he puts his fingers to his lips before making a cutthroat gesture and speeding off as soon as the lights turn green. Frozen in shock, my mouth still hanging open, I peer down to find my lap covered with soggy, half-chewed Maltesers. Did that actually happen?! The cars behind begin to blast their horns in fury at me when the lights turn red again.

No sooner had I pulled up outside Nanny Bradshaw's quaint little bungalow than I find myself on my online banking app, cancelling the weekly Direct Debit in the name of Barry Larkin. Well, I can't very well go on being trained by a psychotic ABBA fan who just threatened to kill me, can I? I'd been looking for an excuse to quit since my first session and I'm not sure I'll find a better one than this.

I ring the doorbell and stand back in anticipation. Nanny Bradshaw's murky figure appears in the frosted glass of the front door. Then disappears. Oh no, she's back, fumbling and faffing with her keys. I glance at my watch as she drops them, muttering obscenities. By the time she even gets the key in the lock, I've already read an online news article and replied with an emphatic "no" to a text from Levi asking if I got a belly full of Dan-Marrow last night.

'Ooh! Ello! Which one are you then?' she coos, smiling broadly as she opens the door.

'Lizzie,' I remind her, trying not to roll my eyes.

'That's it! My Des's girl. D'you know, I've got that many grandkids, it'd be a bleedin' wonder if I could remember 'em all, even if I wasn't losin' me marbles!'

'It's alright Nanny. I'm used to it by now.'

She looks me up and down.

'Well, *you've* put on some timber! You used to be right skinny,' she says disappointedly.

'Nanny, I've never been skinny in my life, even as a foetus I was probably fat,' I remind her as she pulls me into one of her vice-like hugs, squishing me with her massive bosom; a bosom which earned her the secret nickname "Nanny Jugs" among her many grandchildren.

We venture into the sitting room, where what starts as 'Ow's work?'" somehow evolves to a full-blown account of the holidays she used to take with Grandad, all the restaurants they ate in and the many people they met along the way – tales I've heard a thousand times over. Funny that she remembers things from fifty years ago with such vivid detail but couldn't tell you what she'd had for breakfast that morning. Doesn't stop her chatting, mind you; an hour in and I still haven't got a word in edgeways!

'You pregnant yet?' she suddenly asks out of nowhere, her face beaming.

'No Nanny, not yet.'

'You sure? You look like you might be.'

'Charming! Well, if I am, then it was an immaculate conception.'

'Oh yes of course, cos you've never 'ad a fella, 'ave yer?'

'Well, actually Nanny, I've just started seeing somebody. We had our second date last night.'

'Really? 'Ow wonderful! 'Ave you had coitus yet?' she asks, her eyes wide in delight.

'No, not yet. But we did have our first kiss,' I say, trying not to think too much about how Dan's lips felt on mine.

'Just a kiss? What, on a second date? What's the madder, you frigid or summin?'

'No, nanny. I think he's a bit—'

'What, gay?' she says.

'No. Er. Well, I did at one point, but he's not,' I confirm with a shake of my head.

'Sounds ter me like you've gotch yaself a gentleman there, Lisa! Any other bloke would've been in yer knickers before yer can say Jack Robinson!'

'He's a proper gent, that's for sure,' I agree, dreamily. Hang on, Lisa? Who the fuck's Lisa?!

'Well, I'm delighted for yer darlin'. You deserve some 'appiness,' Nanny Bradshaw concludes. 'Yer wanna 'old onto him, mind, someone with your track record.'

Delightful.

'What do you mean, my track record?'

'Well, you've not 'ad the luck with fellas, 'ave yer? There was a time not even a sniper would take you aat!' She begins laughing hysterically, a sound not dissimilar to a machine gun.

Nice! So, my dementia-plagued grandmother can't remember my name but she does recall perfectly well that, where men are concerned, I'm as useless as tits on a bull. The shame.

Chapter 7:

It's Official!

If I wasn't disappointed enough to learn my prince is in training all day in the upstairs meeting room, imagine my disappointment to learn that Rachel will be there with him, sat next to him no doubt with either her legs or her pert, ample breasts on display, flicking her hair and being all touchy-feely. Just the thought of them up there together fills me with rage. I know Dan has chosen to date me, whether that's voluntary or involuntary, but I can't say with any confidence he'd stay true to a walrus when someone like her offers it to him on a plate. Still, at the end of the day, I'm the one who's had his tongue down my throat, not her!

The above statement is immediately called into question when I bump into Fat Ann in the loos.

'So ... you're dating Dan,' she remarks, a hint of poison in her tone.

'Yes. Yes, I am actually,' I reply smugly.

'Going well is it?'

'Yes, actually. I think it rather is,' I reply.

'Hmmm,' she mumbles, raising her eyebrows suggestively as she pumps the soap dispenser.

I stare at her for a few moments before a sudden burst of anger kicks in.

'If you've got something to say, say it!' I demand, locking eyes with her in the mirror.

'Sorry?'

'Well, you've clearly got something to say,' I continue.

'No?'

'Well, that's a bloody first!' I exclaim as her head wobbles in outrage.

'Pardon?'

'Come off it, it's obvious you were alluding to something.'

'No?' she repeats, not even trying to sound convincing.

She hesitates for all of three seconds before the urge to spill overcomes her.

'Well, I think you should know that Dan and Rachel were seen getting into a cab together last Friday night. The night of your date.'

I stare at her with furrowed brows.

'So? I … left early and she was there at the same restaurant. Doesn't mean anything.'

'I thought you were asked to leave and banned for life?' Fat Ann sniggers.

'No? No! Who told you that?'

'Rachel did.' The bitch!

'Well … well, she's bloody lying!' I practically shout before viciously turning on the tap.

'Well, I'm not getting involved. All I can tell you is it was very late and it was just them two, all alone, in a cab!' she adds, stirring the pot *and* licking the bloody spoon!

I think back to my moment of departure and how I'd longed for Dan to chase after me. But he didn't, because the whole time he was with *her*!

I feel like I'm going to cry, but I'm not about to let Fat Ann see.

'So, what? It doesn't mean anything,' I snarl. 'Dan and I are fine! For your information, we went on to have a wonderful second date at his place. He cooked "coq au vern" … or whatever the bloody hell it was and we kissed *and* he put his tongue in my mouth *and* he touched my face and we're fine, ok?!' I blurt out before furiously shutting off the tap, storming out of the loos and returning to my desk where I sit questioning everything.

What is Dan playing at, sharing cabs with

raven-haired temptresses? Why did they leave so late? Is he leading me on? Am I part of some bet? I think back to Nanny Bradshaw's crude honesty yesterday. She's right, not even a sniper would take me out, so why would Dan Elliott?

I skulk into the staff room at lunch, flying into an instant rage as I spot her sat next to him.

'I'm starting to wonder if you're growing out of Dan's arse!' I exclaim, storming over.

'Not again!' she groans, rolling her eyes.

'If I throw a stick, will you fuck off?' I demand, livid.

'Calm down, Lizzie,' a confused-looking Dan tells me.

'No, I won't. I'm entitled to know what's going on.'

Dan looks at me, his eyebrows furrowed.

'Sorry? I've no idea what you're talking about,' he says slowly.

'Did you, or did you not share a cab with *her* the night of our date?'

'I do have a name!' Rachel points out.

'Shut it, bitch!' I tell her. Her mouth falls open and I turn my attention back to Dan. 'Well? Apparently, you left a lot later than I did. Together!' I probe.

'Well, yes, the food arrived and I hadn't eaten

since lunch so I figured as I was going to be paying for it anyway, I might as well eat it. And yes, we did share a cab Lizzie, but only to save on the fare. We live close to each other and we went our separate ways after that,' he explains.

I glance at Rachel, who raises her HD brows suggestively in contradiction of both the girl code *and* everything Dan just said. Seeing red, I point my finger sternly in her face, going to speak but hesitating when I can think of nothing cool or clever enough to say. Ugh! What was I thinking? There's just no competing with the cow.

'You know what, I don't think this is going to work Dan,' I huff, trying to panic him.

'What do you mean?'

'I mean us,' I say, hesitating slightly as I realise the full meaning of that tiny, little word. Dan picks up on it too.

'Us? Lizzie, we've only had two, well one full date. There isn't really an "us" yet,' he says.

And that was it. The statement that told me all I needed to know, straight from the Sex God's mouth. There *is* no "us".

Perfectly humiliated, and without another word, I turn and storm out.

After feigning a migraine and asking Sue if I could leave early, I'm reminded of my poor attendance record – which apparently stays poor even if you *were* the star seller of the day a few weeks ago – and told to see how I feel in a bit. What is this, junior school? Well, I can tell you how I feel right now Sue: pissed off, humiliated, stupid, deluded, unworthy, a laughingstock ... and that's just for starters. It's already the hardest thing in the world to be at work when shit's going down in your personal life, but it's even bloody harder when the root cause of said shit is actually here in the building, sashaying around with a Cheshire cat grin on her smug face.

I eat my lunch in the loos, staring into space as various dramatic fight scenes play out in my mind – all of them involving Rachel and all with *me* victorious ... obviously. I spend the rest of my shift ignoring everyone and somehow make it through the day without beating anyone to death with an office chair.

'Lizzie, wait up,' comes Dan's voice from behind as I'm leaving.

I ignore him, continuing to walk.

'Lizzie? Hey, wait up!' he repeats.

I continue to ignore him, clicking my heels louder in demonstration of my overwhelming anger.

He jumps out in front of me, grabbing me by the shoulders.

'Oh, come on, Lizzie! This is silly!' he says, a hint of a laugh in his voice.

I look at him directly before turning and walking in the other direction, making it clear that I do not wish to talk. God, a few weeks ago I would be a gibbering wreck if Dan Elliott deigned to talk to me outside of office hours, but *now* look at me!

'Lizzie, talk to me!' he pleads as I continue to walk away. I close my eyes momentarily, trying to turn my anger into words I can throw at him. Shit. I've just walked right into the bloody bins. Looks like I'm still a clumsy twat.

'Lizzie, this is madness. Will you just talk to me, please?'

I stop in my tracks and turn to face him.

'I did, earlier. You told me all I needed to know,' I sniff, breaking my staunch silence.

'I told you the truth. Nothing happened with Rachel!'

'What does it matter? There's no "us", remember? If you want to take cabs with tarts, that's your business.'

'Oh, come on! I never meant it like that,' he says.

'Oh, really? The phrase "there isn't really an us yet" has some other meaning I don't know about?' I ask mockingly.

'Look, all I meant was it's early days. You were acting like we're engaged or something. It spooked me a bit. I mean, I have a lot of female friends and clients. You can't go shouting the odds at them like you do Rachel the whole time,' he explains.

'I know that, but surely you see what she's doing? Don't tell me you haven't noticed that she flirts her tits off with you!'

Much to my annoyance, Dan lets out a short laugh.

'Lizzie, she's like that with most blokes! Women like her usually are.'

'You've not noticed that wherever you go, she's there?! Oh, and let me guess, you don't find her the slightest bit attractive, either!' I accuse, his laugh lighting a fire inside me.

'Well, of course she's attractive. But that doesn't mean I want to date her. She's all fur coat and no knickers. She's not the kind of woman I'd choose to date,' he says.

'Jeez, and I am? Tell me, out of all the women you could choose Dan, I'm dying to know, why me?' I challenge him, making a babyish gesture toward my size.

He pauses, his eyes moving from my face down my body before returning to meet my eyes, taking in everything about the gesture I had just made. But then ...

'Why *not* you?' he asks.

I stare back at him in disbelief.

'I felt so humiliated today,' I tell him, fighting against my bottom lip which has gone into an erratic spasm.

'Well, if I made you feel like that, then I'm sorry. That's the last thing I'd ever want,' he replies, his voice dipping with emotion.

'Ok. Well, whatever,' I say, attempting to walk off and regain my former stoicism. But just as I turn to leave, his arm lands on mine and grabs me, pulls me back towards him and he snogs me. The stubborn half of me wants to resist and break away from him, but the other half is kissing him back and loving every second – Dan Elliott and Lizzie Bradshaw, kissing like teenagers outside the office! As we eventually come up for air, I notice Fat Ann's shitty little car lurking behind us in the carpark. Though it's getting dark, there's enough light from the streetlights to make out her round nosey face staring out at us. Ha!

'Lizzie, will you be my girlfriend?' Dan asks suddenly.

I pause, unsure of how we've moved so quickly from arguing to this.

'Don't say it if you don't mean it,' I say, hoping with every sodding fibre of my being that he does.

'I *do* mean it. I … think you're magic, Lizzie,' he stammers.

Hmmm, well, *I'm* not … but all this probably is!

'Well in that case, yes!' I reply, glancing back in Fat Ann's direction with a smug smile creeping up my face. When I see that she's still there, I pull Dan closer and we go for round two of tonsil tennis.

I don't know if it's the high of Dan having made things official or just plain stupidity but I've invited him to mine to spend the weekend together. Quite how I'd forgotten I'm penniless, living off of 15p noodles and that it's still a fortnight until I'm paid, I don't know. In my mind I was seeing candlelight, two star-crossed lovers and a three-course banquet but in reality, it'll be two star-crossed lovers with my last crust of bread between us.

I spend the next hour Googling "how to make a meal out of nothing" and contemplating a trip to the food bank. Luckily, Mother makes a typically unannounced weeknight appearance and, having waited a lifetime to be offered a cup of tea and finally resorting to make one herself, is left appalled by my empty fridge and cupboards and subsequently thrusts forty pounds at me to buy some groceries, which, after a short period of resistance – around five seconds – I snatch like a scavenging seagull, while firmly reminding her that I am an independent woman and can take care of myself.

I spend the week busier than a one-legged man in an arse-kicking contest bringing my living quarters to an acceptable standard of cleanliness and making forty pounds stretch to record lengths.

Saturday morning dawns and I've been up since sparrow fart. I've hoovered, I've mopped, I've de-cobwebbed, I've de-pubed, I've polished, I've scrubbed, I've primped and I've preened – and not all in that order. Finally, I'm ready to let the crown see the jewels! Or in my case, the prince see the pauper.

The buzzer goes a little before lunchtime and Mr Wonderful arrives outside my door armed with his weekend bag, a bunch of pink peonies and a sexy smile – a vast improvement on the last sight I observed through my spy hole! No offence, Pervy Bob.

We re-acquaint with a kiss.

'I'm taking you to lunch, beautiful!' he smiles. 'Then I thought we could go see a film after. My treat,' he adds. It would have to bloody be!

'Perfect!' I reply, going in for another kiss just as the buzzer takes us both by surprise.

'Are you expecting somebody?' he asks.

'No, nobody,' I reply casually on my way over to the intercom.

'Hello?'

'Elizabeth Bradshaw?' the disembodied voice asks.

'Yes, who's this?' I ask brusquely, conscious that I am wasting vital seconds that could be otherwise spent with Dan on the sofa. Or kitchen table. Or bed.

'We're bailiffs. We've been instructed to visit your property to remove goods and furniture to the value of £285 in settlement of your long-standing debt owed to the city council.'

My heart stops, my blood runs cold and time seems to stand still as I take this in. Here I am, about to spend the weekend with my newly, miraculously and painstakingly acquired hot boyfriend whom I've invited over for a romantic weekend stay and the fucking bailiffs have just arrived to take the furniture. You couldn't make it up. This cannot be happening! I didn't think I could top the disaster date at Luigi's, nor the mammoth shit at his house, but this is off the bloody scale. This is the nightmare of all nightmares!

'There must be some mistake. I don't have debts!' I tell him in a high-pitched voice, going all hot.

'No, there's been no mistake, madam. It's your debt and you will have received several letters about it up to now.' An image of unopened letters thrust into one of the kitchen drawers surfaces in my mind's eye. Oh, is that what they were about?

'Well, now is really not a good time. Could you come back later?' I ask.

'I'm afraid not. We have a court order,' he replies, his tone suggesting he's less than five seconds away from physically breaking down the door.

I glance behind me at Dan who looks horrified.

'Er ... this is a little awkward, but I've just got to let the bailiffs in before we can go out. They have a warranty,' I tell him.

'A *what*?' he remarks, confusedly.

∞∞∞

I've been Dan's girlfriend for less than a week and already I owe him £285! Oh, the shame.

'You really didn't have to do that,' I tell him as we stroll hand in hand in the city en route to lunch.

'Yes, I did. We wouldn't have had anything to sit on when we get back if I hadn't!' he laughs.

'How can you laugh about something like this?' I ask.

'How can you not?' he replies, squeezing my hand.

'Well, my furniture's old and crap anyway. They'd have been doing me a bloody favour taking it away,' I whinge as we enter the restaurant.

The one thing I have been able to take from the nightmare bailiff situation – aside from Dan's money – is that I no longer need to put on a pretence. In the short time we've been seeing each other, he's already seen the worst of me and the worst has already happened in front of him. So, I figure there's no point in trying to be someone I'm not and, thus, I find myself a lot more chilled in his company.

As we share a massive cookie dough sundae together, laughing about our school days, I find myself feeling a strange sense of déjà vu. Not in the sense that I'm about to be kicked out of the place and banned for life, but in the sense that I've known him a lot longer than I actually have, like in another life or something. I can't quite put my finger on it. Lunch is rounded off with a cosy cinema film. Cosy but not "kinky cosy", rather "falling asleep and having to be woken up by Dan at the end" cosy. That's another thing I've learned about Mr Wonderful, he has a supremely comfortable shoulder on which I just left a large patch of dribble. I've no idea what the film was about but Dan tells me it was pretty good.

After being treated to the perfect day, I was keen to return the favour with a blinding meal for two, which turns out to be exactly that when the electric meter runs out and we're plunged into darkness. After scurrying around on all fours trying to find the meter box to push the emergency credit button, dinner finally resumes.

'That was delicious. Really worth the wait. Where did you get the recipe?' Dan asks out of interest.

'Er, it's one of Gordon Ramsay's,' I lie, clearing away the plates and forcing all evidence of the Marks and Spencer meal for two containers as far down into the kitchen bin as I possibly can.

I'm suddenly all overcome with nerves as I recall that the MILDOS is actually staying over and bouncy-bouncy is almost a given. Though I've imagined it a million times over and it's pretty much all I've thought about for the past year, I've actually been living like a nun – aside from the swearing and gluttony – during the many years that have passed since my first and only time with Asperger's Andrew in his Nan's bed. Don't ask, it was not my proudest moment.

Someone like Dan, on the other hand, is bound

to have shagged countless women. I'm totally out of my depth here. I don't even know how to suggest us going to bed without it sounding like I'm asking for him to fill me in like an application. The nerves worsen as I look up from my position curled into his side observing his eyes growing more and more red and hooded as the hours go on.

'Um … shall we … er? Shall we …'

He looks down at me in anticipation.

'Journey up the wooden hill to Bedfordshire?' I finally manage. Bloody Mother and her sayings.

'You have stairs?' he asks in surprise.

'Duh, no! It's a flat, silly!' I reply, getting up to switch off the television.

I make nervy small talk en route to the bedroom where Dan begins taking off his shirt as I busy myself picking my jaw up off the floor, pretending not to have noticed his amazing body. Jesus Christ! Am I really seeing this? How in the hell is someone like me about to get in bed with someone like *him*?

I take myself off to the bathroom where I pour myself into the one and only pair of sexy undies I own, brush and floss my teeth, discreetly freshen my make-up and conceal a spot I notice on my left tit. Taking a deep breath, I put on what I hope is a sexy walk and venture back to the bedroom, where I promptly observe Dan is already in bed ... fast asleep! Bugger, bugger, bugger! I get into bed and stare at the back of his head; the very head I've been staring at from my desk for nigh-on a year, hoping, praying and wishing I could merely get within touching distance of and now, here I am. Here *we* are. I shimmy closer to him, wrap my arm around him, cuddling him like a favourite childhood teddy, breathing him in. I eventually fall asleep with a very silly grin on my face.

Having woken repeatedly during the night to check my prince was still there and not just a figure of my dirty imagination, I wake with gritty eyes and a sense of relief when I observe the back of his beautiful head still present beside me in my bed. *My* bed; the loneliest place in existence and birthplace to some of my lewdest fantasies of this man. My sense of relief soon gives way to dread when I consider the following: 1. I look rough as arseholes, and 2. I have morning breath.

I slip out of bed to deal with both issues before he wakes. He's still asleep by the time I'm done and, after a brainwave, I decide I'll wake him with a romantic breakfast in bed, wowing him with my sweet thoughtfulness and Nigella Lawson-like appeal.

Flinging open the kitchen cupboards in search of ingredients for said romantic breakfast, I quickly determine two options: bugger all or sweet FA. Hmm, what do you eat when you've got nothing in? Eggs! I check the fridge and am relieved to note there are two left in the carton. Boiled eggs and soldiers for two it is then! I need to be quick so I can go in and surprise him before he wakes.

Deciding it'll be quicker to boil the eggs in the microwave, I shove them into a glass bowl, half fill it with water and set the microwave off for five minutes before taking out two plates, some cutlery and the bread and butter for the toast. Quiet as a mouse, I go to take out a serving tray before jumping clean out of my skin when, around three minutes into cooking time, a sound I can only describe as the biggest fucking bang ever comes from the microwave behind me. I screw my eyes shut and freeze, rooted to the spot in utter shock. I eventually open them, turning slowly behind me to find the explosion has blown the microwave door off its hinges, as well as left it powerless.

Dan skids into the kitchen, still in his tighty-whities, to find myself, the kitchen, and now his feet covered in bits of boiled egg. I don't know how he likes his eggs in the morning but I'm guessing *not* on the floor or up the wall.

'What happened? I thought a bloody bomb had gone off!' he gasps, his eyes wide in panic.

I remain open-mouthed, totally speechless and feeling pretty fucking far from Nigella Lawson.

Just as I conclude the day could not have got off to a worser start, the buzzer alerts me to an unannounced early-morning visitor. Nope, not the bailiffs. Worse than the sodding bailiffs. It's Mother.

'I'm really busy, could we do this another time?' I plead down the intercom.

'No, we can't. I'm here now,' she replies in the authoritarian tone notorious for reducing Dad and I to total doormats.

'Oh, okay. Come up then,' I say grudgingly, proceeding to sweat like a pig in heat.

I turn to Dan, still in his pants, who is valiantly trying to clean up the remnants of breakfast with a towel.

'Quick, go and hide somewhere!' I order him in a panic.

'Hide? Is that really necessary at our ages?' he asks in surprise.

'Trust me, it *is* where my Mother's concerned,' I tell him.

He gives me a funny look before hurrying off to the bedroom.

'What on earth has happened in here?!' Mother cries upon bursting into the flat and observing the aftermath of romantic breakfast in bed-cum-nuclear blast.

'And go and put some clothes on, your father will be here any minute. He's just gone to fetch teabags, milk and sugar from the corner shop so we can have a cup of tea.'

I hurry to the bedroom where Dan is causally taking his time to select clean clothes from his holdall, blissfully ignorant to the severity of the situation.

'Hurry up!' I urge in a shout-whisper. 'I thought you'd have been dressed by now!'

'Who are you talking to?' comes Mother's voice from outside the door.

'Er, nobody! Nobody!' I reply, a fraction of a second too late.

A pointless, single knock follows before the bedroom door bursts open. Dan makes a hasty dash behind the curtain as Mother brazenly strolls in.

'Good grief, it smells like a kennel in here. Get some air into the place for heaven's sake,' she barks, striding over toward the window in what feels like dramatic slow motion.

I screw my eyes tightly shut, cover my face with hands and brace myself for the inevitable.

'Gahhhhhhhhhhhhhhhhhhhh!' she screams, upon pulling back the curtain to discover a terrified looking chap stood in his underpants.

I gulp, clearing my throat.

'Mother, I'd like you to meet Dan. Dan, meet Mother'.

Though my sorry life has been one awkward incident after another, I've never felt more awkward than now as the four of us sit drinking tea; Mother with a face like a pickled onion and Dad picking bits of boiled egg off the sofa around him.

'You didn't tell us you were in a relationship,' Mother remarks, having finally – and regrettably – found her voice. 'I'd have much preferred to meet your gentleman friend in a more suitable setting.'

'Well, we've only really been a couple since Monday,' I stupidly blurt, observing her subsequent look of horror.

'I hope you used protection!' she grunts at me quietly through gritted teeth.

'We'd best make a move, Petunia,' Dad announces, clearly sensing my anguish.

'Nice to meet you mate,' he says, reaching across to shake Dan's hand.

'You too Mr Bradshaw'.

'Call me Des,' he says, smiling.

'Nice to meet you too, Mrs Bradshaw,' Dan adds. His face falls slightly as she walks off with her back to him.

'Yes,' she replies unenthusiastically over her shoulder.

I wince in shame as I turn to face Dan the minute the front door is closed behind them. Paying my debt, cleaning up the pig's arse I made of breakfast and then being made to feel like a naughty schoolkid really should be the final nail in the coffin of this unlikely relationship. A moment of silence ensues, before we both simultaneously burst out laughing.

Whether it's down to my scary mother having been the ultimate turn-off or Dan just being a gentleman, bedtime cuddles are, once again, of the non-coital variety! Bugger!

Chapter 8:

Worst Foot Forward

A fortnight on from Mother having discovered Dan hiding behind the bedroom curtains in his smalls, I have two concerns: A. we still haven't moved past first base, and B. I'm about to meet his family!

Although A is fundamentally the most concerning concern, B makes it less concerning and given that I'm shitting my pants at the prospect of B, I deem B the most concerning concern of the two ... well I know what I mean, anyway.

'Relax, they're very normal people,' Dan assures me loudly over my blaring *Ultimate 90's Dance* album as I follow his directions and steer us through the sweeping, leafy country lanes to his parents' barbecue.

'Are you implying my parents aren't?' I challenge him, suspiciously.

'No. Of course, not. With the exception of your

mother, of course.'

'And do you think *I'm* normal?' I bite. Hmm, think it might be PMT week.

'Don't be silly Lizzie, of course I do!'

'Hmmm! Silly-normal then?!' Am I spoiling for a fight with the man I adore? Yep! It's definitely PMT week.

'Do a right here and it's the third house on the left.'

We arrive at Dan's parents' modest four bed semi, outside which several cars are crammed onto the drive and adjacent pavement.

'Christ! How many cars do they need? There's nowhere to park.'

'Only two of them are Mum and Dad's, the rest belong to the family guests who got here on time. We're late, remember?' he adds.

'So, it's *my* fault we're late?' I retort, immediately regretting it.

'I never said that,' he replies. 'Look, you'll just have to park at the side of the house, down this cul-de-sac.'

As we get out the car, I hear Dan's family chatting and laughing in the garden from the other side of the fence. They do all sound very normal, thankfully. And aww, bless! I can hear Dan's nephew. Dan's told me so much about him, he sounds like a proper little love. Kids make for great conversational icebreakers too.

I find myself starting to relax as we head for the front door where Dan ascends the steps and rings the bell which triggers instant, incessant barking. An overly made-up ageing blonde, disguised as someone far younger, answers the door and squeals in delight as she forcibly grabs Dan and pulls him toward her ample bosom in a massive bear hug.

'Oooooooooooooh, my darling Danny Boy! Come to mummy!'

No sooner has this happened than an enormous Great Dane comes flying out of the door, leaps up and knocks me straight down on my arse with an almighty thud. From here, it turns and reverse-mounts me, slobbering all over my face and moving down my chest to my stomach. As I lie back on the gravel, aghast, I find my eyes fixed on its colossal balls which are swinging dangerously close to my face.

'Help', I plead pathetically as I continue wrestling the hellhound, watching in dismay as that bloody hug goes on ... and on ... and on ... and on.

'Er, Mum, this is Lizzie,' comes Dan's muffled voice from between her cleavage.

She nudges Dan aside – finally – and peers down at me. It's either my PMT-induced paranoia or her face definitely did just fall a bit as she clocked me, lying awkward as arse on her gravel driveway with her enormous dog on top of me.

'Hee hee, come away now Norbert, leave the poor gal alone,' she chuckles, walking toward me.

'Here, boy!' Dan whistles, prompting Norbert and his almighty balls to finally get to fuck.

'It's so lovely to meet you. I'm mummy ... Sharon,' she tells me, giving me a far briefer bear hug.

'Hi Sharon, yes and you,' I smile, bending down to retrieve the hoop earring she just knocked clean out of my ear with her massive tits. She leaves me on the driveway scrabbling to get it back in as she returns her attention to darling Danny Boy, whom she grabs around the waist and marches straight into the house, chattering incessantly as she goes.

'How've you been squidgems? Not working too hard, I hope! Are you getting enough sleep? Eating enough?'

Their voices trail off as I wander in behind them like a stray kitten, wide-eyed and dazed. I didn't realise "they're very normal people" was synonymous with "my mother still breastfeeds me". Ooh, that was bitchy but then again it is *that* week.

I walk zombie-like through the kitchen and out the back door into the garden where his family stop talking to stare at me as if I'm some sort of ghostly apparition that has just manifested before their eyes. The prolonged pause only serves to confirm their shock that Dan is romancing a fatty.

'You must be Dan's girlfriend,' his apron-clad dad finally manages, stepping away from the barbecue to shake my hand vigorously. 'Hungry?' he adds.

Christ, let me get in the place first! I may be overweight, but don't assume I'm constantly hungry. I mean, yeah, I *am* hungry 99.9% of the time but that's not the point. You don't just assume an overweight person has a stomach like a bottomless pit! Before I can even reply, his back is turned to me and he's loading a plate with food.

'Come and sit down,' Dan urges from over on the lawn.

I nod in agreement as I wander up the garden steps, my look of relief quickly replaced by disappointment as I note Mummy Sharon has parked herself on one side of him and a yet-unidentified bloke is sat on the other.

'I'm Mark, Dan's bro,' he says, shaking my hand. 'Pleased to meet you!'

There's a prolonged pause as neither of them get up to allow me to sit next to my boyfriend, forcing me to return back down the steps and take up a seat next to the scowling old woman, who I assume is Granny, sat by the fence near to the barbecue.

'Hello, I'm Lizzie,' I greet her.

'Aye. Ye'er Danny's wee wench are ye?' she remarks, taking me by surprise with her heavy Scottish accent. 'Nay so wee, mind,' she brazenly adds, taking me by even greater surprise. Cheeky bitch!

'Here we are! Tuck in!' Dan's dad urges, handing me an enormous plate piled high with food. I stare down at it, my heart sinking as I spot a massive lamb kebab staring back at me. I don't eat lamb. Just the smell of it makes me feel sick.

'Thank you, Mr Elliott.'

'No, no. Call me Rob,' he urges.

I nod, peering down at the giant corn on the cob which I can't imagine is going to be at all possible to eat elegantly in front of these people. I begin to pick at the heap of chicken wings, relieved as a woman wanders over with Dan's little nephew and introduces them both.

'Hi, I'm Lucie, Dan's sister,' she smiles. 'This is Toby, Dan's nephew.'

'Hello, aren't you cute?' I smile, reaching forward to give him a playful pat. He backs away in fright as though he's just been introduced to the bogeyman.

'You're not going to eat me, are you?' he asks,

looking worried.

'Toby! Don't be so rude!' his mum scolds him as Granny unashamedly laughs her arse off next to me.

'No, definitely not,' I assure him, my cheeks reddening. I look over toward Dan, willing him to come over and sit with me, but he's far too busy drinking beer and laughing on his phone with his brother to even notice.

'Do you and Uncle Dan rub willies together?' Toby asks out of nowhere as he pelts me with the biscuits Lucie has just given him.

Chance would be a fine bloody thing I think to myself, dodging the many Oreos sailing my way while noting decidedly that Toby is definitely less "little love" and more "little shit".

'Oh, God. I'm so sorry! He's been coming out with that sort of stuff lately. I've no idea where he gets it from. Nursery probably!' Lucie blathers, grabbing Toby's wrist and prising the packet of biscuits from him.

'That's alright, he's a kid. That's what kids do,' I politely reassure her, my head jerking violently as Toby runs behind me and starts to kick the shit out of the back of my chair.

'So, how long have you been with Dan?' Lucie asks, steering both the conversation and attention away from her badly behaved child.

'Around a month now,' I tell her, recoiling in shock as Toby puts a half-eaten Oreo down my back.

'Well, I'm fair surprised! Dan doesnay usually go fae lassies like you,' Crabby Gran tells me, unapologetically.

'Lassies like me?' I ask. She should've just said "fatties", I know it's what they're all thinking.

'Do you need the toilet, Toby?' Lucie asks, awkwardly trying to reroute the conversation again.

'No,' he replies, looking up from the side of my chair where he's been quietly raking through my handbag.

'I think you do,' she insists, grabbing him by the shoulder and marching him away. It's all I can do to not give him the finger as he retreats towards the house, but then I remember that he is only a kid. Still. Little shit.

'Eat up, Lizzie. There's plenty more where that came from,' Rob winks from the barbecue.

Ugh! Even with my stomach being the bottomless pit it is and me as polite as I am, I still can't bring myself to eat that lamb kebab. I look up at Dan, hoping I can catch his attention, beckon him over and sneak it onto his plate, but I think he's quite forgotten I'm here by the look of it. I peer around the garden – it looks like everyone's forgotten I'm here! Even Crabby Gran's attention is placed fully on the enormous cigarette she's battling to light in the wind. I seize the moment and toss the kebab over the fence next to me. I peer down at the giant corn on the cob. That's got to go too. Between them they've managed to make me feel like Jabba the Hutt enough already without me adding to it, sitting crammed into a plastic garden chair with my gob around a fuck-off great corn on the cob like some vastly overweight gerbil. I look around for somewhere to put my plate.

'Oh, finished already? My, you are a hungry girl. I'll do you seconds,' Rob announces in his jolly sing-song voice as he clocks my empty plate.

'I don't want anything else, thank you,' I insist firmly, taking him by surprise.

'Alright. Well, how about a drinkie then?' he asks, holding out a wine glass. Now you're talking. Bloody fill her up!

'Oh, yes please. That'll be lovely,' I reply, hoping his wine measures are as enormous as his food portions, before swiftly recalling I'm driving and subsequently finding myself forced to begrudgingly decline. As Dan, who seems to be very much enjoying himself, slowly gets drunk on lager, I'm fast becoming drunk on apathy. Why did I bring the bloody car? I should've let Mr Wonderful live up to his namesake and bear the responsibility, leaving me to sit and switch off and get pissed, which I find is the only thing to be done in these situations.

Oh, Christ! The hellhound's back. I've tried not to make eye contact, but it's too bloody late. He lollops over and plunges his snout straight into my crotch as I grab his face and desperately try to steer it away.

'Go away!' I mutter quietly under my breath. 'Get!'. He ignores me, sniffing aggressively and forcing his head further and further between my legs.

'Ha ha ha,' I laugh pathetically as all eyes begin to turn in my direction. Why are they just bloody sitting there? Bastards! If they want to keep enormous, rampant hounds, they ought to at least keep them under control. Just when I think I've reached the peak of total twat, Rob walks out from the house with a camcorder.

'Here she is! The lovely Lizzie, Danny Boy's new girlfriend!' he announces to the recorder dramatically as I go all stiff. Toby proves to be an unlikely saviour when he blasts Norbert with his super-soaker water gun before immediately undoing all good by turning the gun on me, leaving me pissed off and panda-eyed. Obviously, everyone laughs and the camcorder pans away to the barbecue and other, drier members of the family, leaving Toby and I in a staring battle.

'Are you having a baby?' he enquires, prodding

my spare tyre with the end of his gun. 'UNCLE DAN, IS SHE HAVING A BABY?!' he shouts over to Dan, who pretends not to have heard.

I roll my eyes, exasperated, as Toby takes a tampon from my bag and begins unwrapping it. Jesus, this kid doesn't stop!

'Could you put that back please?' I ask him, politely. He continues taking it out and proceeds to pull off the applicator, dangling it upside-down and swinging it like a pendulum in my face, completely ignoring me. A sudden pent-up rage explodes within me.

'Put that back now, you little fucker!' I tell him through gritted teeth, looking up in horror to see Rob's camera pointing in my face. Yep. He just caught all that on film.

'What?!' I challenge, noting his shocked expression. 'I think I've done bloody well to keep it together up to now!'

'Lizzie, he's just a child!' Rob gasps in disbelief, still filming.

Everyone falls silent around me. I gulp as I observe their shocked expressions. Oh, but it's about to get worse. A man's head appears above the fence next to me brandishing the lamb kebab in one hand and the massive corn on the cob in the other. Rob directs the video camera in his direction.

'Watcha playin' at chucking these over me fence!?' he roars. I wince as Rob directs the camera back in my direction and all eyes fall on me.

'For goodness' sake. Turn the camera off Rob,' Mummy Sharon calls over at him.

'You didn't throw those over the fence, did you Lizzie?' Rob challenges me.

I clear my throat.

'No!?' I lie, 'I must've dropped them by accident'.

'What, over a seven-foot fence?!' he answers.

Shit.

'Well, *yes*, actually, I did throw them,' I admit. 'I happen to have a high regard for fluffy little lambs which I think should be frolicking in meadows, not cruelly snatched from their mums when they've barely lived to be made into lamb kebabs and covered in mint sauce!'

Silence.

'But you ate the chicken wings though, didn't you?' Rob argues.

'Yes, yes. But that's different. Chickens aren't … chickens aren't that cute beyond being chicks,' I add, wishing the ground would swallow me up. There's only one thing for it. 'I'm going to leave now,' I announce, rising from my plastic garden chair which rises with me. I forcibly prise it from my arse and glance over at Dan who looks on frozen in shock as I storm out. I let myself out of the front door and make my way back to my car where I put my ear to the fence to see if they're slagging me off. Which they are.

'He could do so much better than her'.

'Aye, the lassie's aff her heid.'

'Mummy are you sure she's not having a baby?'

Shaking my head in anger, I climb into my car and slam the door as hard as I possibly can. I start the engine just as I observe Dan through the wing mirror, running toward me. I look up out the window at him as he stands on the path gesticulating with his arms and shouting something incomprehensible. I ignore him, turning up the already blaring music before proceeding to do a very bad three-point turn in the road, which ends up being an eight-point turn and concludes with me reversing into a hedge and leaving a bit of a hole. I wheelspin off, leaving Dan stood on the path observing the hole in the hedge and shaking his head in my wake. I have no idea where I'm going, but it feels good speeding off like this, violently changing gear as the bass pounds through my chest. Do I think I'm better off alone? Yes, I bloody well do! At least I will until the PMT subsides and then I shall miss him like the deserts miss the rain. Bloody dance album.

'Very normal? Pah! That's a bloody laugh!' I shout to nobody. 'And squidgems? Bloody squidgems?!' I'm not sure which of our mothers is worse and as for that little sod of a nephew *and* the bloody Gran! Hang on. Why am I seeing signposts for places nowhere near home? Shit, I must have taken the wrong M25!

After much panic, I spot a slip road, leave the motorway and stop in a layby where I download and consult a free sat nav app – yet another reason why Dad should've let me get the better model of this car. You'd have thought he'd have known someone as directionally challenged as me would greatly benefit from sat nav. Perhaps he gives me too much credit.

Eventually, with a quarter of a tank less fuel than I'd accounted for, I arrive home exhausted, weary, pissed off and, as ever, alone. I've done it again, haven't I? I've attended and left an event in record-breaking time without my boyfriend. Oh, and made a total arse of myself as well. What must Dan think of me? Did he actually witness me losing it and swearing at his small nephew? Well, if he didn't, he likely has now. The whole debacle was caught on camera, after all. They're probably all sat round the TV watching it in horror this very second! Oh, God. What a disaster. There's only one thing that can help me now: chocolate, and an industrial sized bar at that.

Other than a cheeky text asking if I had

calmed down yet, which I treat with the contempt it deserves by ignoring it, Mr Wonderful has given me a wide berth since all the unpleasantness. He certainly didn't show up on my doorstep with the flowers and apology I was expecting. Is this it? Is this the beginning of the end? Has he finally come to his senses and realised he can do so much better? Am I that much of a nightmare that I'm an antidote to Mrs Birch's love charm?

Monday morning gets off to its usual dreary start. No sooner has the alarm sounded than I find myself in the usual cycle of contemplation:

1. What can I do to have an extra half hour in bed?
2. God, I wish I went to bed earlier night last night. Definitely need an early night tonight.
3. Shall I phone in sick? *Don't be a twat!*
4. Do I really need a job? *Lizzie, don't be a twat!*
5. What do I need an income for, anyway? *Get up, you plum!*

The PMT seems to be lifting as I've gone from despising Dan to thinking about sex with him the whole journey to work. Why hasn't it happened? When will it happen? And, is it likely to ever happen after my latest performance?!

Moments after walking into work, Dan

corners me.

'Lizzie, I need to talk to you. Can we meet at lunch?' he asks.

'W-what do you want to talk about?'

'Now's not really the time. We'll talk later, yeah?' he says dismissively.

Oh, fuck! He's going to dump me, isn't he? This is it. I've gone and done it now! His family have got to him and convinced him that I am not and shall never be good enough for their squidgems! I can barely think. I'm going out of my mind sat at my desk staring at the back of Dan's head, looking for the slightest visual sign that he's a man on a mission to dump – the ending relationship kind, not the toilet kind.

The phone hasn't stopped ringing all morning which is great for Trip Hut's greedy pockets but not so great for someone who can't remember their own name right now, let alone retain the ability to cunningly screw every penny out of umpteen, unsuspecting holiday seekers. I'm a bag of nerves as lunch finally arrives. I've glassy eyes, a permanent lump in my throat and Toni Braxton is already playing on loop over and over in my mind. I couldn't bear for Dan, or anyone else for that matter, to see me cry but it's looking inevitable.

I head into the staff room, pretending to be engrossed in my phone instead of my impending rebuttal. Shit, there he is! Here he comes.

'Hey. How've you been?' he asks pleasantly.

'Alright, you?'

'Glad to hear it. Yeah, fine thanks ... um, Lizzie —

'Don't!' I interrupt. 'I don't want to hear it. At least not here at work, anyway. Could you not just wait for God's sake?'

'Pardon?'

'Well, I get that you're keen to get it over with, but here? Now? Are you deliberately setting out to humiliate me or something?' I ask, aware that my rising voice is earning me a few stares.

'Me humiliate you? Come on, you don't need any help doing that!' Dan scoffs.

'Excuse me?'

'Well, your performance at the weekend, I mean—'

'My performance?! That's a laugh! What about your bloody family? I was made to feel unwelcome and unworthy for the duration of the very brief time I was there. Not to mention being bullied by a bloody pre-schooler!'

Dan raises his brows in surprise.

'Wow! I think you ought to calm down Lizzie, people are looking over.'

'I don't care!' I say. Well, I do but it's too far gone for that now.

'Look, this is getting out of hand. What's got your back up so much? I was only planning to ask you to come away to the Cotswolds with me this weekend, but jeez, just forget it!' he says, his hands falling to his sides.

What? I pause and look at him, raising my eyebrows.

'Well, I thought we could use some time alone to get away from it all, just you and me,' he explains.

'Oh … Ooh! I thought you were going to chuck me!' I say, the realisation dawning that no chucking is happening. Well, at least not today.

'What? Of course not! I wouldn't have done that … not here in the staff room.'

'But you're saying you might still?' I say, as if he hasn't just told me he's whisking me away for a romantic getaway. Thankfully he laughs.

'No, Lizzie. I can categorically tell you I have no plans to chuck you. If anything, I thought you were going to chuck me! You've been really off with me lately.'

'Oh? What on earth made you think that?' I joke.

In the space of a mere few hours, I've gone from "in a relationship but fucked-off", to "probably no longer in said relationship and bereft", to "back in said relationship and ecstatic". I know right, it's a miracle I'm still sane! Or maybe I just think I am? But never mind all that now, the point is I still have my Adonis boyfriend and he's whisking me off for a romantic weekend break, just the two of us, with absolutely none of the following: Brazilian supermodels, bailiffs, overbearing mothers, filmographer fathers, irate neighbours, cantankerous grans, pre-schooler bullies or crotch-sniffing hounds from hell!

This is a wondrous opportunity for lovemaking, assuming he makes a move on me this weekend. And if he doesn't? Well, I haven't really thought that far ahead yet, but I do still have that fuck-off great gaffer tape to fall back on. Not that I'm some sort of sadist nympho or anything, God, no! It's just that I'm nearly thirty, I've only ever had one remotely sexual experience in my lifetime and even my old and past it parents are having more sex than I am. Things are getting desperate!

I estimate that I have spent two thirds of every waking hour since Dan asked me to go away with him thinking about shagging. When will it happen? Where will it happen? And more to the point, how might I bugger things up this time?

As much as I'm keen for it to happen, there are so many things to worry about, like who takes the lead? Lights on or off? Fully or semi-naked? Will he end it when he sees my arse? Will I be crap?

There is also the small issue that I've no experience. Well, I can't very well call lying on my back grimacing while a spotty twerp pounds me for three minutes an experience, can I?

I thought it might be helpful to ask the advice of someone who knows the male anatomy better than most, but let's just say, Levi Hilton's sexual technique has absolutely no place in any quaint cottage setting. There's only one thing to do when the time comes: I'll just have to consult my only other friend Mr Jack Daniels because, as I've always said, if all else fails, get pissed!

Chapter 9:

Copulation in The Cotswolds

Finally, the weekend arriveth and I'm running late – as per. Dan will be here at any moment to pick me up. I run through a mental checklist. Calls diverted to answerphone? Check! Cat litter tray sorted? Check! Slow, demonstrative pep talk with cat about using it rather than having movement on sitting room rug? Check! Water and cat biscuits left out? Check! Bowels emptied as much as possible insofar as to avoid repeat of floater incident? Double Check! Sexy undies packed? Checkety-check! Unruly growler tamed? Check!

Just as I contemplate digging out the Gutbuster 2000, I hear a beep. My chariot awaits! No time for Gutbusters now … which is probably for the best since I still have the welts from last time.

Grabbing a can of hairspray from the end table, I give my hair a liberal blasting and a zhoosh and I'm off! Other than for Dan strangely keeping asking if I can smell lemons, the car journey en route to the Cotswolds has, thankfully, all been very normal and uneventful.

We arrive at the gates of the cottage in the mid-afternoon. Dan steps out to open them back as I quietly wonder how it can be that, not so long ago, I could only dream of getting within a mere foot of this man and now he's brought me here for a weekend of copulation in the Cotswolds. Ah, yes ... I did a spell on him, I recall, looking shadily from side to side. We ascend the sweeping gravel driveway. The air is sweet, the skies are clear, the flowers are in full bloom and, hopefully, romance will soon be too!

Dan takes our bags from the boot and we make our way to the rear entrance, our footsteps crunching the gravel in tandem. I survey our weekend hideaway – a pretty, olde worlde chocolate box cottage with storybook architecture and fairy tale charm – and conclude that, right now, there's no place I'd rather be.

'I thought we could unpack, freshen up and go for a late pub lunch. There's a great little place not far from here,' Dan suggests, fumbling for the door keys.

'Sounds great.'

He unlocks the door and opens it back, revealing the interior cosy character.

'Wow, this place is unreal!' I gasp. 'Must've cost

a bit with it being peak season.'

'Not entirely, no. Got a great discount through work,' Dan replies, accomplished.

'Ah! So, there *are* perks to working for Shit Hut, then.'

'It has a hot tub, you know,' he adds with just the slightest hint of suggestion in his tone. 'Maybe we could sit out in it and watch the stars this evening ... glass of bubbly and that.'

Suddenly I feel a lot better about working for Trip Hut.

We put away the bag of grocery cupboard staples we'd stopped off to get along the way and venture upstairs to the master bedroom to unpack, with Dan behaving very much the gentleman having taken my bag and myself behaving very much the pervert with my eyes boring into his arse as he climbs the stairs in front of me.

The first thing I spy on entering through the doorway is the mahoosive king size four-poster bed. Wow! I'm going to feel like fucking royalty in this tonight – literally. Ordinarily, I would've excitedly dropped everything in favour of leaping on it, but it would be one thing for Dan to lose his damages deposit for a bed broken by vigorous bonking and another for Dan to lose his damages deposit for a bed broken by his tonne-weight girlfriend having dived on it.

We unpack and, reaching the bottom of my weekend bag, I discreetly take out my undies to place them in the drawer, being careful to keep them folded so as not to reveal their full magnitude in viewing range of Mr Wonderful.

'You just about done?' Dan asks, walking up behind me and pulling me into him. 'I'm getting peckish.'

'Almost,' I reply, confused when he begins sniffing my hair ... what the fuck? Weird seduction technique, but hey, I'm game...

'Er, Lizzie ... What the hell have you used on your hair?' he asks, pulling away.

'Eh?' I gasp, spinning around in surprise.

'Smells a lot like furniture polish to me,' he says, making a guess.

Pulling my hair forward, I give it a sniff. Oh, shit! I must've picked up the Mr Sheen off the end table instead of the hairspray this morning. I've always left a can out on the side somewhere in anticipation of Mother arriving at the flat unannounced to give the impression I'm in the middle of cleaning. Damn.

Dan bursts out laughing.

'Oh bugger! It's gone all greasy and limp,' I groan, checking myself out in the en suite bathroom mirror. 'God, whatever must you think of me?'

'Well, I did think I could smell lemons in the car, but I'd never have guessed it was because my girlfriend uses furniture polish as hairspray,' he laughs, ruffling my hair playfully.

After a frantic triple shampoo and blow dry, we set off hand-in-hand down the gravel driveway and out onto the charming little street lined with similarly quaint cottages. The grass is greener and the air cleaner outside of the big, bad city and the picturesque scenery makes for a perfect backdrop for love and romance. The late afternoon sun beats down on us as we approach the Coach and Horses pub. With it now being too late for even a late lunch, thanks to Mr Sheen, we decide to have dinner early. I scan the menu meticulously in search of something that: A. Makes for reasonably elegant eating, and B. Is not going to play merry hell with my unpredictable bowels.

We both end up settling on quintessentially British pie and mash. They say couples who've been together a long time begin to develop similar tastes, don't they? Well, here we are, making the same food choices already! This is major. I can *definitely* see us winding up with a mortgage, a couple of kids and a Golden Retriever!

Dan goes off to the little boys' room. The minute he's out of sight I pull out my phone and get straight on Facebook to tag myself at this idyllic Cotswolds drinking establishment to keep frenemies guessing and update Levi on proceedings.

Me: *Sooo, cottage is awesome, only has a frigging hot tub! You wanna see the four-poster bed! Just in village pub having dinner. He's even chosen same food as me! Give it a month and he'll be fucking proposing!!!*

I hit send and sit back dreamily plotting our perfect future together, my mind awhirl with visions of tiaras and tuxedos. Moments later, Dan returns to the table and sits down, a markedly strange expression upon his face.

'What's up? You look like you've just been propositioned by some sheep-shagging weirdo in the lavvies,' I laugh.

He's not laughing. In fact, he looks quite serious.

'You haven't, have you?!' I probe, still giggling.

'What you just sent on Messenger, well you ... um ... sent it to me by mistake, I'm guessing,' he explains.

I'm not laughing now. I've gone all hot and stiff.

'Oh, er ... shit! Did I? Sorry, it wasn't meant for you, obviously!'

'It's okay, but Lizzie, you should just know that marriage is a hell of a long way off in my life plans.'

'What? Oh, God! I know, I know! It was just a figure of speech, honest! I'm like you, *totally* not ready for all that,' I lie, thankful that Pinocchio is just a fairy tale because that was a whopper and I really should be sat here sporting a metre-long conk with leaves and branches sprouting from it by now.

'Seriously?'

'Christ, yeah!' I insist, adding the would-be bird's nest to it.

'Phew! Thank God for that!' he laughs in relief, as all former visions of tuxedos and tiaras are promptly snuffed out.

Oh, God! Me and my big bloody mouth! When am I going to learn? When *am* I going to learn? Not anytime soon as it goes, because my next monumental fuck-up is to inadvertently let him know that he's dating his Facebook stalker when he casually mentions his cousin, whom he's never spoken of before, and I absent-mindedly ask, 'Which one? Kieran, Max or Brad?'

We visit the village shop for fresh fruit and local produce for the cottage. Downcast and dejected at the earlier calamities of the Coach and Horses, I ask at the counter for a small bottle of Jack Daniels while Dan browses.

'Are you twenty-one, madam?' the old bag behind the counter challenges me.

'I'm twenty-*nine*,' I scoff. In normal circumstances, I would have been thrilled to have been challenged about not looking my age, but since I was planning to slip the bottle straight into my handbag without Dan seeing it and have a few sneaky ones for Dutch courage back at the cottage without the assumption that I'm a raging alcoholic, time is very much of the essence!

'I'm going to need to see some identification please,' insists the overly-anal assistant.

Sighing, I reach into my purse and pull out my credit card.

'*Photo* identification,' she adds, sternly.

'Ugh! Well, I don't have any with me,' I mumble under my breath, rolling my eyes.

'Then I can't serve you I'm afraid'.

'Look,' I groan in a hushed tone, 'I can promise you I am twenty-nine. Cross my heart and hope to die!'

'I can't serve you without photo ID, it's the law.'

'No, it's not. It's only illegal for under eighteens to buy alcohol! Name me one seventeen-year-old *you* know with a credit card!' I argue through gritted teeth, waving it in her face.

'It's twenty-one,' she insists.

'It's eighteen.'

'It's twenty-one!'

'IT'S EIGHTEEN!' I yell, forgetting myself and attracting the immediate attention of the other customers in the shop ... including Dan. Shit.

'Lizzie? What's going on?' he asks in surprise as he walks over to the counter.

'Look, I just fancied a teeny-weeny little evening tipple, but *she* thinks I'm underage and won't serve me,' I explain, annoyed.

'I'm not prepared to break the law, sir. No photo ID, no sale,' she informs Dan in her defence.

'Well, she *is* twenty-nine, but it's alright, I've got photo ID. I'll buy it,' he tells her, taking out his wallet.

I stand smugly as she's forced to sell my bottle of Jack to Dan. I watch in satisfaction as she begrudgingly scans and packs our groceries and, petulant as it is, poke my tongue out at her in victory as we leave.

'I didn't know you were a whisky drinker,' Dan exclaims outside the shop.

'I'm not!' I bark, defensively. 'Well, I like a Jack and Coke now and again but I'm not a drinker at all. God, no. I can take booze or leave it,' I insist, nodding sincerely with no immediate recollection of that night in the club.

'I wasn't implying anything,' he laughs, 'I just thought you might be interested to know there's a distillery not far from here. They do taster sessions and stuff. Maybe we could go check it out tomorrow?'

'*Oh* ... ha ha ha! Yeah, why not?'

'Fancy a game of scrabble?' Dan asks back at the cottage. 'There's a whole bunch of board games in the sitting room sideboard.'

Scrabble? Bloody Scrabble? I've come for a weekend of debauchery, not to play fucking Scrabble!

'I'm crap at Scrabble,' I whinge.

'Oh, come on. There's sod-all on TV, we might as well.'

The game gets off to a surprisingly good start, but an hour in and several Jack and Coke's later, my former intellect has reduced to immature words like "dogging" and "boner". I'm fully aware that I have reached the point of no return in terms of intoxication, but similarly I'm also fully aware that: A. I've got to climb into a hot tub in front of Dan at some point. B. Sex is inevitable – providing A *isn't* the passion killer I suspect it'll be.

Keen to ease the last of my nerves, I go to pour another drink.

'Maybe you'd be better with water now?' Dan suggests.

'Sorry?' I gasp confrontationally.

'Well, you look like you've had enough already.'

'Who are you, my Daddd?' I slur.

'I'm not trying to tell you what to do, it's just I've seen you wasted before, remember? You tend to walk into walls and that,' he reminds me.

'I dooo not! I can h-handle my drink perfectly well thhhanks.'

'Hmmm ... If you say so.'

∞∞∞

Grimacing, I open my eyes. I've a pounding head and a mouth as dry as Gandhi's flip-flop. I don't remember getting into bed and how is it even morning already? The last I remember was pouring another drink and suggesting a game of naked Twister. *Fuck*! I sincerely hope we didn't!

Flinging back the bed covers, I go to make a swift dash to the loo, tripping over the washbowl from the kitchen I assume was thoughtfully left on the floor at my bedside by Dan. Realising I've only my underwear on and my rolls are visible in the early morning light of the room, I immediately drop to the floor. Like a dishevelled meerkat I slowly rise up, peering over the edge of the bed to see if Dan's still asleep. He is, but it's only a matter of time before he stirs. I've *got* to make myself decent before he wakes! Gingerly, I creep on all fours around the bed, peep my head out on Dan's side to check the coast is clear, then make an inelegant high-speed dash for the en suite door ... still on all fours.

'Lizzie?' comes Dan's puzzled voice from behind me.

Startled, I freeze for a moment, having not quite made it to the bathroom door, before swiftly realising Dan has a full and uncompromised view of my large and unsightly hide. In panic, I throw myself at the door which opens back, causing me to tumble, rolling onto my side. I forcibly fling the door shut with my foot and the last thing I observe is Dan's confused expression as it closes on him.

One long and lethargic shower later, I head downstairs in my dressing gown to the kitchen where Dan is fixing breakfast.

'Morning,' I greet him, cringing for all I'm worth.

'Oh, hey. Morning. Are you alright now?' he asks, concerned.

'*Alright* now?'

'Yeah, last I saw of you, you were on the bathroom floor.'

'Er ... yeah. Thought I was going to be sick,' I

blag, blushing a little.

'Ah!'

'Dan, can I just ask…?'

'Yeah?'

'Did we play naked Twister last night?'

He bursts out laughing. 'No, we didn't. But you were adamant we should.'

'Oh, God, I'm so embarrassed!' I sigh, covering my hands with my face.

'*Don't* be,' he assures. 'You were actually really amusing.'

'Did we … did we … *you* know?' I ask, feeling very juvenile.

'Oh! No, we didn't,' he replies, clearing his throat.

'Ah! Then er, how did my clothes come off?' I probe, hoping to God it was nice and dark when they did.

'You took them off yourself,' he replies, appearing suddenly awkward as he plonks an omelette down in front of me.

'Really? I can't have been in as bad a state as I thought, then.'

'Er, well not quite. You attempted a striptease, but you only got as far as your underwear before you passed out and I had to put you to bed,' he tells me, trying not to laugh.

'Please tell me you're joking!' I gasp, clasping my hands over my mouth in shock.

'Nope.'

'Oh, fuck. Oh *fuck*!'

'Chill! You looked pretty hot to me, all woman.'

A surprised grin creeps up my face and I begin to melt a little. All woman? He just called me all woman!

'So, you still fancy checking out that distillery then?' he asks casually, sliding omelette number two onto his plate.

Slamming down my fork, I spring from my seat, rushing over to the kitchen sink to expel the gob-full of omelette that had been doing laps around my mouth. Er, not bloody likely! I don't *ever* want to touch a drop of whisky again in my life!

Dan suggests a walk and picnic in the countryside to help clear my head. Not being an outdoorsy person in the slightest, a walk in the countryside is the *last* sodding thing I want to do, but I have to do *something* to shift this bastard hangover and get Operation Copulation in the Cotswolds fully back on track, and so I find myself begrudgingly agreeing. He sets about making sandwiches and loading them into a picnic bag along with some posh looking carrot cake, strawberries, champagne and a selection of crockery and glassware from the kitchen cupboards. I watch in fascination, concluding he really could be the most perfect man on earth.

Taking myself upstairs to dress, I opt for a floral maxi dress and light cotton cardi: summer picnic chic. We set off on foot together, arm in arm. I have no idea where we're heading, but Dan clearly does. The fresh, country air does seem to be helping the hangover, I'm relieved to note. We stop at various idyllic backdrops for cute selfies together and I have already identified and chosen the optimum envy-inducing shot of us leaning against trunk of large oak as my new Facebook profile pic! I get to feeling that in the reasonably short time we've been together, I can't imagine where I would be without Dan. I also get to feeling that in the unreasonably long time we've been walking, that I can't imagine where Dan and I actually *are*!

'Dan?'

'Yeah?'

'Do you actually know where we're going?' I probe.

'Sort of. Well, not entirely. I just know that there's a lake somewhere round about here and I thought it would be nice to eat there.'

Hmm! Two young-ish lovers picnicking by a lake, how very Jane Austen!

We arrive at a gated field of cattle. Great, now what?

'After *you*, madam,' Dan gestures, pushing open the gate.

'What? We're not walking through there, surely! I don't fancy getting shot at by some angry farmer.'

'Of course, we are – we're ramblers! There's no 'keep out' signs, so as long as we close the gate, we won't be getting shot anytime soon,' Dan laughs.

'Well, I wish you'd have told me we'd be walking through fields of cow shit,' I whinge, 'I can't imagine *these* are the everyday shoes of choice for ramblers.'

Dan peers down at my baby pink wedge sandals and raises a brow. 'Why on earth did you come out in those?! Didn't you bring any walking shoes?'

'I don't own such a thing!'

'You don't go out walking, ever?'

'Not if I can help it.'

'Well, there's not a lot we can do about it now, you'll just have to watch where you're walking.'

Rolling my eyes, I link his arm as we make our way through the field, dodging molehills and cow pats as we go. A lot less Jane Austen, more

Farmer's sodding Weekly!

For the most part, the cows couldn't be less bothered with our presence, but all of a sudden a nearby reddish-brown female looks up from grazing and stares at us inquisitively. She begins walking over lazily in our direction, stopping within a couple of metres of us.

'Aww, bless! She's come over to say hello,' I coo. 'Ahh, cows are so sweet with their ... cow eyes and that. I really don't know how people can eat cows.'

'Hang on, didn't you have steak pie at the Coach and Horses yesterday?' Dan challenges.

'Well, yes. But I hardly ever eat beef,' I reason.

'*Hardly ever* being yesterday!'

'Yes, but from now on, I *don't* eat beef,' I declare determinedly, stepping forward to give Mrs Cow a pat.

'Lizzie, don't get too close. They can get really protective of their young,' Dan warns.

'Oh, she's ok! You just want someone to wuv you, don't you Mrs Cow?' I coo, putting a hand up to give her a fuss.

Without warning, Mrs Cow makes a sudden lunge forward towards me.

'Gaaa!' I yell, darting backwards and immediately attracting the attention of the rest of the herd.

'Lizzie, we'd better...' Dan begins, before trailing off as he observes the massive bull bounding towards us from out of nowhere, 'Fucking runnn!' he yells, dropping the picnic bag at his feet, shattering the crockery and glassware within it in the process. There goes his security deposit!

Hoisting up my maxi dress, I mirror Dan in turning tail and legging it back the way we came – well, as much as one *can* leg it in summer-chic wedge sandals!

Alarmingly, I can hear the bull hot on our trail, tearing up the field behind us, its snorts and grunts growing louder by the second. Dan makes it to the gate, but with no time to waste with the faff of unlocking it, he scales and clears the surrounding fencing with the poise and elegance of an athlete.

Hindered by my footwear, complete lack of stamina and 42G rack, I'm a little farther off!

'Hurry! Faster Lizzie, he's closing in!' Dan calls across to me.

In between running for my life on treacherous uneven ground in wedges and dodging cow pats, I feel somewhat pissed off that he's skedaddled and left me. It's not very fucking Superman is it?

'Fuuuuuuuuuuck!' I yell as I approach and arrive at the fence, flinging myself over it with all the poise and elegance of pig on ice, landing heavily in an unsightly heap on the ground behind it with an enormous thud.

'Oh my God, are you okay?!' Dan pants, rushing over as I lay there groaning.

'Well, I think I might've broken my back ... *and* my femur ... *and* my fibula *and* my tibula *and* my coccyx *and* my pelvic girdle, but apart from that, fine. You?'

With the picnic hamper and its contents lying smashed in the middle of mad bull territory and neither of us stupid enough to attempt to retrieve it, the lover's picnic is now untenable. Feeling cursed we head back to the cottage at a snail's pace, me hobbling and clinging onto Dan like an invalid, the final blow delivered when the heavens open and it starts pissing down.

Eventually, we arrive back at the cottage soaked to the bone and exhausted.

'Well, that was a hell of a pointless trek,' Dan sighs, closing the door behind us. 'And I don't know about you, but all it's done is make me fancy a steak!'

'Yeah, me too. Extra rare!' I huff.

'I thought you didn't eat beef as of today?' Dan points out.

'Oh, I don't. It's revenge!'

'So, you're going to eat the beef of an entirely different animal, possibly not even British-farmed, as revenge on that bull for chasing us, all while not eating beef?'

I stare back at him. 'Oh, er ... I see what you mean. Should I call for a Chinese?'

'Fancy trying out that hot tub then?' Dan suggests after supper. 'It might just help that broken back. And the femur and the tibia and the fibula and the coccyx and the pelvic girdle for that matter.'

'Sure, yeah,' I reply, trying to hide the anxiety in my voice as I peer down at my belly, bloated from dinner.

Nervous, I strip down to my underwear in the bathroom upstairs before putting on a dressing gown. Willing Dan not to be in the hot tub already and, consequently, able to observe me getting in, I make my way downstairs to the outdoor patio area. Breathing a sigh of relief, I'm pleased to observe he *hasn't*. He's only just removing the lid.

'Glass of Prosecco?' he asks, observing me in the patio doorway as he turns on the jets. 'Couldn't quite stretch to two bottles of Champagne I'm afraid. Slightly annoying that we didn't even get a sip of the one we did have, which is lying in the middle of a field somewhere as we speak. Couldn't make it up, could you?'

'Yeah, love a Prosecco,' I reply, my mind focused on far more major issues like how I'm going to get into the bloody hot tub without him seeing me!

'I'll get the drinks then,' he says, heading inside.

Seizing the moment, I grapple furiously with the belt of my dressing gown, whip it off and throw it to the ground before making a frantic, shaky ascent up the plastic steps to the hot tub, which consequently topple over, causing me to fall in face first with a loud splash!

'Fuck!' I yell underwater, flapping and splashing about in the manner of a shark attack victim in my struggle for composure before Mr Wonderful returns.

Hearing the kerfuffle, Dan rushes to the patio door. 'Lizzie? Lizzie, are you ok?' he asks, concerned.

'Yep, Yep, all good!' I pant, scraping my saturated hair away from my face. 'You couldn't grab me a towel, could you? I can't er ... see,' I inform him with tightly screwed up panda eyes.

'Sure. What happened out here?' he enquires as he picks up a towel from inside the door. 'How come there's water all over the patio? And why are the steps lying on the grass?'

'I ...slipped.'

'Christ! Are you alright?'

'Yeah! Yeah, fine! Just dandy,' I lie in a high-pitched voice, grabbing the towel from him.

'Okay, I'll just grab the drinks then,' he says, returning to the kitchen and leaving me to dry off, wondering if I've shattered my knee on the side of the hot tub. I hurriedly rub at my panda eyes, claw through my sopping wet hair and tighten the straps of my bra to give the girls a boost.

Dan returns with the drinks. He places them down on the side of the hot tub before untying the belt of his dressing gown and removing it, leaving me visibly swooning and slightly open-mouthed at the sight of his amazing body as he stands there in his smalls like some fit as fuck Calvin Klein underwear model. Bypassing the plastic steps, he places his hand down on the side of the hot tub and hops in next to me, sinking down into the bubbles. We gaze at one another in silence for a few awkward moments before he turns and picks up his glass.

'Well, cheers' he says, chinking it with mine and taking a long sip.

'Cheers!' I say, mirroring him.

It's a warm, clear night despite the earlier rain, with very little breeze. The balmy summer evening air is infused with the aroma from the pine trees at the bottom of the garden. The steely blue sky is subtly highlighted with the very last of the sun's peachy-pink hues and the first stars of the evening flicker and twinkle subtly within it. Everything – apart from my knee, which is throbbing like a bitch – is calm.

'This is nice,' I remark, trying to keep the conversation flowing.

'Yeah, it is,' he agrees.

'I know it's gotten off to a ... dramatic start, but er, thank you. Its lovely here,' I tell him.

'My pleasure. I wanted to take you away and have some quality time together. We haven't really had the luck so far, have we?'

'No, we haven't,' I agree, recalling the many farces and fuck ups of the past few months.

Before I know it, I've drained my glass. He pours me another without judging, probably sensing I'm totally out of my comfort zone.

'You ok?' he asks, observing me wincing in pain.

'Well, I kind of bashed my knee as I slipped earlier,' I confess.

'Which one?' he asks.

'My right.'

He takes me by surprise as he places his hands under the water, lifts my knee up and begins bending and squeezing it with his strong, warm hands.

'It's bruised already,' he remarks, 'but you haven't broken it.'

'How do you know?'

'Because you can move it in both directions, see?' he says, demonstrating. 'And it's not swollen.'

I sit in a starey, trance-like state in the manner of a very happy dog, hypnotised by its master's belly rubs.

'Did I ever mention I'm trained in sports massage?' Dan asks.

'Oh? No, you didn't,' I reply, suddenly back in the room.

'I learned it as part of my personal training course, for sports injuries and that.'

'I can't imagine you've treated many people with injuries sustained from falling into hot tubs and running from bulls,' I remark.

'Can't say I have!' he laughs, grabbing my shoulders, pushing me forward and sliding behind me so that I'm sitting between his legs. I tense up and go stiff as I feel his hands on my shoulders. Note to heart: please calm yourself at this crucial moment and stop beating out of my chest!

'Wow, you're so tense! Just relax,' he instructs.

Relaxing is no easy feat as a salad dodger in a state of undress with an Adonis pressed up against me. Taking an ultra-long swig of Prosecco, I wince my eyes shut and lay my head back against his hunky shoulder. Even though I've wanted and willed this to happen for so long, I'm *still* the girl nobody wanted on the school sports team. The girl who never got a card on Valentine's Day, unless it was for a joke. The girl who had a zillion school crushes but never a boyfriend. The girl whom, up until now, only Asperger's Andrew wanted to get his leg over. Is there any wonder I can't catch my breath and I feel like I'm hallucinating?

You'd think someone like Dan who can have practically any woman he wants would exude confidence to the point of arrogance, but it's funny, even Mr Wonderful, as perfect as he is, isn't all that confident either I notice as we sit in awkward silence.

Time seems to stand still as I feel him suddenly lean forward and begin kissing my neck. My toes curl under the bubbles as a million tingles journey from my shoulder all the way down the whole of my right side. Gradually, I turn my head to meet his lips and we kiss; slowly at first, then more urgently.

I flinch as his hand comes to rest on my waist

under the water, as though he might pull away in disgust the moment he feels my squishy waistline. But he doesn't. In fact, he opts to feel even more of me ... and more ... and more, having his fill like a kid in a shop where the sweets are free and nothing's off limits. Knowing I can't very well be repulsing him as I'd feared, and with a year-plus of pent-up lust for this man exploding within me, I turn around and we drink each other up as he holds me in a vice-like grip.

Sometime later, he takes my hand and we kiss our way out of the tub and up to the bedroom where we fall onto the bed, soaking wet but oblivious, unaware of anything else but each other.

At this point, the very worst of my lumps and bumps are concealed and contained within the sexiest (and now sopping wet) underwear I could find to fit me, but unfortunately in order to engage in wonderful lovemaking, one cannot remain in their underwear!

My sense of awareness makes an abrupt return when I feel Mr Wonderful begin to tug at said underwear, filling me with a sudden terror. No man has ever seen my Mary ... not even *I* have seen my Mary! Well, certainly not from a standing position for a while, anyway. And from what I *have* seen of it, I hate it! I'm sure Dan has seen many a perfect Mary in his time, but now he's about to come face-to-face with the worst yet. If anything should kill this unlikely romance, it will be the sight of my aesthetically displeasing Mary, I'm sure of it!

I tense up, stiff as a board. Dan pauses for a moment before getting up from the bed and flicking off the lights. My heart! I could cry. Just when I think this man can't get any more perfect, he yet again exceeds expectations. He goes on to surpass all fucking comprehension during the hours (yes, hours!) that follow ... sheesh!

I've always said that something bad usually follows anything good in my life. Like the time I won a ton on a scratch card only to, moments later, get an on-the-spot speeding fine of a ton. As I lay entwined in the arms of the man of my dreams, having just experienced actual heaven, I can't help but quietly ponder the inevitable calamity heading my way.

I doze off, only to be awoken by the ping of a text sometime later. I reach lazily across the bedside table for my phone, perfectly unaware that this new level of bliss I've been experiencing has peaked and is now heading into rapid free fall. Then, I read the text that would change everything:

'Lizzie, been trying to reach you urgently but our calls are going straight to answerphone. Nanny's passed away. So sorry. Call me. Dad x'

I lay frozen, just staring at the screen, re-reading those words over and over. Nanny Bradshaw, gone? She can't be! I think back to the last time I saw her, only a week or so ago. She was stood in her doorway, wearing her favourite baby blue jumper. She was larger than life, full of beans and as crude as ever. Her eyes danced as she told me about her win at bingo. She didn't look like someone who'd be gone forever in a matter of days. She was getting better. I was sure she was getting better. We'd all thought so.

It must be starting to hit me because my enormous sobs have woken Dan. I wasn't even aware I was crying.

'Hey! Hey, what's wrong?' he asks, putting an arm around my shoulder.

Unable to speak, I pass my phone over my shoulder to him. He reads the text. 'Oh, God. God, I'm so sorry, come here.'

He holds me tight against his chest as my world comes crashing down, but not even Dan Elliott and his amazing guns can make it better.

We leave the cottage early and journey home in silence. Not knowing what to do or say, Dan keeps a rigid focus on the road ahead. My mind is somewhere else, stuck in some sort of limbo land with only the distant hum of the car radio keeping me somewhat present and vaguely alert to my surroundings whizzing by in a 60mph blur.

Nanny Bradshaw was such a big part of my

life; always there, always around. We all know death is inevitable, but she was such a big personality. In my mind, she was going to live forever. As daft as it sounds, I'd never really contemplated her death. I certainly hadn't planned for it – how *do* we plan for someone we love dying? I guess we don't. Like most of the painful parts of life, we cross that bridge when we come to it and now, here I am. I've arrived at that bridge, but I'm still not ready to cross it.

'Will you be okay?' Dan asks as we draw up outside my parents' house.

I nod, forcing the tiniest of smiles.

'I'll call you,' he says as I begin to get out. 'And Lizzie?'

I turn to face him.

'I'm really sorry.'

I nod, reaching for his hand, holding it in mine for a few moments before letting go. He drives away as I walk toward the front door where Mother is already waiting with her arms crossed.

'Where are his manners?' she complains.

'Sorry?'

'That ... boyfriend of yours. Driving off like that with not so much as a hello.'

'I don't think he saw you, Mother'.

'Now don't make excuses for him, dear'.

'I'm not. He would've said hello if he'd seen you. He's a gentleman.'

Mother pulls a face as though she just smelt a fart. 'Hmph! Some gentleman.'

Dad appears in the doorway behind Mother looking downcast, his eyes lacking their usual sparkle. Bypassing Mother, I fling my arms around him and we stand and sob as she races to close the door, terrified the neighbours might hear.

We sit in the front room in silence, other than for the ticking of the old grandfather clock, as our teas go cold on the coffee table. Mother drains her cup in between making unhelpful comments here and there, her words of comfort not spanning beyond:

'We all knew it was coming at some point.'

'It's a blessed relief.'

'It's all for the best.'

'She had a good innings.'

I had expected as much from Mother. She and Nanny Bradshaw had never seen eye to eye. Whether it was down to the clash of two, strong personalities, Mother being unable to stand Dad answering to anyone but her, Nanny having 'no time for stuck-up arseholes' (her own words) or a combination of all of those things, I'm not sure.

'I just can't believe she's gone,' I remark to

Dad as Mother sits fondling her Filofax as she calls around to break the news to people who barely even knew Nanny. What starts with 'Desmond's Mother has sadly passed away' quickly progresses to 'That blasted Delia Davenport! Smearing a sponge base with shop-bought icing and passing it off as homemade baking is pure deception!'

'Nor me,' Dad mumbles, taking his glasses off every few minutes to dab at his eyes.

Mother insists I should stay in the spare room for a few days as though it would be some kind of therapy for me. In needing Mother's therapy on a similar level to needing a hole in the head, I respectfully decline until around the fourth time she asks when I get a bit sweary.

The following days pass in a blur. To my surprise, Trip Hut have shown some actual humanity in allowing me a few days' paid leave for bereavement. I've taken the rest of the week as annual leave to give me some time to get my head together. It means I don't get to see Dan through the week, but it also means I don't have to sell overpriced holidays to suckers, which is a blessing because right now I couldn't sell water in a bloody desert! In normal circumstances, I'd be wondering what Rachel is up to; is she flirting her tits off with Dan? Has she flashed her G-string at lunch yet? For the first time ever, I find myself unperturbed. Everything feels different;

pointless almost.

Chapter 10:

The Hardest Goodbye

'Are you sure you want to do this?' the lady assistant at the funeral home asks me, looking concerned.

I nod, unconvincingly.

'It's a pretty big deal you know and it's not for everyone. You don't have to go in if you don't want to.'

'I'm sure I'll be fine,' I say in an attempt to reassure us both.

'Alright well, take your time. Take as long as you need. I can come in with you if you'd like?'

'Um, no. I'd rather be on my own. You know, to say my goodbyes and that, but thank you.'

'That's fine. I'll give you some privacy. She's in the third room on the left whenever you're ready.'

'Thanks'.

'Okay, I'll be just out here if you need me.'

I stand, just staring at the wall ahead for a time. Both Dad and Dan had offered to come with me today, but I had been so insistent that this was something I needed to do by myself. Suddenly, I'm not sure if I can. I've been mulling it over for days. I've never done this before, never seen a dead person. What if I can't handle it? What if it gives me nightmares? But on the other hand, this is the last chance I'll ever get to see her. If I don't do it, I might regret it later and it'll be too late by then. I can't let her go without having said goodbye. I *have* to do this.

Taking a deep breath, I slowly ascend the swirly-patterned carpeted corridor. It smells freshly painted. There are purposefully placed pictures on the wall of calming oceans and beaches. I stop to look at them, recalling fond memories of the many trips I'd taken to the seaside as a kid with Nanny and Grandad Bradshaw, such as the time Nanny's chair toppled over backward in the sand with her in it. She had lain in a heap, laughing, with her legs up in the air. It had taken her ages to get back up, she had been laughing that hard. She was always laughing that machine gun laugh of hers. Then there was the time she got mobbed by this massive, angry seagull. It didn't bother her, even when it shat all over her top. That's what I loved about her; nothing phased her. She didn't take life seriously, was always upbeat. She had such wit and dry humour and always had a funny tale to tell. How can she be gone? Gone forever?! It still doesn't seem real.

As I turn the corner and observe the numbered white doors, the enormity of what I'm about to do starts to hit. I arrive at her door and stand staring at it for a while, trying to summon the strength to push it open and go through. Just the knowledge she is on the other side of it is overwhelming in itself. I'm getting upset already.

Reaching up to the door, I hesitate. It takes all the fight within me to overcome the immense anxiety I'm feeling. Somewhere in the depths of my angst-ridden mind, I can hear Nanny's thick cockney accent saying 'Just open the bleedin' door yer tit!' I give a slight chuckle – that's *definitely* what she would say if she were here now.

Well, here goes! Taking a deep breath, I push open the door, peering slowly around inside. It's a small room. There's a table with a vase of fresh cut flowers on it, a box of tissues placed nearby. It's perfectly still and calm, other than for the sound of the whirring air conditioning.

Nanny's coffin is over by the wall at the far side of the room. It's open, but I can't see inside from where I'm standing. I hesitate by the door. I can't bring myself to take the necessary four or five steps toward it, because if I do then I can't un-see what I'll see and I'll know for certain she's gone. Half of me wants to turn back and just remember her standing, smiling in her doorway, but the stubborn half of me won't allow it.

Bracing myself, I edge toward the coffin, keeping my eyes fixed on my feet the whole time. I can't bring myself to look just yet. I don't know why. I know I've got to look at some point, just not yet. Moving closer still, I use my hand as a sort of visor against my forehead to shield my eyes. When the wheels of the coffin stand come into view, I come to a stop. Wincing, I take a deep breath and take away my hand.

My mouths falls open in shock as I peer into the coffin. I blink and blink again. Well, I'll be dipped in shit! It's *not* Nanny Bradshaw at all! It's some old Sikh dude in a turban!

'Holy fuck knuckles!' I gasp in a whisper. 'God, sorry! Sorry, I'm really sorry ... er ... looks like I got the wrong room, sir,' I explain, bowing before him. 'Do excuse my language, it's just that it was quite a shock t-to see a bearded man lying here instead of my Nanny,' I add, pausing as though waiting for him to speak (he's not going to, he's a corpse). 'Anyway, best be going now. Er ... rest in peace,' I gabble, making a sharp exit.

Cringing, I head back to the reception desk where I'm shown to Nanny's actual room. Sometime later I leave, having left a small part of me behind.

I've spent much of the past week staring at, but not actually watching, the television while picking my feet. It's surprising how therapeutic peeling off great chunks of dry skin while staring into space actually is. Other than for drifting from bed to lavatory to kitchen to sofa – and opening the door to the Deliveroo guy with my flies undone – I haven't moved much in a week.

Flicking aimlessly through the music channels on TV, I pause on MJ's "Smooth Criminal" music video, finding I've a sudden and unexplained wish to master the moonwalk. Having mastered only a stiff sort of crap, backward shuffle, I try the infamous, gravity defying lean, which doesn't end well.

Just as I've swept up the last of the broken glass from the coffee table, the buzzer goes. It's Dan … and I look like shit! *Shit!*

'Oh hey, you er … never said you were coming over?' I say into the intercom.

'Yeah, thought I'd surprise you.'

He's done *that* alright!

'Well, I wasn't really expecting you. The place is a tip and—'

'I've brought Chinese.'

'Ok, come straight up.'

'So, how have you been, or is that a stupid question?' Dan asks, taking the food into the kitchen where he observes the sink full of dishes.

'It's a stupid question,' I mumble in reply.

'Well, I come armed to the teeth with prawn balls and I'm even prepared to sit through *Pretty Woman* if it'll make you feel any better,' he announces.

'You know me so well,' I remark, touched at his thoughtfulness.

'Alright, you're on!' he announces, flashing that sexy smile of his which drops suddenly. 'Have you got any clean plates and cutlery or is it all in the sink?'

'All in the sink.'

After tackling the mountain of abandoned washing up, Dan brings through the plates.

'Oh, the coffee table's gone,' he remarks, looking puzzled. 'Not the bloody bailiffs again, surely?'

'No. *God*, no.'

'So, where is it then?' he probes.

'Er ... it's in that bin bag to the side of the door.'

'Why?'

Because I crash-landed onto it impersonating

MJ.

'Er, because I dropped something on it and it smashed,' I lie.

'Oh. We'd better have these on our laps then.'

Observing what is essentially an empty shell of someone you love is quite a mind-fuck. Even though grief subsides with the passage of time, nothing is ever quite the same again, not even prawn balls. Having uncharacteristically wasted the majority of dinner, we curl up on the sofa where I discover my appetite for Dan remains insatiable.

'I feel guilty,' I announce as we lay in bed together having only made it to the famous "no pantyhose" scene in *Pretty Woman*.

'Why?' Dan asks.

'It just feels disrespectful having orgasms, well, *multiple* orgasms, actually, when you're supposed to be grieving.'

'Grieving's not a duty Lizzie, it's a process. Anything that helps you through that process isn't a bad thing. Quite the opposite, actually.'

'Yeah, but, what if...'

'What if what?'

'What if she can see me? I mean, she's not been gone a week and *I'm* lying here getting shagged!'

To be fair, Nanny Bradshaw was no stranger to

getting shagged. Dad is one of six children, after all.

By the time the day of the funeral comes around, I still haven't returned to work, instead opting to take more emergency annual leave, although, from the tone of Sue's voice on the phone and the flippant remark she'd made about it not being an immediate family member, I can tell I've reached the limit of Trip Hut's humanity.

I didn't want Dan to come to the funeral. Not least because it doesn't help my overall appearance in the slightest when I cry, but because Mother has made it abundantly clear that she doesn't like him and I can't be arsed with the inevitable questions to come from nosey relatives whom, in their shock at my bagging such a catch, would assume he's some unconventional sort of gigolo.

Standing outside the church among the throng of mourners, none of whom are in black at Nanny's request, we could almost be gathering for a wedding or christening. It's not until the hearse draws up that I begin to lose my composure as I'm reminded of why we're here.

Dad and his brothers stand in line, preparing to carry the coffin into the church as I dab at my eyes, quickly disappearing inside behind Mother's fuck-off great hat. Hushed voices give way to a series of sniffs and a brief, pre-emptive pause follows before Wham's "Wake Me Up Before You Go-Go" rings out from the church sound system. Along with just about everyone else, my mouth falls open in shock as I assume there's been the mother of all fuck ups for which heads will roll. I should have known it was played at Nanny Bradshaw's request; it was the single last thing she could do to make Mother cringe. She was a bugger, God love her.

As the coffin passes in a disorderly manner with Dad and his brothers each making their own clumsy, inharmonious attempts to walk in synchrony with the music, then slowing the pace again when they realise it's impossible, I place my hand over my mouth in an attempt not to laugh; something I totally didn't envisage myself doing today, nor in fact, any time soon.

The laughter doesn't last long before I return to being numb and switch off throughout the ceremony. The vicar's long, monotonous religious spiel fades to a distant hum as the voices in my head take centre stage. Where is she now? Is she reunited with Grandad? Does heaven even exist? Dad sits with his head hung beside me. Mother appears to be more worried about how her hat's sitting versus how her husband might be feeling. She looks on in horror as, without warning, I stand and hurriedly make my way out of the church, feeling as though I might suffocate at any given moment if I don't get some air.

'Lizzie,' comes a voice from behind as I step outside. I turn my head to see Dan stood at the side of the entrance door.

'Dan! What are you doing here?'

'I'm on lunch. I couldn't stop thinking about you, so I thought I'd come and see that you're okay.'

'*Oh*. Well, not really, but thank you.'

He's come all the way here from the city in his lunch hour just for me! I could hug him and I do, just as Mother exits the church with a face like a bulldog licking piss off a nettle.

'Could you not have had the decency to wait until the end of the service before frolicking off to your boyfriend?' she shrills.

'Actually, I just came out for some air. I didn't know he was going to be here.'

She looks down her nose at Dan. 'Well, it's family only I'm afraid.'

'Oh, er, of course. I'm just on my lunch break, I should really be heading back, I just wanted to...' His face falls as she turns around and walks back inside, completely ignoring him.

'I'm so sorry. Please don't take it personally,' I tell him, mortified at Mother's icy hostility.

'Its fine, I'll call you,' he says, planting a kiss on

my cheek.

Even in my grief-stricken state and though I'm within the house of God, I still ogle his arse as he leaves.

The hardest part comes as Nanny's coffin is lowered into the ground. So, this is it. Goodbye forever. It's so quick. So final. I find myself deeply questioning life as I stare into the grave plot, my eyes blurred with tears. One minute you're here, the next you're just a memory; what then, is life's purpose?

Around a fortnight on from burying Nanny Bradshaw, I have plunged to new, unfamiliar depths while my body hair has soared to new heights … well, lengths. Suddenly, everything is pointless. The nights seem longer and darker and the days are passing me by in a dreary blur of grey. I'm paranoid. I'm questioning everything. Sinking in dark thoughts I am a prisoner locked up within the darkest caverns of my own mind; my only respite wasted with endless angry Facebook scrolling and scoffing at the following:

Morons who log their runs. (Oh, aren't *you* good?)

Preachy blood donors. (Omg! So selfless!)

'Celebrate my birthday with me by donating to x/y/z charity'. (Would I normally be celebrating your birthday with you?!)

Be kind! (But you're *not!*)

Starey, pouty 'wasn't going to post this BUT' selfies (Here, take these three fire emojis.)

Another fucking fundraiser. (Now that you've skint me out, how about arranging one for me?)

Hospital check-ins. (OMG are you ok?!)

Celebrity death broadcasts (Congratulations on being the first to drop that RIP!)

Silent copycats (So, you're far too busy to hit "like", but have all the time in the world to copy stuff I do?)

Filter fanatics (Ooh look at you, all pore-less and flawless with no nose!)

I spend twenty minutes psyching myself up to walk the short distance downstairs to fetch the mail. I've been avoiding it for days, knowing a plethora of bills lie in wait like vampires waiting to bleed me dry. At the top of my hefty mail pile lies a formal looking letter. On closer inspection, I spot Trip Hut's annoying, depressing logo – it's a letter summoning me to a meeting to discuss my return to work. My annual leave was up several days ago but I went off sick immediately after, the mere thought of returning to *that* dump having become too much of a daunting prospect. I don't even know why they're so keen to have me back. I was as useless as a nun's tits before all of this, scheming and blagging my way through the working day. I can't imagine I'd be doing a roaring trade in my present, self-destructive, feral state.

I open the kitchen drawer and ram the letter inside where it shall remain tucked away in oblivion, along with the multitude of others I simply can't face.

The last contact I'd had with Dan was my texting him to say I needed some space to come to terms with my grief. I know right! What better remedy for grief is there than him? But with showering a huge accomplishment it is right now, Dan seeing me unwashed and at my worst day after day is something I wish to avoid at all costs. Besides, I'd only make for crap company. Having waited hours for a reply, I was worried I'd offended him, but when a worried text back from Dad eventually arrived saying 'We're all in this together, Lilibeth. I really think it's best you don't isolate yourself. Mother's worried, she wants to call the doctor x', I realised I'd sent yet another text intended for Dan to Dad, doh! With the one letter difference between their names proving dangerous, I conclude it might be best to change Dan's name in my contacts before the inevitable day comes that I text Dad thanking him for all the orgasms last night. I duly change Dan's name to Sexy Pants.

With so much time on my hands, I've gotten to feeling guilty. It's one thing to pursue somebody and quite another to do a love spell on them. What I have with Dan is the stuff dreams are made of and that's just the point, it's not real. It's an illusion. All this time I've had my head in the clouds as though living out some charming romantic novel plot: *The King and the Scullery Maid: a tale of love against the odds*, or similar. When, in reality *The Hunk and the Munter: a tale of love by sorcery* is far more fitting! Perhaps this is my karmic payback? My punishment for dabbling in the occult. Shit ... I hadn't thought of it like that until now.

Ever since I was a little girl, I would daydream about my wedding. What would my future husband look like? What kind of dress would I wear? I would plague Mother for hours to let me dress up in her wedding dress, which was only gathering dust in the attic, but she would always refuse, forcing me to improvise with old and yellowing net curtains. Funny, but back then I'd never imagined that I would have to force someone into merely dating me at almost thirty! It was always a foregone conclusion that love, whenever it came along, would be real.

Chapter 11:

Gone Girl

'Dear Elizabeth,

I write to inform you that, as of today's date, your employment has been terminated without notice to you as per the terms and conditions of your contract.

The business has acted sympathetically towards your recent bereavement in allowing you paid time off work. You were also given the opportunity to attend a meeting to discuss your return to work, which you did not attend and failed to notify the business, neither in advance nor thereafter, of any reason for your absence.

I have been unsuccessful in my many attempts to reach you by telephone to discuss the matter and, as such, the business has duly taken the only means of action remaining.

As you have failed to provide a doctor's note for beyond the self-certification period of your absence, your final salary payment shall only include statutory sick pay for the eligible period.

Additionally, it has been calculated that you have taken more annual leave than you were entitled to at the point of termination of your employment. This will therefore be deducted from your final salary.

Thank you for your service to the business and I wish you luck in your future endeavours.

Yours sincerely

Pissface'

I place the letter down upon the arm of the sofa with a long sigh. Well, that's *that* then, I am now officially a jobless bum! I'm cool with the having no job part, it's just the no income whatsoever part I'm totally not cool with. What the hell am I going to do? My significantly reduced, final salary payment is due in a matter of days and it won't be enough to cover all my bills and outgoings for the month. And what about beyond that when I'm destitute? I'm not likely to land another job anytime soon – nobody's advertising for a useless tit – and, even if I *wasn't* too proud to live off the state, I would be impoverished before the claim was even finalised. There is also the small matter of the many letters threatening disconnection I've received from the gas company having still not settled that outstanding debt from ages ago.

I have three options:

1. Call Trip Hut, plead insanity and beg for job

back. (Sod that!)

2. Go cap-in-hand to Mother. (Fuck that!)

3. Prostitute myself! (Nobody wants me for free, though? Well, not unless under the influence of one of Mrs Birch's love charms.)

I'm doomed!

I take some time – less than five minutes – to evaluate everything I own as potential eBay listings and quickly conclude that nobody in their right mind would part with their hard-earned cash for my wares, which are definitely more "shabby shit" than "shabby chic".

Sometime later, I find myself grovelling in the manner of seven-year-old me on the phone to Mother.

'I just need a little help till I can get another job, that's all.'

'Well, I hate to be the one to say I told you so, but I'm going say it anyway; I told you so! I warned you time and time again, didn't I? You simply don't have the necessary life skills to live alone, Elizabeth. It was always going to end in disaster!' Mother gabbles down the phone from up on her high horse.

'Well, it won't end in disaster if you'll help me out. I just need some help with bills till I can get another job,' I reason.

'But that might not be for months! Especially

for somebody with *your* IQ. We're not made of money, dear! And now that you've gone and got yourself the sack, you'll not be able to use your last employer as a reference. Good grief, nobody's going to touch you with a barge pole!'

Story of my life, that.

'So, what are you saying, Mother?'

'Well, isn't it obvious, dear? You have no choice but to give up your flat and move back home with Daddy and I, just for a while till you're back on your feet.'

'NO! *FUCK*, NO!' Shit. Just said that out loud.

'I beg your pardon?'

'Er … left the oven on, gottagoloveyoubye!'

To be forced to move back in with my parents at almost thirty would finish me off. There's no bigger indicator that you've failed in life. Living with Mother for any longer than a week would send me around the twist but, though it pains me to say it, I really can't think of any other option.

Having emailed the landlord notice of my intention to quit my tenancy on the flat (Mother wins) I spend the week packing and deep cleaning, feeling an overwhelming sense of sad disbelief that things have come to this.

Casting my mind back to that trip to the Cotswolds, I recall how buzzing I was as I was packing my weekend bag. I had it all at that point: a job, my independence, the man of my dreams – who is still "giving me space" – and, of course, Nanny Bradshaw. One minute I was on the road to the rainbow's end, the next I'm on the highway to hell. Either I'm the world's unluckiest person right now, or I'm on the receiving end of some pretty bad karma.

I decide to pay Mrs Birch a visit with regards to the latter. She appears like a spectre in her doorway and ushers me into the incense-filled flat.

'Ah! It's you. Didn't work then?'

'Oh no, it worked alright. It's just that my whole life has been turned upside down ever since!' I say, noting that the room is still filled with tiny bottles of who knows what.

'Well? You got your man, didn't you?' she points out.

'Yes, and lost everything else in the bleeding process!'

'Well, sometimes you have to empty your cup a little to allow for a fresh top-up from the universe.'

'Well, I think my cup got smashed. I need a whole new bloody cup and a full refill!' I complain.

'Nonsense. You'll be sitting pretty within a week. Life's like that, up and down and up and down.'

'No, it's *more* than that. This is bad karma, I know it! Listen Mrs Birch, I need you to reverse that love charm at once.'

From the wry chuckle that follows, I conclude I must have amused her in some way.

'Who do you think I am, Harry bleeding Potter?!'

'Well, you do spells so, as good *as*.' Definitely more Slytherin than Gryffindor though I think to myself, as her cat jumps down from the arm of the chair and arches its back.

'I'm a holistic therapist, I do *not* do spells! And should anyone ask, I never gave you that candle, you don't know me and you've never set foot in my flat,' she says over-defensively, ushering me out and slamming the door in my face, before it tears open again moments later.

'Now that I know it works, I'll do them for a tenner a piece. Tell your friends!'

I load my car with the last of my things before forcing a very unwilling Smudge into the back.

'And don't even *think* about pissing on the seats!' I warn him, sternly.

'Lizzie?' comes a voice from behind me.

I bang my head on the roof of the inside of the car in surprise before inelegantly shuffling out backwards.

'Dan? What are you doing here?' I ask, flustered at the sight of him standing there.

'Well, since you haven't replied to my texts, I figured I'd come and see you,' he replies, appearing puzzled – but looking fit as fuck – as he observes the loaded car which is shaking slightly as Smudge does anxious laps inside of it.

'Er ... is that the cat in there?'

'Yes. Dan, listen...'

'What's happening. You're not ... moving out, are you?' he asks, frowning.

'Yes.'

'What? Why? Where are you going?'

'Well, I've lost my job, Dan. I can't afford to stay here anymore.'

'I know. I tried to get Sue to hold out a bit longer but she said it was out of her hands. Listen, you should've said. You can stay at mine,' he offers.

'I've already made plans, but thank you,' I tell him.

He nods, pulling an expression as though sensing there's more to come.

'Dan...' I begin, before trailing off as those piercing blue eyes of his get to work on me, making my heart flutter and turning my legs to jelly. All I want to do is take him back into the flat and pick up from where we left off like none of this ever happened. To go back to the Cotswolds when I was lying ensconced his strong, masculine arms, feeling luckier than a leprechaun and safer than a baby in utero.

There's a saying that goes, 'If you love someone, set them free. If they come back, they're yours. If they don't, they never were.'

Well, I love him alright. More than words could ever describe, but he was never mine to begin with. I have no choice – especially if I want to stop this bloody karma. I have to let him go.

'I ... can't be with you anymore' I mumble.

'What? *Why*?' he gasps, looking shocked.

'It's not you, it's me...' I utter the age-old cliche, 'I just can't do this.'

'But, why? I thought we were good.'

'We were. We were better than good, but it's not real,' I mumble, in a fluster.

'Sorry? Lizzie, you aren't making any sense.'

'You can do so much better than me,' I tell him, turning to get in the car.

'What? But I'm not looking to do better than you!' he insists, grabbing and turning me around to face him. 'Lizzie, you've got to stop doing yourself down. I really care about you.'

'No, you don't. You just think you do.'

'I *know* what I feel, Lizzie.'

'No. You don't.'

He appears completely baffled. I wish I could tell him truth. He deserves that at least, but there's no easy way to tell him he's under one of Mrs Birch's love charms!

'I've got to go,' I tell him, battling against my trembling bottom lip.

'Where are you going?' he asks.

'It doesn't matter. Just forget about me.'

He steps away from the car, confusedly, allowing me the space to turn and get in. It's overwhelmingly hard to resist getting out, throwing my arms around him and telling him it's all just a wind-up before snogging his beautiful face off, but I manage not to … *just*.

Staring straight ahead through a teary mist, I pull away out of the car park, leaving behind both my independence and the love of my life.

'Good grief, what on earth is the matter? Get inside, quicky!' Mother barks, grabbing hold of my shoulder and yanking me inside before the neighbours see.

'Lizzie? What's wrong?' Dad asks, appearing in the hallway looking shocked.

'I've j-just e-ended it with D-Dan!' I sob, falling to the floor and howling like a werewolf.

'I'll make us some tea,' Mother announces with the tiniest of smirks. 'Desmond, get her away from the door and for heaven's sake shut her up!' she tells him discreetly through clenched teeth.

'It's alright love. You'll patch things up, I'm sure,' Dad soothes, putting an arm around me and leading me into the sitting room.

'N-no we w-wont. It's o-over for g-good.'

'Were things that bad?' he coos.

'I...d-did a s-s-spell on him.'

'*Oh!*' he replies, his face falling in shock.

'Well, I rather think it's a blessing,' Mother announces, breezing in with the tea. 'Holiday salesmen don't make for good husband material dear. He had nothing to offer you.'

I spend the rest of the evening trying *not* to think about what Dan had to offer me, but it's a trying task with such lasting, erotic memories forever imprinted on my mind.

Before I can blink, a week has passed. I'm still no further to getting a job or getting over Dan. Mother has started putting the word around her well-connected, entrepreneurial chums as though one of them would actually be looking to take on an undisciplined simpleton when they're in the business of hiring the best of the best.

As she appears in the doorway of the spare bedroom with a typically glum expression, I assume Mother's come to goad and badger me again about looking for work.

'Elizabeth, I'm afraid Mr Kempton-Smythe has run over your cat,' she announces matter-of-factly.

'*What*?! And who the fuck is Mr Kempton-Smythe?!' I roar, springing up from the bed.

'Language! He's been our neighbour for the past twenty years, dear.'

'Well, is he ok?' I ask, anxiously.

'He's a little shaken and he was terribly worried about coming over to tell us, but…'

'Not *him*, the bloody cat!'

'Oh no, the cat's dead, dear.'

And that was it. The cherry on the cake. The final nail in the coffin. I've lost Nanny Bradshaw, my flat, the love of my life and with Smudge now added to the list, I've officially lost everything. They say things come in threes. Well for me, it seems they come in fours – and counting, probably.

'Lizzie? Can I come in?' comes Dad's voice from behind the door later in the day.

'Uhhh,' I mumble in response.

'I'm so sorry about Smudge,' he says, plonking himself down on the bed next to me. 'Now you know I'm not one for swearing, but life can be a bloody ... bitch sometimes,' he manages, looking relieved to have got all those years of pent-up blasphemy out of his system.

'Well, you're definitely going to hell now,' I chuckle, not looking up from my tear-stained pillow.

'Just know that when you've hit rock bottom, up is the only way left to go, love,' he soothes.

'Thanks Dad, but I can't see things improving anytime soon.'

'Hmm. Well, *this* might just help things along,' he says, waving a piece of paper at me.

'What's that?' I ask, sitting up.

'It's your Nanny's will, love.'

I shrug, staring back at him.

'You're listed as a beneficiary. Er ... you might want to brace yourself a bit before you read it,' he advises, handing it to me.

I unfold it and almost fall off the bed in shock. I've never seen such a sum with my name beside it. Mrs Birch was right, a week on and I *am* sitting pretty. Looks like Nanny Bradshaw must have been too!

I've survived a fortnight living with Mother, but surviving should not in any way be confused with having any sort of life. When I say I've survived, this merely means I am not dead *yet*. The constant nagging and assumed ownership of my life is suffocating:

'What are your plans for today, dear?'

Whatever you've organised on my behalf.

'When did you last shower?'

Would it help you to sleep tonight to know?

'I hope you're looking for work on that contraption!'

Nope. Watching someone make a cake in high speed on YouTube.

'Is that *another* packet of crisps?!'

The third *and...*?

∞∞∞

There! I've deleted Facebook! And not as some week-long, attention-seeking protest. I've wasted far too much of my life scrolling through cliched, ostentatious guff and, since nobody ever likes my posts or engages with me beyond wanting me to aid in their shameless self-promotion with my likes and shares, I doubt my absence will be noticed. Even by Levi, who is so terribly busy being popular that I haven't heard from him *once* since Nanny passed away, or indeed very much before then unless I'd been the one to reach out to him first. My only sense of regret comes from the realisation that I shan't be able to stalk Dan any longer, but I figure perving over his selfies and monitoring his every move probably isn't conducive to getting over him anyway. Nor, I conclude, is having the option to call him at all practical. Rather, it's a situation akin to a toddler armed with a black permanent marker being given free, unsupervised run of the house. Accordingly, I acquire a new sim card and mobile number. The drawback to this, of course, being that anyone else who has my number, including Levi, shall no longer be able to reach me – would they notice, though?

With little else to do, nothing holding me back and money to my name, I've been thinking *a lot* about the future...

'I'm moving to America,' I announce out of nowhere at the dinner table.

'That's nice dear. Now, don't forget to call and thank Auntie Val for putting a word in for you at Marks and Sparks along the high street. It was jolly decent of her and...'

'I won't be working at Marks and Sparks along

the high street, Mother, I'm moving to Ameri—'

'And Auntie says there's a bus stop right outside the store, so you won't have to travel on that dreadful undergroun—'

'Handy ... Anyway, about my move to Ameri—' I try again.

'Auntie says it's a lovely working environment and—' 'That's nice for her,' I quickly interject, 'but as I was saying, about Ameri—'

'Yes *and* she was telling me she gets a great staff discount, you know and—'

'MOTHER! I COULDN'T GIVE A FUCK ABOUT AUNTIE VAL *OR* MARKS AND SPARKS. I'M MOVING TO BLOODY AMERICA!'

The room falls silent. Mother slams her cutlery down with a chink. '*You*? Moving to America?' she chuckles patronisingly. 'You couldn't even manage living down the road, dear! How could you possibly live in America?'

'I'll rent an apartment and I'll get work there, like anyone else,' I tell her defiantly.

Mother almost chokes on a Chantenay carrot. 'But you can't even manage that *here*! Besides, you'd need to apply for a work permit which can take months!'

'I know! I've got my inheritance to support me while I'm waiting' I reason, leaving her looking even more horrified.

'This is all a bit sudden, love. Have you thought it through properly? Why America?' Dad asks with his usual Buddha-like calm.

'Why *not* America? I need a clean break. A brand-new start. There's nothing holding me back now. There's nothing left here for me,' I argue.

'Charming!' Mother huffs, her face like an angry ball sack.

'Everything is so much bigger and better in America,' I continue, looking at Dad and perfectly ignoring Mother, 'And I think I could really *be* somebody there, build a totally new life.'

'Well, it's your life. If it'll make you hap—'

'Desmond! Don't encourage her!' Mother scolds. 'This is all silly talk. It won't come to anything.'

The silly talk comes to something, when, three weeks later, we stand saying our goodbyes at the airport.

'It's not too late to change your mind,' Mother repeats for the ninth time.

'I won't,' I scoff, rolling my eyes

'Now you *do* remember how to work that rape alarm I bought you, don't you?'

'Yes Mother, I pull the pin out,' I sigh exasperatedly.

'Good. Where is it then?' she demands.

'It's in my suitcase ... somewhere.'

But you've checked that in! What use is it in there? You're meant to keep them on you at all times!'

'Mother, I'm sure I'm not going to be raped between now and baggage claim on the other side,' I groan. 'Besides, I'm quite certain nobody would be desperate enough.'

'Call us as soon as you get there,' Dad, squeaks, removing his glasses and dabbing at his eyes.

'Oh don't, you'll start me off,' I groan, my voice wobbling as he pulls me into one of his bear hugs.

'Look after yourself.'

'I w-will Dad.'

'And *don't* squander your inheritance!' Mother barks, pulling me into one of her rigor mortis hugs.

I give them one last wave as I head through departures. Oh my God. This is it. I'm really going.

∞∞∞

My heart sinks as I spy the hyper pre-schooler sat in my window seat onboard the plane – the window seat from which I had intended to have unencumbered views and a chilled flight experience. I feel instant regret at not having gone business class. I could've afforded it for once in my life, why didn't I? Oh God, there's his brothers *and* his newborn sister, along with their even noisier, happy-clappy "Wheels on the Bus" singing Earth Mum sat in the row behind.

I stand in the aisle waiting for him to get his arse out of my seat. He doesn't. A tailback soon forms behind me.

'Oscar, let the nice lady sit down,' Earth Mum eventually shrills in her sing-song voice, before immediately picking up with 'the wipers on the bus.'

By take-off, when the baby on the plane goes whaa, whaa, whaa, waking me abruptly from an involuntary ten second slumber at which point I jump out of my skin to find Oscar staring through my soul, I find I'm feeling much less "nice lady" more Cruella De Ville as I secretly picture them all being sucked out the window – well, *you* want to try enduring that while maintaining a smiley essence of calm on a mere two hours broken sleep!

A couple of hours into the flight, I decide an

alcoholic beverage (or four) might aid me in my coping skills and dampen the urge to give Oscar a Chinese burn. As the effects hit, I feel a sudden wave of melancholy at observing our position on the TV screen in front of me. I've done it! I've officially left my home country *and* the love of my life. I can't believe Dan and I are going to be living five thousand miles apart. How can we have been so close and now so far away? Suddenly, my eyes begin to well and tears spill uncontrollably down my cheek. I turn my head as far toward the window as possible, crying silent tears for lost love.

'Mummy, why is that lady crying?' Oscar asks Earth Mum, loudly. 'Is it because she's fa...'

Before he can quite finish humiliating me and totally without thinking, I give him a hard pinch on his arm.

'OUCH! That hurt!' he yells, 'I'm telling my mu...'

Before he can grass me up, I instantly buy his silence by handing him my phone to play games on. What is it with kids having no bloody filter?! Ramming my earphones in and making a mental note that I *never* want to have children of my own, I crank up the volume of my iPod in order to lose myself in my nineties dance album and also to get James Brown's "Living in America" out of my head, which has been stuck on loop for the past week. As the music soars through me, my sadness is replaced with an enormous sense of accomplishment. I am here. I am doing this! I am a strong, independent woman and I don't need anyone.

The former statement is soon called into question upon landing at JFK airport when I suddenly feel very alone and bewildered, a rabbit caught in the headlights among the hustle bustle of the crowds, queues, non-stop ding-dongs and unintelligible last calls. What am I doing here? Now what? Oh, yes! *Facebook!* I must check myself in at JFK airport on Facebook to let my frenemies know that I've just touched down in New York. Ha! Imagine their faces ... Ugh, forgot! Deactivated my bloody account, didn't I? Bugger.

Negative thoughts begin circling my mental image of the American dream like vultures, waiting opportunistically for me to crack and have a meltdown. What was I thinking? How can I start a whole new life in the Big Apple when I can't even change a lightbulb?! I shall almost certainly be shot dead – so Mother says – or spend the rest of my life on death row in an unfortunate case of mistaken identity. On the other hand, things might just work out. After all, only in America can one acquire fame from nothing and go on to develop their own multi-million-dollar beauty line all while having a very large bottom. There's hope for me, yet!

Having spent a good hour standing at the

wrong baggage reclaim and very nearly starting a fight trying to claim a total stranger's case, the American dream hasn't gotten off to the best start but is fully back on track less than an hour later when I find myself with my gums around the biggest hamburger I've ever come across in Jumping Jack's, a downtown diner. I so wasn't wrong when I said everything in America was bigger and better.

'*Yes* Mother, the rape alarm is in my handbag,' I lie in between gob-loads of said burger while on the phone to her.

'*No*, I haven't been shot yet.'

'Ugh, No! I *haven't* bumped into Clint Eastwood, Harrison Ford or any other of your ancient fancy men.'

'Okay, loveyoutoobye.'

During the very short time I've been here, I'm amazed at how nice American people are. So much more friendly and far less antisocial than us Brits. People talk to one another instead of keeping their heads down, eyes down, hoods up and earphones in. I feel like royalty every time I open my mouth, mesmerising Americans everywhere with my London accent rather than feeling like an arse every time I open my mouth, appalling *everyone* everywhere with my lack of social intellect.

As I leave the diner, the noticeboard by the

door catches my eye and, in particular, an advert written in fabulously chic, looped writing upon pink coloured card:

Roommate wanted:

Mature, professional interlect (female) seeking female of simular background aged 25-30 to share rent and bills of downtown modern 2 bed apt. Should be feminist, have great sense of humour and no aversion to cats and/or music of following female soul legends:

Etta James

Urethra Franklin

Gladis Night.

If this is you, call me, Brooke Nelson: 718-516-4811

Chapter 12:

Twin Strangers

'O-M-G, you're British!' squeals the petite blonde over the din of Aretha Franklin's "Don't Play That Song" as she stands grinning in the doorway of the apartment.

'Yes, that's right,' I yell back at her over the music, wishing she would do as the song title suggests. I notice that the thick-rimmed glasses perched wonkily on her nose have a missing arm and the one that's *not* missing is overly bound in Sellotape, drawing the conclusion she's a girl who likes to get her money's worth.

'I'm Brooke, it's sooo amazing to meet you,' she coos, shaking my hand vigorously. As well as thrifty, she's pretty in a geeky, librarian sort of way.

'Lizzie. And you,' I smile, confusedly inspecting my hand which is now slightly orange and smells distinctly cheesy.

'Sorry,' she giggles, 'I just ate a whole tonne of Cheetos.'

Cheetos, yes! *Totally* forgot they were a thing. Must call and get some on the way back to the hotel.

'Well, come on in! Excuse the mess,' she says, gesturing toward the many empty water bottles, soft drinks cans and food wrappers strewn about the place. I spy a tub of Betty Crocker chocolate cake frosting on the coffee table complete with spoon standing to attention within it.

'Oh, er, I have the worst sweet tooth,' she explains. 'Well, *sweet teeth* really, as in all of them are sweet, get it?' she explains, laughing hysterically.

'Yeah, same,' I reply, forcing a laugh nowhere near the magnitude of hers.

'Believe it or not, I did just do a big clean this week,' she exclaims awkwardly. 'It just never seems to stay tidy for very long.'

'Oh, I know exactly what you mean!' I agree, unperturbed by the mess and feeling quite at home.

'I don't know about you, but I just think life is waaay too short to be doing housework all the time,' she says, excusing the slobbery.

'Or indeed *any* time!' I agree.

I notice her perfect figure as she leads me from room to room and begin to wonder how it is that she can scoff Cheetos and gorge on tubs of Betty

Crocker cake frosting and *still* look like that. Obviously, she works out like a bitch.

'Just get this out of the way,' she mumbles, wheeling a mobility scooter out from the hallway. 'It was my late grandmother's,' she explains, noticing my puzzled expression.

'Oh, I'm sorry,' I rush to tell her, 'my Nan passed away recently too.'

'Er, well, it *was* like, two years ago now,' she adds, looking awkward.

'*Oh.*'

'Yeah, I couldn't bear to let Mom get rid of it, so I thought I'd keep it and use it myself,' she explains while I look her up and down, inquisitively. She doesn't look disabled and she's definitely not sporting any sort of limp. 'It comes in real handy, you know? Like for whizzing from room to room, doing the housework, going out to the shops in it. Everything's so much quicker,' she adds, nodding sincerely.

Okay, she's nuts, I quietly conclude. And clearly, she *doesn't* work out like a bitch. Exactly *how* she's stood there in cut-off denim shorts with a washboard stomach is what I'd bloody well like to know. Has she been dabbling in sorcery too?

'Sooo, kitchen,' she says, leading the way through. 'There *is* a dishwasher, I just haven't gotten around to unloading it yet,' she adds, gesturing toward the sink full of dishes.

'Oh, you get those fresh meal kits delivered?' I chirp. 'I thought about starting those up but they're expensive,' I remark, noticing the company logo emblazoned upon the large cardboard box perched on top of the heap of rubbish which has long surpassed the confines of the kitchen bin.

'Yeah, totally. At least it *is* for what I actually used from it,' she tells me. 'I had the lemon in my gin and tonics and used the cucumber on my eye bags. Other than that, the rest of the ingredients went outta date. Didn't get around to cooking any of it. Probably ate a shit tonne of fast food instead,' she tells me sincerely.

'Ah!'

'So yeah, totally not worth it, unless you're going to cook it.'

'So, have you had many people interested in your ad?' I ask, spying the murky goldfish bowl on the countertop with no actual goldfish in ... *oh*, wait, there's one floating dead on top. Well, half of one ... it's obviously been there a while.

'Oh yeah, tonnes. Just no takers yet.'

'Ah.'

If I couldn't already see why Brooke hasn't had any takers for her ad for a roommate, I definitely do as she leads me into the spare bedroom where her cats are.

'This one's Cleo,' she says adoringly, 'I've had him since I was like, eighteen.'

I stare wide-eyed at the stiff-looking tortoiseshell staring coldly through my soul, along with the rest of her many other equally statue-like feline friends dotted about the room.

'They're stuffed,' she adds, cool as you like after noticing my confusion.

'S-stuffed?' I repeat in horror.

'Yeah, I mean, I'm in a high-rise. It's much easier this way.'

I stare at her open-mouthed, not quite believing what I just heard.

'Oh, they all died of natural causes over the years. I didn't have them done ecspecially,' she reassures me, 'but this way we get to be together forever. Way better than the worms getting at them, right?'

I suppose she's right – just not in the way she says "especially".

'Oh! And this would be *your* room by the way,' she smiles, 'that's why the advert says any takers should have no aversion to cats.'

'It didn't say they were stuffed,' I gulp.

'Well, I would have them in my bedroom, but

I just don't have room in there,' she quickly explains. 'Besides, I find it hard to orgasm with them staring at me, you know? It's kinda like getting yourself off in front of your children.'

'Well, what about if *I* ever want to er ... to er, you know, orgasm?' I ask.

'Ha-ha! They won't see you, silly! They're stuffed!'

I must be out of my mind but within ten minutes, I've given her a cheque for half a month's rent and I move in tomorrow. I suppose that in the short time I've been in her apartment I've quickly established that there are no skeletons in the closet where Brooke Nelson's concerned: there are just cats. *Several* stuffed cats which are going straight in said bloody closet as of tomorrow!

Mother calls at 5.20am next morning to let me know there's an earthquake in California and that I should get under a sturdy table at once.

'You do know it's like 5.20am here?' I point out.

'Well, it's after ten here and don't say "like" in that context, it's frightfully common. Now, have you a sturdy table close to hand?'

'No, Mother. I'm over 2,900 miles away from California, you really needn't worry.'

'Well, it might still ripple across to New York.

Better to be safe than sorry dear,' she trills.

'Ugh! Is this the sole reason for your call?' I ask, yawning.

'Not entirely. I thought you might like to know that Auntie Val has had her hysterectomy.'

Why the fuck at 5.20 in the morning would I like to know that Auntie Val is now womb-less?!

'Oh!' I reply.

'Stop shouting Desmond! I'm trying to find the button!' Mother roars down the line.

'Ouch, *what?*' I ask, holding the phone away from my now ringing ear.

'It's your father, he wants me to put you on loudspeak—'

And she's gone!

Ten seconds later, my phone starts ringing with "Mother's ring"; I haven't assigned a separate ringtone especially for her, I'm talking about the way the ring sounds extra annoying whenever *she's* calling and the sixth-sense I seem to have which tells me it's her without even looking.

'Oh, *there* you are. I don't know what happened there. Blasted telephone's packing up. I knew we should've gone for that new, modern set I saw in John Lewis last month. There was money off too but, oh no, *you* know best Desmond,' she waffles.

'Mother, do you actually want anything? It's just, what with it being not even half five in the morning...'

'Lilibeth? It's Dad. How's the Big Apple, love?'

'Er, yeah, great, Dad,' I yawn, picking at the crusty bits wedged within the corners of my sleep-deprived eyes.

'That's good. Listen, that Dan stopped by yesterday to ask where you were.'

'Oh?! Well ... what did you tell him?' I ask, sitting bolt upright, suddenly alert.

'Not much, your mother sent him pack—'

'I hardly think I sent him packing! I simply told him you were thriving in your fabulous new life without him,' she interjects.

'Oh, Mother! You *didn't*?'

'No point beating about the bush dear.'

'What did he say, then?' I ask, my eyes wide and stomach doing somersaults.

'Well, what does it matter now? Whatever silly little romance you had is, thankfully, done and dusted. The man's a pseud, nothing between the ears. You're well rid if you ask me,' Mother replies.

'I *didn't* ask you.'

'Goodness, I almost forgot to mention!' she announces, dramatically.

'What? *What*?!' I probe desperately with just the tiniest flicker of hope that he might've asked Dad for my hand in marriage.

'Daddy and I have picked out the new conservatory. It's being fitted next week. Wonderful isn't it?' she announces with glee, instantly obliterating said tiny flicker of hope.

'Yeah, *great*.'

Thanks to the utterly pointless early morning wake-up call, moving day gets off to a lethargic, slitty-eyed start and I can't stop thinking about Dan. Up to now, America had proven to be the perfect distraction, but knowing I'm on his mind has put him firmly back on mine. Should I call him? Ugh, no. Hearing his chocolate voice would only serve to plunge me further down this rabbit hole of melancholic contemplation. What if I'd stayed? Could we have been something? Of course, we couldn't. It was pure sorcery. Oh, but the guns, his kisses, the lovemaking (which too, was pure sorcery). Ugh! Well, sorcery or not, even if I were to perish in a Californian earthquake in New York in the absence of a sturdy table, at least I knew love with Dan Elliott. The question is, can there ever be life after love with Dan Elliott?

∞∞∞

'Brooke? Is that *you*?!' I blink and blink again at the sight of the indescribably gorgeous being stood in the doorway of what is to be home for the foreseeable. Her silky, shoulder-length icy blonde bob gleams brilliantly against her firm, bronzed skin. Her make-up is flawless, airbrushed almost, and her killer body perfectly accentuated in the red bodycon dress she's totally rocking. That megawatt smile and those eyes: massive, vibrant, green eyes, marvellously free of any one-armed, Sellotape bound, thick-rimmed specs. She's like some kind of female, non-fictional Clark bleeding Kent counterpart! What the actual fuck?!'

'*Yes*, it's me ... I just, cleaned up a bit,' she shrugs.

Cleaned up a bit? Give over! It's like she's had a visit from Cinderella's fairy godmother! She's perfect! Beyond stunning! And the most beautiful part of it all is that she doesn't appear to know it, unlike Rachel De Souza whom I might add isn't a patch on this American beauty standing before me. Ha! I'm sure it would shatter her perfect little world to know she most definitely *isn't* the fairest in the land.

I soon observe that when Brooke says she's "cleaned up a bit" she merely meant herself and not the apartment, which is in even more of a tip than yesterday. How can one woman make so much mess? I thought I was bloody bad!

'What are you doing,' Brooke gasps from within the doorway of what is now my bedroom, a look of horror on her aesthetically-thrilling face.

I freeze within the closet door, a statuesque Cleo dangling by the tail in my right hand. 'Er, well I thought I'd put them away in the closet. You know, for safekeeping. I might … break one or something.'

'No, silly! I mean, why are you unpacking?'

'…because I need to,' I reply, wondering if it's a trick question.

'Jeez, you Brits! You're so, I don't know, *meticulous*, with your need to organise. To form orderly queues and stuff. Have you never heard of the saying "always put off until tomorrow what you can do today?" she asks, leaning against the door, her hands rested on her slender hips as though mid-shoot for some high-end glossy mag.

'Er, I think it might be the other way round,' I tell her.

'Whatever! Come on, get cleaned up and let's hit the bars!'

My "cleaned up" is on a much less radical and way more disappointing scale than Brooke's. Oh, why can't I look like a frigging supermodel? Why? Life would be so much better and simpler all round if I could only look like a supermodel. I mean, imagine having a face of such perfect proportions and so aesthetically pleasing that you can skulk about looking your absolute worst in full confidence that your very worst is better than some people's absolute best?! Imagine being able to wear anything you like without needing give a flicker of thought to the size of your arse or belly? I can't even begin to imagine the bliss that comes from being free of the burden of more or less lifelong issues. Whatever Brooke Nelsons secret, I must become privy to it at once!

'So, how come you live alone? Someone like you?' I ask over a Cosmopolitan in Rudey's, a chic little downtown bar in which the entirety of its male patrons' gazes is firmly fixated on Brooke.

'Someone like me?'

'Yeah, I mean you turn heads like the bloody Exorcist! How in the hell are you even single right now?'

'I've always been single,' she shrugs, gormlessly crunching the ice at the bottom of her glass having quickly drained it.

'Come again?'

'I've never had a boyfriend.'

'You're shitting me?!'

'No, straight up! I've never even kissed a guy. Not beyond high school, anyway,' she reveals.

'Whaaat?!' I gasp in disbelief.

'I don't know, it's like, guys just don't approach me and I'm too shy to approach *them* so…'

'So, you're a virgin then?!' I gasp, wide-eyed and not quite believing that out of the two of us I'm the only one to have had sex! *Me!*

'Yeah,' she nods. 'I mean, my hymen's probably long gone with all the sex toys but, yeah. What about you?' she asks, instantly triggering incessant, unrelenting, misty-eyed Dan-talk for the rest of the night which gets louder and more emotional in tandem with cocktails consumed.

'H-he was the lovvve of my liiife,' I slur.

'Yeah, I can imagine. I've never even seen the guy and I'm literally sat here wet just hearing about him!'

I fish my phone out of my bag, knocking both our drinks over in the process.

'Thisss is himmm,' I announce, holding out my phone. 'Gawjusss, ain't he?'

She leans toward it, squinting her eyes in an attempt to focus. 'Oh! Well, er, that's not how I'd pictured him,' she remarks, her face falling.

'You don't go for pretty boyyys?' I ask, shocked.

'Oh, yeah. Love a pretty boy! Just like them younger. Well … quite a bit younger actually and with more hair and less grays.'

Frowning, I turn my phone around. Shit, it's Dad!

'Ugh! That's not him. Hang on,' I tell her, swiping through my photos.

'T-this is h-him,' I sob, my face screwing up at the mere sight of him.

'Phwoooooar!' she gasps. 'Girl, you gotta be out of your mind to move away from that. What a hottie!'

'I l-love him s-sooo much!' I howl, oblivious to the eruption of laughter breaking out in the bar around us.

∞∞∞

Unable to move my head an inch without triggering unwithstandable pounding, I am reduced to an unsightly, bed-bound heap, from beneath which I am frantically scrolling through the call logs on my old sim card having had a momentary flash recollection of several drunken attempts to get the old sim back in my phone and call Dan last night. Luckily, I was too pissed to manage it – I have enough trouble managing it sober in daylight hours! I breathe a sigh of relief, not just because I would have almost certainly made an arse of myself, but because it was 4.50am UK time which is what Mother likes to do to *me*. With the hourglass of my twenties at the very last dredges, I absolutely refuse to become her a clone of *her* in my old age! As well as relieved, I am also extremely despondent to note the absence of the string of incoming texts I had been quietly anticipating. I realise I told Dan to forget about me, but come on, not even *one*? Not from *anyone*?! Bastards! They're all utter bastards, the lot of them! The lot of them as in Levi and Dan.

Eventually, I am forced to withstand said unwithstandable head pounding in order to ingest the copious volume of water necessary to see off this sodding hangover. I walk in on Brooke in the kitchen, eating Nutella straight from the jar with her fingers while staring into space.

'I'm thinking we might have to unload the dishwasher at some point,' she murmurs in a daze, smacking her lips. 'We've got, like, no cutlery or anything to eat off.'

'We could toss a coin?' I suggest, clutching my head and lapping water straight from the kitchen tap like a dog.

Having spent most of the day watching Brooke eat her way through the kitchen cupboards, I'm keener than ever to learn how it is that she is able to scoff like a gluttonous bear without gaining weight.

'Oh, well it's actually very simple,' she tells me.

'*Do* tell!'

'Eating in modulation,' she winks, proudly.

'Eh?' Isn't that something to do with audio?

'Well, for five days of the week I eat like a mouse, then at the weekends I eat like a horse. Simples.'

And that was it! Such simple words within a simple sentence that would go on to bring about the end of my tumultuous, torturous, weight battle and the start of life as a slim, slinky sex goddess! Well, not quite, but I'm getting there. During the lengthy wait for my work permit to come through, I have achieved the following:

Thighs no longer touch or rub when I walk

Arse is significantly smaller

Knickers actually stay up rather than roll down over belly

Can see (most of) Mary

Hair a sexy, multi-tonal blonde and Rapunzel-like.

I have since acquired job interview at top Manhattan finance firm along with whole new brightly coloured wardrobe of clingy tops and fitted pencil skirts, which I have discovered give the illusion of even more streamlined bod without need for Gutbuster 2000 or similar.

And, owing to all of the above, head is higher, smile wider and life great! Even *with* Dan-shaped hole in.

Chapter 13:

Straight Up

Some people go to great lengths to prepare for job interviews, undertaking thorough research of the company, sourcing the perfect, professional attire, carefully rehearsing their answering technique in front of a mirror. I, on the other hand, have always tended to treat job interviews like my eyeliner: I wing it.

Winging it gets off to a stressy start as I discover what looks like – but isn't, given the lack of men in my life – a semen stain on the left tit of my executive, royal blue shift dress. The highly suspect stain in fact originated from the trendy but crap steel-cut oats I unknowingly spilled down my front this morning while engrossed in extreme TV makeovers. After a frantic scrub and blast with the hair dryer, it dries to what looks like leaked breast milk. Oh, fuck! Cannot have potential future employer assuming I am some strange, lactating British chump. *Must* source alternative, laundered professional attire at once, which proves to be difficult since neither Brooke nor I have quite mastered the art of putting a wash on. Well, they don't make it bloody easy, do they? Why have so many complex-looking buttons on a washing machine when all you really need is a start button? Why?! There's absolutely *no* need to design washing machines to look like spaceships, it's ridiculous! And then, suddenly, a lightbulb moment: a brooch! I could cover the offending stain with a brooch! Do I even own a brooch?! Well, being under the age of seventy, *no*, but I'll bet Nanny Bradshaw did … and I have her jewellery box! You, beauty! Tottering at speed into the bedroom, I fling open the closet doors, jump out of my skin at the array of stuffed cats glaring back at me from within the shadows and begin rummaging frantically through Nanny's jewellery box just as my phone pings to alert me to my waiting cab. Ugh! There's plenty in the way of pearls and brash, clip-on earrings, but not much in the way of brooches. In fact, there's just a bunch of badges from birthday cards she'd kept throughout the years, some rusty with age. Bugger, bugger, bugger!

With the cab meter running and no alternative laundered professional attire to hand, I conclude pinning a birthday badge over the ghastly stain on my dress and having to smile and thank anyone who notices and subsequently wishes me a happy birthday a mere, mild inconvenience and, actually, an all-round bloody good solution. Who knows? It might even land me the job! I grab the least-rustiest badge and hurriedly pin it to my dress, being particularly careful to ensure its positioning conceals the circumference of the stain. There, done!

I've no regrets – other than for not having a pee before I left – at the lack of interview preparation as I climb out of the yellow cab and step into the bustling centre of Manhattan among a series of clip-clopping heels, honking horns and petrol fumes. I always think you're far better off just going in there, taking it all in your stride and being yourself. Stressing beforehand over every minute detail only serves to make you anxious. Besides, they always ask the same old cliche questions anyway, such as:

'Why should we hire you?'

Er, because you need to fill your vacancy and I need to work!

'Tell me about you?'

Do I have to? I really need this job!

'What are your strengths?'

Hmm, let's see: falling over, scoffing and fucking things up!

'What can you bring to the company?'

Disarray and destruction no doubt, but please

hire me still!

'Where do you see yourself in five years?'

In bed with a hangover, probably!

Three minutes later, I'm taking it all in my stride and being myself alright by striding straight through a secured fire exit which triggers a loud alarm, causing the majority of the ground floor to come a-running. Good God! This highly reputable financial firm is *never* going to employ me. I might as well just turn around and walk out now.

'Elizabeth Bradshaw?' comes a voice from behind me.

'Er, yes, hello?'

'Ooh! Love the accent! Follow me would you please, ma'am?'

I'm not even slightly nervous as I follow the smart, camp-sounding, headset-clad dude from reception along to the ambience of the saxophone music playing quietly in the background to a meeting room where two, senior, important-looking men in grey suits sit awaiting me. It'll all be over and I'll be out of here in minutes and back at the apartment with my feet up in front of the Ellen DeGeneres show before you can say rejection letter.

'You must be Elizabeth. Come on in and sit yourself down', interviewer one greets me as they both stand to shake my hand.

'I am, yes, thank you very much. Pleased to meet you, hello!' I grin, trying to appear posh.

'Get a load of that accent,' interviewer two remarks. 'Where in the UK are you from?'

'East London,' I reply in as regal a tone as possible, smiling with pride as I go to take off my jacket and freeze in horror as I read for the first time the words displayed upon my borrowed birthday badge: Another year older, another year wider. Happy Birthday you fat c**t!

'A-ha-ha-ha, yes, yes,' I chortle in panic, swiftly closing my jacket and tightly folding my arms. Jesus Christ, Nanny! How didn't I guess her birthday badges *wouldn't* have been of the nice, pleasant kind that normal people gift to each other?!

'So, it says here you worked as an investment banking manager back in the UK,' interviewer one remarks, peering down at my application and causing me to rock nervously on my chair.

'Yes,' I squeak.

'And you've got a university degree, great!'

'Uh-huh.'

'And what was your reason for leaving your last job?'

'I left because I, er, came here to America,' I tell him, putting on the same crap, hoity-toity, high-pitched tone I always use when I'm either flogging a dead horse or in trouble. What me? Oh, no, I'm just an English rose. I swear down, my career history in investment banking is one hundred percent legit, I have never worked in holiday sales and have *never* been sacked in my life!

'Well, your resume is very impressive and you're actually pretty over-qualified for what is essentially an entry-level position,' interviewer one muses, fondling his beard.

'Yes, well, you know, I've done a lot of er, leading and managing, but I'm happy to work my way up. We've all had to start at the bottom to get where we want to be,' I chuckle executively, unphased by the fact that Hedge Fund Analyst is in actual fact, a giant fucking leap for someone of my actual experience

'Love your thinking! Well, Lizzie ... can I call you Lizzie?'

'Sure, go ahead, sir.' Ooh! Get me with my newly-garnered Americanisms!

'Well, there's no point beating about the bush, Lizzie. You're more than experienced for the position, when can you start?'

'You *what*?'

∞∞∞

I meet Brooke for a quick lunch at Delilah's, a bistro close by to the accountancy firm she's temping at.

'Holy cow! You landed a job at Wilson Garcia & Co?' she gasps, spraying me with her oat milk latte.

'Yeah!'

'What did you do, suck off the interviewer?'

'No, why?'

'Nobody gets hired at Wilson Garcia! I've applied there like six times and never even scored an interview'.

Well, you wouldn't, if you've words like "interlect" on your resume.

'Er, well, I did exaggerate my work experience a little,' I confess.

'Wait, you lied on your application?'

'A bit.' More like a fucking lot! 'I'd read in their ad that the candidate should have experience in investment banking so I just put on my resume that my last job was an Investment Banking Manager,' I shrug.

'Shit, Lizzie! An Investment Banking Manager? Do you know how much they earn per hour?! I mean, I can't do the maths, but it's a lot.'

'No? Anyway, so what? Nobody ever got anywhere in life being completely honest. Besides, they're not going to go to all the trouble of following up my references, are they? Not with me being from the UK.'

'I don't know, I hope not,' she says in a hushed tone, cautiously looking about the place.

'They won't, will they?' I repeat, suddenly nervous, imagining my future fraud conviction and excessively long US jail term.

'Well, it's done now, so I say you just ... I don't know, go by my favourite life motto,' Brooke suggests.

'What's that?'

'Celebrate now, worry later!'

And we do just that – once the weekend parole from eating like mice comes around, that is.

'Hope you don't mind but I invited a few of them from work,' Brooke announces around the open door of the toilet from where she demonstrates a new take on multitasking: combining painting nails a matte, contemporary grey with taking a dump.

'Oh no, the more the merrier,' I declare from within the kitchen fridge where I've spent the past three minutes administering heavenly bursts of spray cream into my mouth straight from the can, just the sort of desperate action arising from five out of seven days of eating like a rodent.

A little before eight, the apartment buzzer sounds in the manner of a hyperactive wasp and swathes of revellers of all ages armed with bottles pour inside from off the street. When Brooke said she'd invited "a few of them from work", what she really meant was the entire bloody workforce. The place becomes a hive of raucous pleasure seekers, each on their own types of parole: parole from professional responsibility, parole from him or her indoors, parole from the kids, parole from the mundanity of everyday life. I can't see that any of them are here to celebrate my fraudulent landing of a spectacular job in finance, they are merely people on a mission to let loose and, in the words of a true Londoner, get absolutely wankered.

'Right, everybody! If I could say a few words,' Brooke announces to nobody. Well, nobody who's listening, anyway.

'Er, everyone, listen up!' she attempts again, clapping her hands together.

The pissed-up gabbling continues.

'OGGY, OGGY, OGGY!' I take the sudden initiative to roar which does the trick, though it gets me some strange looks and I'm not altogether sure anyone here, myself included, knows what it means.

'Okay, so you guys have all met my fab new roomie by now,' Brooke announces to a chorus of drunken whoops. 'Well, people, tonight we celebrate, because not only did she just land a job at Wilson motherfucking Garcia, *but* … and I know she's been trying to keep this a secret … SHE JUST TURNED THIRTY!'

My face falls into a confused frown as the room erupts into cheers.

'I saw the badge! I saw the badge!' Brooke yells, pointing toward me from the other side of the room before they all needlessly launch into a rowdy rendition of "Happy Birthday". I go to correct them before swiftly deciding it will be far easier to just go along with it.

Much of the following day proceeds in accordance with the usual hangover recovery procedure: lie in feral state of hibernation beneath blanket in front of trash TV, eating a shit load of junk food. That is, until the day starts drawing to a close and I decide I had better undertake some sort of preparation for my first day in the new job tomorrow.

To do list:

Launder executive work outfits for week ahead

Prepare healthy work lunches and ensconce in orderly fashion in fridge overnight

Ascertain what hedge fund is

∞∞∞

It has taken me twenty minutes to simply get into the building of my new place of work this morning – twenty bloody minutes! I had thought it would be a mere case of breezing through the open front entrance doors in the manner of Beyoncé or similar independent woman, rather than wasting precious time waving my arms erratically in an attempt to activate the secured automatic doors before realising said doors require the input of a secret code into a scary looking intercom which does nothing beyond making a series of unnerving bleeps when I attempt to ring for help! Eventually, I pluck up the courage to ask the first person in the lengthening queue of workers forming on the steps behind me for the code before I am forced to ask them to input it on my behalf when the intercom refuses to co-operate. It works first time for them, leaving me red-faced and gabbling about machinery and I not mixing.

Suddenly, I'm a bag of nerves. I can't even open the door at my new place of work and I'm still not altogether sure what a hedge fund is. I imagine I'll be let go by lunchtime and shall be reduced to begging for work flipping burgers at Jumping Jacks diner, though I doubt I'm even up to scratch for *that*; I'd probably set the bloody place on fire! Oh, God, help!

Beyond being shown to my desk on the trading floor by that same camp chap on reception, nobody knows I'm here, not even the workers around me whom are either yapping executively on their telephones or typing manically on their computers with slightly mad – and possibly cocaine-induced – game faces on. Where is my induction complete with tediously, boring health and safety video? The issuing of my locker key and staff pass complete with fancy company lanyard? My ego-boosting VIP tour of the building with friendly introductions to all staff members ranging from cleaners and maintenance to company director? The issuing of my new starter pack, complete with number to call should I be struggling with my mental health? I know Americans are far less anal than us Brits, but the lunch I went to great lengths to prepare will spoil in my bag unless I'm shown to a fucking fridge as a minimum! Surely this highly reputable firm has a staff fridge?!

Just as I contemplate slipping out and heading down to Jumping Jacks, some dark-haired Latino-looking guy in a suit on his way to the coffee machine spots me sat staring in open-mouthed confusion. His presence strangely causes the workers around me to talk even louder on their telephones and type even faster on their computers.

'Hey there! You look a little lost,' he remarks.

Not fucking half!

'Er, yeah, it's my first day today,' I tell him, trying to appear cooler than I am.

'Excellent! In that case, welcome to the firm. I'm Brian,' he says, shaking my hand vigorously. 'You're British!' he adds, much like everyone else I've come into contact with since arriving here, as though I might not know it.

'Uh-huh,' I murmur with a discreet roll of the eyes.

'Where are you from?' he asks, again much like everyone else I've come into contact with since arriving here.

'East London,' I reply on autopilot, casually checking my nails.

'Ohhh, *love* London!' he grins. 'We're looking at opening an office over there at some point.'

'Uh-huh,' I mumble, growing seriously concerned for the welfare of my probiotic yoghurt which still has not found its way into a fridge.

'Well, have a good first day!' he chirps, glancing at his Rolex as he breezes off and prompting the formerly perfect postures of the workers around me to slump somewhat.

'Lizzie Bradshaw?' comes a voice from behind.

'Er, yes?' I reply spinning on my chair to find a petite, middle-aged blonde with a clip board and a friendly smile standing behind me.

'Pam Johnson from HR,' she says, reaching out to shake my hand. 'I'm here to give you your induction.'

Halle-fucking-lujah!

To my relief, the majority of my first day working as a hedge fund analyst has been spent analysing sweet FA, having largely been taken up by my lengthy induction. To my utter distress, however, I soon learn during my ego-boosting VIP tour of the building that the guy in the suit I was rude and standoffish with this morning is none other than Brian Garcia, one of the CEOs of the fucking company! Shit, shit, shit!

I'm not sure whether it's down to the success of my various attempts to redeem myself during our re-introduction – over-enthusiastically complimenting anything and everything from his suit to the paper weight on his desk – but he seems jovial enough and, thankfully, hasn't ordered the immediate termination of my employment complete with security escort off of the premises. In fact, dare I say it, he appeared to be rather flirty with me in a polite, executive sort of way.

∞∞∞

Keen to avoid provoking suspicion and a subsequent lengthy jail term for fraud, I spend the evenings trawling through YouTube videos on finance and investment, investigating the stock and bond markets as well as looking up business buzzwords online which I spend the week reciting loudly over the telephone whenever Brian Garcia is in the vicinity of my desk.

My first week in the job has gotten off to a miraculously successful start! A week which has seen me blag not one, but two decent investment opportunities for the company, no doubt aided by my mesmerising British telephone voice. Who needs a university degree? I can do this! I can bloody well do this!

Mother has been telling everyone back home about my high-flying job in a Manhattan skyscraper. I was especially careful to be vague in terms of the actual job title so as to avoid being rumbled by one of her hoity-toity friends who would know I had not been to university, have no experience in investment banking whatsoever and am probably under-qualified to mop the floor of a bank.

A month on and just when it was beginning to look as though I might get away with fraud,

I have been summoned to Brian Garcia's office. Shit, shit, shit! Oh my God the FBI are probably in there waiting for me. Everybody back home will get to know I'm a criminal – Dan Elliott included. A blotchy, red rash creeps up my neck and along the whole of one side of my face. Heart pounding, I apprehensively make my way to Brian's office where I stand outside paranoid with my ear to the door, listening for federal sounding voices. Can't hear any, phew! All I can hear is Brian on the phone using business buzzwords I haven't yet come across and sounding very important and CEO-like. Once he's wrapped up and ended the call, I take a deep breath and timidly knock the door.

He gives an executive 'Yah!' by way of a response, prompting me to pop my head around the door, nervously. 'Er, you asked to see me … sir,' I gulp.

'Oh hey, Lizzie' he greets me. 'Come on in and sit down,' he urges in a markedly cheerier tone than one might expect him to be using in the case of employee fraud.

'How's your day been?' he asks.

'Er … good' I mumble in a monotone voice, wondering if the pleasantries are part of his interrogation technique.

'Good stuff,' he replies, his lengthy gaze making me shift uncomfortably in my seat. 'So, er

Lizzie, I wanted to ask...' he begins, his voice taking on a more serious tone just as the phone on his desk starts ringing. 'Sorry, excuse me,' he says, answering it and getting into a detailed, important sounding conversation as I sit in prolonged agony, twiddling my thumbs and trying to come up with a perfectly reasonable explanation for my fraudulent job application, determining in all of two seconds that no such explanation exists. Well, there's nothing for it. I shall simply have to admit to my guilt and hope he's not looking to prosecute and, if he *is*, beg him the fuck not to!

'Sorry about that,' he says, placing down the receiver.

I nod anxiously as we both go to talk at once.

'I'm sorry, you go,' he says.

'It's okay, you go first,' I reply.

'No honestly, after you.'

'No ... you,' I squeak, going all stiff. Hell, this is awkward as fuck!

'Well, er, I just wanted to ask you about—' he pauses.

'Yes,' I blurt out. 'I admit it.'

'Admit what?' he asks, suddenly looking puzzled.

'Everything. I admit to everything.'

'Right, er, you've lost me,' he says, giving me a strange look.

Turning bright red during the continuing silence that follows and with the swift realisation that he can't possibly have summoned me here to accuse me of anything, I begin wildly racking my brains...

'I, er, admit to drinking more complimentary coffee from the machine than would be deemed a reasonable quantity as per my contract of employment,' I tell him, all in one breath.

'You and me both!' he laughs.

'A-ha-ha-ha-ha-ha' I fake laugh along with him.

'No, er, Lizzie. I wanted to ask if you'd like to go for dinner some time,' he smiles.

'You *what*?' I eventually manage by way of a shellshocked response.

'Well, not if you don't want to or if you're not comfortable with it,' he quickly adds. 'I mean, please don't see this as me hitting on you. I'd just like to get to know you a little better'.

'*Oh*' I gasp in surprise. 'Sure'.

'Great! Well, I'll give you a call and we'll arrange something soon, okay?' he suggests, taking out his phone from his trouser pocket. 'What's your number.'

'My number? Er, it's...it's...'

Oh, fuck! My mind's gone blank! I've forgotten my own phone number! I. Have. Forgotten. My. *Own*. Sodding. Phone. Number. This is it! Dementia does run in the family and it's already taking hold ... and I'm not even bloody thirty!

'Go ahead,' he prompts, poised in readiness to add me to his contacts.

'Er, it's a new phone, I haven't learned the number off by heart yet,' I lie.

'It's okay if you're not comfortable giving it to me,' he says. 'Your number, I mean,' he swiftly adds, realising the double entendre.

'Oh no, honest. It's not that,' I insist.

'Okay. Well, here, take my business card,' he says, selecting and handing me one from the tray on his desk. 'Now the ball's in your court,' he smiles, prompting my formerly broken heart to flutter for what feels like the first time in ages.

∞∞∞

'What?' Brooke gasps, almost choking on her Piña Colada as I break the news over drinks in Rudey's. 'You're shitting me, right? I mean, this is a joke!' she yells over the loud music.

'No, honestly. Straight up,' I yell back, placing my hand on my heart sincerely.

'What the fuck? How the hell did you bag a date with the fucking CEO, girl?!'

I shrug, still not quite believing it myself.

'So, I'm guessing they don't yet know about the fraud,' she yells, prompting the entire table beside us to turn their heads our way.

'Sssshhhh!' I frown, placing my head into my hands in disbelief.

'Shit, whoops, sorry,' she mouths at me. 'Jeez! This is big! So, are you gonna call him? Do you like him?'

'Maybe and, er, I don't know, perhaps,' I tell her, smiling coyly.

'Then do it now!' she yells.

'No, I was going to hold off a while. I don't want to look desperate.'

'The guy's a fucking billionaire, get in there quick before some other bitch does!'

'Wait, I thought you were a feminist?!'

'Yeah, so?' she shrugs, vacantly.

'Well, don't you advocate female empowerment and independence?'

'Yeah, so?' she repeats, even more vacantly.

'Well, wouldn't that be against everything you

stand for?'

'You've lost me!' she frowns.

'Ugh! Forget it, look, I don't think I'm gonna bother calling him. He'll just think I'm after his money and I'm not that kind of girl. Besides, he's a bit older than me and he's not my usual type.'

'Lizzie, are you out of your fucking mind? He's rich and handsome!'

'Yeah, well. I can't see we'll have much in common. It'll be awkward as arse. Plus…'

'Plus, what?'

'Well … he's not Dan, is he?'

'Ah! So that's what this is really about! Lizzie, that bird has flown. You gotta move on.'

She's right. I know she's right. Of *course*, she's right. But my heart still pines for him. I miss him. Ache for him. He was and still is the love of my life. Burying Dan Elliott in the past and moving on is far simpler said than done.

Chapter 14:

Too Good to be True

Not rushing to call Brian must have given him the impression that I'm playing hard to get, which of course I'm not, but he doesn't know that. He's probably thinking I've a damn nerve making someone of his status work to land a date with little old me – yes, little! I can actually say that now and it not just be a figure of speech.

I couldn't bear for Brian to think I'm the type to play silly buggers, but then I don't want to appear overly keen either, suggesting I'm only interested in him for his wealth. Oh, it's all very awkward! The more I try to keep my head down and focused on work, the more I seem to bump into him:

At the coffee machine, 'Hi!'

In the corridor, 'Oh, hey!'

In the staff restaurant, 'Afternoon!'

Outside the toilets, 'Oh, hello.' Getting a bit cringe now.

In the elevator. Really? Aren't CEOs supposed to be permanently unavailable?

'Good morning,' he greets me cheerily as I step in.

'Oh, morning.'

'How's it going?'

'Er, great.'

'Listen, I want to apologise for putting you in an awkward position,' he says the minute the elevator clears, leaving us alone together. 'It's clear you're uncomfortable and, er, it was unprofessional of me. I don't always ask our staff out to dinner I can assure you. It's actually pretty out of character for me. I guess I'm just intrigued by you,' he smiles with both his mouth and eyes.

'No, honestly. I'm flattered,' I tell him, blushing furiously.

'It's okay, shall we just forget it and move on?' he suggests.

'NO!' I blurt out, a little too loud and quickly, taking us both by surprise.

'Er, God this is so embarrassing,' I mumble, wishing the ground would swallow me up. 'Look, the reason I haven't called you isn't because I don't want to go out for dinner with you, I'd love to go. Really, I would.'

'Okay, so what's the issue?' he frowns, intrigued.

I gaze back at him, a bit lost for words as I notice, despite the ten-year age gap and him not being my usual type, how handsome he is. Similarly, I didn't realise up to now how much businessmen in suits turn me on – with the exception of those in the funeral business and the over fifty. 'I just ... don't want you to think I'd only be going because of who you are,' I manage, finally.

'Ah, that's sweet. But you honestly don't have to worry about that,' he smiles, holding my gaze for a few moments and giving me butterflies before the elevator door pings open.

'Call me!' he says, waggling his index finger at me in mock-disapproval before breezing off toward his office, leaving me standing, staring slightly open-mouthed in his wake.

D'you know what? I think I will!

I decide to wait until the Friday night after work once I've a few cocktails in me for Dutch courage before taking the plunge and calling Brian, quietly slipping off to the ladies in Rudey's to do so. Oh, bollocks! It's gone straight to voicemail. I hate leaving voicemails! My voice seems to involuntarily rise an octave the minute I hear the beep making me sound silly and childish. What to do. Shall I leave a message? Shall I hang up? Oh, too late, it's beeped.

'Er, hi Brian, it's Lizzie,' I manage, pausing while thinking of something sophisticated and executive to say, just as the door to the loos bursts open and an exasperated looking Brooke plods in.

'FUCK, I NEED TO GET LAID!' she wails in a strident echo. Horrified, I swiftly hang up the phone. Well, that went bloody brilliantly, didn't it?!

Having spent the rest of the weekend terrified that Brian thinks I'm a nympho and has duly changed his mind about me, I am thoroughly relieved to have received a charming call from him on Sunday night during which he assured me that he knew the nympho-speak couldn't possibly have come from me since it was delivered in an all-American accent *and* that he would still very much like to take me to dinner. Our dinner date is organised for next Saturday night at some ridiculously posh-sounding French restaurant that I cannot even begin to fathom the pronunciation of. On giving it a swift Google, I'm anxious to note that the dress code requires me to wear an evening dress. A sodding evening dress! I don't own – and have never owned – such a garment. Nor have I ever eaten in a Michelin three-star restaurant and, from what I've seen in films, I'm bound to make an arse of myself since I shan't be able to read the posh menu and I've no idea what all the fucking cutlery's for!

In a state of panic, I proceed to make the biggest mistake ever (well, one of many) in calling Mother to ask her advice on fine dining etiquette with the intention of remaining tight lipped about the occasion, but finding myself cracking under pressure a mere two minutes into the phone call.

'By Jove! I've just done one of those Google searches on him. He and his firm had a double page spread in Forbes magazine last month, goodness gracious!' she sings delightedly.

'I don't really care about that Moth—'

'What are you wearing? Something that screams class, I hope!'

'I'm just in my pyjamas,' I tell her, peering down at them.

'No, no! I meant for the occasion. You'll need an evening dress, of course. Shame you're not over here, I could've loaned you that fabulous one I wore to Mr Tiptaff's gala charity ball now that you've lost all that weight.'

'*What* gala charity ball and who the fuck is Mr Tiptaff?'

'I hope you don't speak like that in front of the hedge fund billionaire, dear! *You* know Mr Tiptaff, the philanthropist from West Brompton? He held that fabulous charity ball back in 1982.'

'Never heard of him ... and I wasn't even bloody born in 1982!'

I duly thank my lucky stars that I am some 5000 miles away from Mother and her eighties evening gown.

'You'll need to appear keen, yet aloof dear. Keen, yet aloof! Remember your posture: head up, shoulder's back. Keep your elbows off the table and *no* slumping!'

'It was more help with the menu and cutlery I needed Moth—'

'Call me the *minute* you're back home, the very minute! You hear? Any time, day *or* night! My goodness, just wait until they hear about this at the country clu...'

There's a click on the line and she's gone. Without even a sodding goodbye!

∞∞∞

I spend all lunch hours of the working week in dress boutiques, texting mirror selfies for Brooke's approval. You would have thought me now being slim would make the process a far easier one, but it's no longer a simple case of duly eliminating anything that doesn't hide my belly and arse. I've gone from not being able to wear anything to being able to wear pretty much anything I bloody well like! I'm living my best life, like someone left the gate open and, for once, I have money to spend!

The practically salivating assistants are of *no* assistance, fawning over me and falling over themselves to sell me frocks ranging from the chic to slightly dowdy to the bastard ugly! In the end, I settle on a classy black figure-hugging LBD with Bardot straps, along with a pair of killer Christian Louboutin heels – *genuine* killer Christian Louboutin heels, not a tenner pair of oddly-smelling Chinese fakes from eBay.

By the time Saturday evening comes around and, recalling my past behaviour in restaurants, I'm a nervous, nauseous wreck.

'Stop thinking of everything that could go wrong and start thinking of everything that could go right! Get your positive pants on!' Brooke orders me from the kitchen where she's scoffing Nutella foldies – obscenely thickly-spread Nutella upon a single slice of bread, folded over in half: the lazy person's sandwich, basically.

Oh, my positive pants are on alright, it's just that I'm in grave danger of shitting them! I find myself wishing I was staying in tonight. Scoffing Nutella foldies and staring at the kitchen wall seems so appealing vs sat trembling in a ridiculously posh restaurant opposite handsome hedge fund billionaire ... who is also my employer!

Just as my thoughts drift towards standing him up and leaving my job, my phone pings with a text:

Your chariot awaits, ma'am x

'Oh, fuck! He's here! Help!' I plead at Brooke who says nothing, grabs and unscrews the litre bottle of vodka from the countertop and holds it up to my lips.

I do a double-take as I spot the limousine parked outside the apartment block outside complete with grinning chauffeur stood beside the open rear door. Hmm! I had better make sure this is legit first. Excitedly clambering into someone else's limo would just be me all over! Crouching down and peering inside suspiciously, I just about spot Brian shrouded by the enormous bouquet he's holding. Oh my God, this isn't real! This is like something from a bloody movie!

'You look exquisite!' he tells me from behind the fuck-off great bouquet of red roses.

'Thank you,' I blush, surprised he can see me.

From behind the tinted glass of the window, I observe several heads turning as the limousine draws to a halt outside the restaurant. The chauffer exits the front of the car, moving swiftly to open the rear door in an expert fashion.

The nearby restaurant-goers dither and dilly-dally, hanging around to see who's arrived. It's all I can do not to spring out from the back seat waving my arms wildly, screaming, 'Hello, everybody! It is I! I'm here at last, hello!' Instead, I clamber out being especially careful to conceal my gusset with my clutch bag as I see all the celebrities do at fancy premieres, just as the heel of my Christian Louboutin plunges straight into a drain and becomes stuck fast. You can take the gal outta East London...

Once Brian has removed my shoe from the drain and placed it back on my foot like some sort of cringey Cinderella parody, we venture inside. The restaurant staff can't kiss his arse enough from the minute his designer loafers touch the tiled entrance floor. I watch in awe as they pander to his every whim as though he's the bleeding president! Some people live for this sort of shit ... Mother being one such person. I don't. I just think it shows how pitifully shallow and materialistic some human beings are.

'Cristal, ma'am?' the waiter asks, holding out a serving tray.

'Ooh, *yes please*!' I grin, almost biting his hand off for a glass while kicking myself for deleting Facebook and denying myself the opportunity to be pictured supping Cristal in this swanky-as-fuck Michelin three-star New York eatery!

In normal circumstances, I would insist on going Dutch on dinner dates, but given that I would have to sell a kidney to do so on this occasion, I keep my gob shut. A few Cristals later, I find myself relaxing in Brian's company. He's surprisingly easy to talk to – well, he talks and I listen until such point that I switch off – and, despite his wealth and status, appears to have no airs and graces about him. He is, in fact, quite a nice guy, not as one might expect. Humble and softly-spoken, although his conversation centres mostly around business, he says "fiscal year" more often than I'd like, plus he pulls this strange face sometimes that makes him look a bit geeky, but I find myself overlooking such teeny flaws and sit imagining what he might look like naked as he waffles on about customer acquisition over the main course.

The evening wears on without incident until just before the stroke of midnight when the limousine draws up at my humble abode. I thank him for a wonderful evening, struggle to peck him goodbye over the fuck-off great bouquet of roses wedged between us, stumble, miss and kiss the glass of the limousine window instead. If I can't even manage to kiss the guy on the cheek properly, I conclude seeing him naked is probably a very long way off. However, all in all, the date was a success. I didn't make an arse of myself.

Nor did I think of Dan Elliott once! Apart from just now, upon mentioning him, doh!

Mirroring Cinderella once again, I find myself on the phone to my villainous Mother looking like a scrubber early next morning.

'*Yes*, I did come across classy. *No*, I didn't use the C word. *No*, I didn't offer it to him on a plate.' Yada yada yada.

'You should've seen Delia Davenport's face when she heard that our daughter is dating Brian Garcia of Wilson Garcia and company!' Mother boasts like an excitable child.

'Oh, Mother! Please don't tell the whole of London! It was just a dinner date. I don't even know if I'm going to see him agai—'

'Of, *course* you're going to see him again! I will *not* have you not seeing him again!' she barks down the line, practically deafening me.

She needn't have worried, because I see him again first thing Monday morning at work when, surprisingly, he summons me to his office to tell me how much he enjoyed our dinner date and that we should "pencil something in the diary" in terms of a second one. Why these executive types insist on using that term is beyond me as there were no pencils or diaries involved, we merely agreed we'd meet at his place at eight this Saturday night.

∞∞∞

I begin to wonder if Brian has fooled the world about his wealth and success when my cab draws up on Saturday night outside a pokey, run down three-bed wooden bungalow strangled with ivy.

'This can't be it! He's minted,' I tell the cab driver, aghast.

'Maybe that's *why* he's minted, he's a miserly fuck living well below his means,' he suggests. 'His type usually do'.

'Er, that's not possible,' I insist, 'he buys bottles of champagne at $200 a pop.'

'Well, this is the address and zip code you gave me, lady. I don't know, maybe he pays monthly for his champagne?'

Eventually, we establish the only foolery behind my arrival at this dump is my own, having wrongly read out Brian's zip code to the cab driver when he picked me up.

'Told you he was minted,' I announce as we arrive at the manned gatehouse at Brian's address some ten miles north of Manhattan, relieved that the cab driver can now observe this for himself rather than assuming I'm a gullible fool. Once we've acquired a stern nod from security, the cast iron entry gate slowly opens back to reveal a sweeping tree-lined driveway framed by flickering gas-lit lanterns.

The full magnitude of Brian's stone mansion set before a backdrop of green hills is revealed as we eventually come to the end of the driveway.

'Holy cow, how the other fucking half live,' the cab driver murmurs, his mouth hanging open and eyes on stalks, much like my own.

'Keep the change,' I tell him as I step out beside an enormous fountain and nervously make my way over to the steps and up to the pillared front porch, where a butler in uniform stands waiting beside the massive front door. This is a whole other world! Certainly, a stark contrast to mine which, prior to now, had been plagued with final demands, electric meters running out and bailiffs arriving to take the furniture. How am I even here?!

'Good evening ma'am. Please come in,' the butler greets me as I follow him in through the enormous entrance hall. I hesitate, feeling almost unworthy of walking across the immaculate, high shine marble flooring. Hell! How do you even live in a place like this? It's hard to imagine being able to do much beyond tiptoeing around as though you've a carrot up your arse, being careful not to touch anything. It's certainly not a place for muddy pawprints, crayons or, god forbid, fake tan – everything is far too white!

'Hey there!' Brian calls out from the top of the grand staircase, his voice reverberating across the entrance hall.

'Hello,' I smile, awkwardly, giving a silly wave.

'Can I get you a drink?' he asks, descending the steps.

'Love one'.

He mutters something unintelligible to the butler, giving him an appreciative pat before turning his attention back to me.

'You look stunning, as always,' he says, taking my hand and kissing it as though I were royalty.

I can't believe my eyes as he leads me by the hand outside to the gardens where a table set for two awaits under a large, lit wooden gazebo, from which there are stunning views of the Hudson. My heart sinks a little as I observe another enormous, fuck-off great bouquet taking up the majority of the table space. I didn't have a vase for the last one which I had to divide into four and display in beer glasses throughout the apartment. In fact, I've never actually owned a vase ever! I conclude that the continuation of romance henceforth will only see the further acquisition of yet more enormous, fuck-off great bouquets and consequently make a mental note to pick up a selection of vases from Walmart.

'They're gorgeous, thank you,' I smile as Brian

hands them to me, leaving me practically hidden from view with a muffled voice as I make various, nervy attempts at conversation.

A harpist creates the perfect ambience as the butler serves us Dom Pérignon champagne in cut glass crystal flutes, eventually relieving me of said enormous, fuck-off great bouquet which he carries away indoors. It's unbelievable what money can buy. Brian has everything most people dream of, but I find myself quietly wondering about this highly eligible bachelor. What makes him tick, besides the stock market? Is living alone in a house bigger than an average hotel and having more money than you could ever spend in your lifetime his idea of happiness? My thoughts soon evolve to wondering why he's single. Surely, he has women throwing themselves at him? Is it me? Am I just being traditionalist? Prejudiced? Overly suspicious? Or should he be married to a trophy wife with five kids by now? Does he even want marriage and kids? With it only being our second date, and if I want there to be a third, I should almost certainly refrain from asking. But with the champagne flowing, I decide to quiz him ... carefully.

'Amazing place you have here,' I remark. 'Must get lonely, just you by yourself.'

'You know what? No, actually. I'm away on business a lot and the phone never stops ringing. No time to be lonely!' he chuckles. If this ought to have served as the first sign of a workaholic, I missed it. Perhaps because of the way my heart keeps missing a beat every time he looks at me, or perhaps because of the Dom Pérignon.

'Why would you choose to date me when you could have anyone?' I blurt out suddenly no longer treading carefully and instead, rudely interrupting his excitable FTSE talk. He pauses for a moment, a little taken aback.

'Er, well now, let me see. You're blonde ... I've a thing for blondes', he laughs. 'You're gorgeous, you've a great figure.'

My ego begins to swell as he begins reeling off my qualities.

'You're smart, business-minded, you've a university degree,' he continues.

My face falls somewhat and I attempt to conceal the look of guilt with excessive admiration of champagne glass.

'And the accent is such a turn on!' he laughs. 'It's like I told you in the elevator that time, this is quite unheard of for me. I don't normally do this,' he adds, holding my gaze long enough to prompt a series of little tummy flips along with a sudden urge to kiss him. I decide to hold off, at least until after we're back inside and I've had the chance to "get lost" on my way to the bathroom and hunt for evidence of other women, a wife or divorce. They say if something seems too good to be true, it probably is and at this moment Brian Garcia is definitely looking that way.

Once we've finished eating, the waiting staff clear the table away and Brian draws the curtains surrounding the gazebo to give us some privacy as we sit together on one of the comfy cuddle chairs, sipping champagne, chatting about life and taking in the evening ambience. It would otherwise have been a truly perfect moment for a first snog, but I have to be sure that Brian and his intentions are genuine before I allow myself to fully fall for him.

Back in the house, I take the opportunity to slip off and get lost on my way to the bathroom as Brian fixes us a nightcap. Tiptoeing up the grand staircase, I make my way from room to room, peering around doorways suspiciously like some undercover FBI agent. I venture into what looks like the master bedroom, where the bed has been turned down and the bedside lamp switched on, presumably by the butler before he left off for the evening, and before I know it, I'm rummaging through Brian's underwear drawer! Aside from some nerdy looking, questionably patterned socks, everything looks quite normal and bachelor-like. I move to his dressing table where I begin rifling through his watches and jewellery looking for wedding or engagement rings. Relievedly, there's nothing but when something tells me to check under the bed, I find myself on all fours doing just that.

'Hey, Lizzie? You want ice with your cognac?' comes Brian's voice from downstairs.

A prolonged silence follows. Well, I can't very well shout, 'Oh, yes please!' from upstairs under his fucking bed, can I?

'Lizzie, you okay?' he calls out in a progressively concerned tone.

I hear the footsteps of his posh, leather moccasin-style indoor slippers against the marble flooring downstairs while my mind works overtime imagining his face upon discovering me here, under his bed. There would be no explaining it away. No excuse in the world for it other than total insanity on my part. And, furthermore, there can be no way back from it. I would have to resign immediately and never see him again. Oh, shit. Shit. Shiiit!

Shuffling out backward, I commando crawl toward the bedroom door before hurriedly turning tail and commando crawling straight back the other way when I hear his footsteps on the grand staircase. Oh, fuck! He's coming upstairs! With little in the way of options, I roll myself fully under the bed and remain there with my hand over my mouth and my heart in my throat. I'd expected potential fun and games on my second date with Brian, but I had been thinking more along the lines of love or sex games, not hide and fucking seek!

My heart almost stops as I spot the moccasin slippers at eye level on the bedroom floor to my left. They aren't moving. Shit! Has he spotted me already? Can he see me? Oh Jesus Christ, why do I get myself into these situations? *Why*?! Why couldn't I have just eaten my dinner, drunk my drinks and bloody behaved myself like a normal person?

Just as I contemplate rolling out and telling him that it's not what it looks like, the moccasins turn and disappear out through the doorway. I wait until I hear his footsteps climbing the stairs to the second floor, roll myself out and hurriedly tiptoe back downstairs to the kitchen where I neck my cognac in one gulp to calm my nerves, which are now shot to pieces.

'Ah! There you are! I thought you'd walked out on me,' Brian exclaims, walking into the kitchen minutes later.

'Oh no, I just sort of … got lost on my way to the bathroom,' I gabble.

'Really? It's just out there in the hall like I told you,' he says, looking puzzled and scratching his head.

I freeze for a moment and, having established Brian Garcia *isn't* too good to be true after all and by way of a convenient distraction, I lunge toward him for that first snog!

Chapter 15:

In a Right Empire State

They say that time flies, but I say it bloody rockets! No sooner had I blinked than my twenties are (regretfully) officially over and a year has passed. It is said that the way we spend our time defines who we are. Funny, but though I've spent the past year in a relationship with a billionaire US businessman eating top class nosh and quaffing offensively pricey champagne in the swankiest eateries around, I'm still the same old Lizzie Bradshaw. You can dress me in Gucci and adorn me with Cartier, but beneath all the finery, there still lies a ninny.

I'd never intended for my relationship with Brian to last a whole year. I'd gone into it fully prepared to be gradually phased out or straight-up ghosted the minute he discovered I'm not conventional girlfriend material for a man of his calibre. But incidentally our relationship has truly evolved so that working for him has now become awkward as arse! I mean, fully enriching love and sex with the man who pays my wages is, frankly, untenable. Hence, I find myself leading crisis talks in Delilah's about tendering my resignation in favour of going into business with the least conventional business partner ever.

'Weddings! We should go into wedding planning!' Brooke gushes. 'It's big business and, I mean, we're both so creative and stylish,' she grins delightedly, completely oblivious to her latte moustache.

'Hmm,' I murmur, sucking in my teeth and trying the idea on for size. 'I've always loved a wedding!'

'Plus, they do say that when you do something you love, you'll never do a day's work in your life,' Brooke adds, selling it to me all the more.

'True,' I nod in agreement, 'but we'd need some commercial base to work from. Then we've got all the start up and running costs. We're going to need a whole lotta dough upfront.'

'We could ask Brian? I'm sure he'd love to help out,' Brooke suggests.

'Absolutely no way!' I declare, almost choking on my latte.

'Why? It'd be nothing to someone like him.'

'Maybe so, but I don't want to be forever indebted to Brian, do you? Wouldn't it be great to have something we've built up ourselves from scratch and be able to take all the credit for? Besides, we're supposed to be feminists, remember?'

'Ooh, yeah.'

'Well, if we're serious about this, then I say we do some research and find out what it's going to take to make this happen,' I suggest, holding out my latte glass which Brooke duly chinks with hers.

'You're ... leaving the business?' Brian repeats, his face falling when, a few weeks on, I'm standing before his desk in my "you will take me seriously" pinstripe, tailored trouser suit.

'That's right,' I smile, feeling accomplished.

'So, who are we losing you to?' he probes, stroking his designer stubble thoughtfully.

'Myself!'

He looks up at me from under furrowed brows.

'Well *and* Brooke. We're starting a business together,' I explain, proudly.

'Well, why didn't you say? I could've—'

'No,' I interrupt him hastily. 'We don't need any help.'

'But I can put you in touch with the best advisors, I could organise...' he goes on.

'No, honestly Brian. We've got this. We know what we're doing,' I insist, shutting him down.

He stares at me curiously for a few moments. 'Okay,' he shrugs, 'if you say so.'

∞∞∞

'Brian's being really distant,' I whinge as Brooke and I sit surrounded by flat pack furniture on the floor of our newly acquired downtown business premises a month post-resignation.

'Well, you dented his pride,' she mumbles, frowning and scratching her head at the instructions in her hand. 'It's a guy thing.'

'No, it's more than that. He's been acting really strange lately.'

'How so?'

'I don't know, just distant. Always busy.'

'Maybe he's got a lot on at work?'

'Nah, he's always got a lot on at work. Well, if it *is* down to me denting his pride like you say, then he really ought to grow up a bit. I mean, it's not up to him to fix everything,' I huff, feeling suddenly miffed. 'And you know what? I'm sick of him … with his posh, bloody moccasin slippers, pacing the floor on his phone, thinking his money can just magic everything at the click of a finger!'

Brooke raises a brow while I pause for breath. 'Trouble in paradise?' she asks in surprise.

'Who knows? Perhaps it's the beginning of the end?' I sulk, nose in the air.

'You seriously think so?'

'Ugh ...*No* ... I don't know! I just want us to do this independently, is that so bad? We can totally do this, what do we need a man for?'

'For putting up this filing cabinet, along with all the rest of the fucking furniture!' Brooke scoffs, her face pulled into an exasperated scowl as she holds up the drawer she just screwed together back-to-front.

'Okay, so maybe there's a small place for men in this venture of ours,' I huff.

Brian had promised to come along to our launch night and I'd spent the whole night looking over the guests' shoulders for him, I guess because I'd wanted him to see me doing well. To be a bit proud of me. And then, ten minutes to closing, he bursts in clutching a bottle of champagne when the place is half empty. Great! Now he's going to assume that, like himself, nobody showed up!

'Hey, so sorry babe. I was held up with work.

The place looks great!' he pants, looking around.

'Hmm,' I manage by way of a response, wondering what could've been too important to delegate to one of the many people employed by him.

The first day of being my own boss doing something I love was meant to be totes amazeballs but instead in between meeting what I now deem to be sickeningly loved-up couples, my mind is working overtime imagining that, in keeping with his stereotype, Brian must be cheating on me. The distance, the worsening punctuality, the more or less standing me up on my big night last night, suddenly it all adds up! Having spent a good half hour Googling "signs your partner is cheating", a text pings:

'Hey. Could we meet tonight? Need to talk x'

I sit, staring at those words, dissecting them. The first part reads reasonable enough, if a little cold and business-like. It's the "need to talk" part that feels like the dreaded "please see me" scrawled on your homework. This is it! He's going to let me down gently, insist we should still be friends, then be gone, never to be seen again ... other than when on the front cover of Forbes. The end is nigh! Ah well, I did well to last a year, I guess.

I make a frantic call to Brooke who is out with one of our sickeningly loved-up couples, checking out a wedding venue.

'Well if you're going to be dumped, make sure you go down in style!' she advises all matter-of-fact, not doing much in the way of reassuring me.

'*What?*'

'You wanna rock up looking a million dollars,' she tells me. 'Make him see what he's throwing away!'

Hmm, maybe she has a point. Vivienne Westwood and Manolo Blahnik's ought to do it.

Later, another text arrives:

'*Sorry, running late. Just finishing up a business meeting at the Empire State Building. Could you meet me there in say, a half hour? x*'

The cheeky bastard! Does he seriously expect me to go out of my way running to him and his terribly important business meeting to be dumped? Well, he can swivel! I'm done. As of this moment, I, Lizzie Bradshaw, no longer run after men and shall think twice before giving away my heart so easily in future. Further bloody more, I shall acquire myself a toy boy and live out the rest of my days a feisty cougar! I will *never* let another man make a fool of me, even if I don't yet know for certain what it is that Brian wants to discuss. But still, a woman knows the signs.

Approximately twenty-two minutes on, my phone rings. It's Brian

'He can go to hell,' I mutter, ramming my fingers into the Nutella jar.

Five minutes later, Brooke calls.

'How did it go? Did they settle on the venue?' I ask in a glum tone.

'Um, yeah, they did. Anyway, where are you?' she asks.

'Back at the apartment,' I huff.

'Aren't you supposed to be meeting Brian?'

'Nope! I'm not going!' I declare.

'What, *why*?'

'Because, like most men, he's a wanker and I'm done.'

'*What*?!'

'He was running late, as ever. Cheeky bastard only asked me to go out of my way to the Empire sodding State Building while he finishes up his precious little meeting,' I tell her in the manner of Veruca Salt.

'Lizzie, you need to get over there and sort things out.'

'No! Why should I go rushing off to him when he clicks his fingers? I told you, I'm done.'

'Ugh, look, Lizzie, you absolutely *must* get over there,' Brooke blurts out after a long pause.

'*What*?'

'I can't say any more than that. All I can tell you is you must go! Get over there now. Hurry!' she orders, hanging up the phone.

WTF?

'Keep the change!' I yell to the cab driver as we draw up outside the Empire State Building. Hurrying inside, I can't see Brian anywhere among the crowds of people. He probably thinks I'm not coming now because I ignored his call. Oh, bugger! Did he leave already? I totter over to reception.

'Can I help you ma'am?'

'Yes, I'm here to meet Brian Garcia of Wilson Garcia & Co,' I tell the chap on the front desk. 'Has he left yet?'

'Er, no ma'am. Mr Garcia and co are still here. He's expecting you.'

'Oh, good. Do you know which floor?'

'That would be the 102nd floor, ma'am,' he replies, over-smiling slightly. 'Jerry, could you take this lady up to the 102nd floor please? She's with Brian Garcia.'

'Possibly not for much longer,' I mumble under my breath, hurrying over to an empty elevator where the attendant takes me up.

As my ears begin to pop from the ascent, I

spend what feels like forever wondering what on earth Brian can be playing at and how Brooke knows so much about whatever it may be. Perhaps it's her! Perhaps *she's* his mistress! No, don't be so bloody stupid, Lizzie!

'Follow me, ma'am,' the attendant instructs as we reach the 86th floor, leading the way toward a glass elevator.

'Jesus bastarding Christ!' I yell, grabbing onto him for support upon observing how freakishly high we are.

'If you've a fear of heights, ma'am, then you probably shouldn't be heading up to the 102nd floor of the Empire State Building,' he scoffs.

'I don't have a fear of heights!' I declare defensively. 'I just … well, I didn't realise how high up the 102nd floor was.'

He shoots me a strange look.

'So? I've never been to the Empire State Building before. I'm a Londoner, how should I bloody know?' I huff in my defence.

'Well, you're pretty much right at the top, ma'am,' he appears to delight in telling me as the colour drains from my face and I come over all dizzy.

What the hell is going on here? Why would Brian choose to conduct business meeting-cum-relationship crisis talks in outer space?

As we hit the top, I wonder if I've passed out and am now dreaming as I spot Mother, done up to the nines with a very silly expression on her face stood beside Dad alongside a small gathering of ex-work colleagues, all standing before a spectacular backdrop of the New York skyline, holding glasses of bubbly. I spot Brooke, grinning from ear-to-ear, among them.

'What's ... happening?' I ask, wide-eyed.

Brian steps out, appearing uncharacteristically nervous before dropping to one knee in front of me.

'Lizzie, will you marry me?' he asks, prising open a ring box to reveal a dazzling rock of enormous proportions.

All at once, it dawns on me. The secret allegiance with Brooke, the distance, the worsening punctuality, the more or less standing me up on my big night last night. Brian hasn't been cheating on me, he'd been planning to effing propose!

Beyond clutching my chest and gasping repeatedly, I haven't yet managed to speak. Mother coughs loudly causing me to look in her direction. Oh! I'd quite forgotten she was here. 'Say yes!' she mouths at me, looking horrified.

'Yes! Yes, I will!' I reply as the room erupts into cheers and applause.

'I love you,' Brian mouths up at me, sliding the

ring onto my finger.

'Congratulations!' Mother shrills, forcing herself between us.

'Thanks, future mother-in-law,' Brian winks, provoking the reverberation of her pompous fake laugh to ring out around us.

'Welcome to the family, mate,' Dad smiles, shaking his hand.

'Well, no need for introductions then I guess,' I remark.

'Oh yes, we're well acquainted by now,' Mother purrs. 'Brian flew us out here first class!'

'You did?' I remark, raising a brow.

'Oh yeah, I've been organising this thing for weeks.'

'What If I'd said no?' I laugh, prompting the silly grin to fall right off Mother's face.

'Well, I guess I didn't really plan for that outcome,' Brian laughs.

'So, where are you staying?' I ask Dad.

'At the Four Seasons,' Mother replies before he can, patting down her hair, nose in the air as though it's not on Brian.

Brian's mother, Veronica, whom I've met just the once – and found to be a stuck-up cow – saunters over. Oh, fuck! I'd quite happily forgotten she existed. Now she's going to be my mother-in-law and then I shall have not one, but *two* stuck-up, pain-in-the-arse mother figures in my life. The ensuing look on Mother's face tells me they're already acquainted and there's a mutual dislike between them, as is usually the case between feisty women. Good lord! The ring hasn't been on my finger five minutes and we already have infighting among our families.

'Congratulations, darling,' she says, kissing Brian and needlessly brushing down the shoulders of his suit jacket as though he has a dandruff problem.

'Thanks, Duchess.'

'Welcome to the Garcia family,' she says to me, almost as an afterthought. I smile and thank her before mumbling something about needing to mingle and making a dash toward a congregation of my ex-work colleagues.

When Brian later pulls me aside and tells me in a hushed tone in that he's booked us a table at a nearby restaurant, I had assumed he'd meant just us and was looking forward to some alone time with my future husband. That is, until he tells me he's invited his bloody mother and my parents along! Oh, FFS! My arising expression must have spoken volumes as he promptly asks if it's okay with me. Well, what if it wasn't? Which it isn't. It's a bit bloody late now!

'No, it's fine,' I lie, 'but please could Brooke

come along? I feel bad her going back to the apartment alone,' I tell him, in truth *myself* being the only person I feel bad for having to endure dinner with ~~Maleficent~~ Veronica.

'Yeah, sure thing.'

'Ooh, let me see the ring,' Brooke coos at dinner while the others sit deep in conversation. 'Fuck me,' she mumbles under her breath as I hold my hand out, 'that's some sparkler!'

'I know, right!'

'So, how do you feel about it all?'

'Er, good. Good,' I smile, trying to put my future mother-in-law to the back of my mind – no mean feat when she's sat opposite in her sickly-green two-piece like Lady Muck. 'I mean, it's not going to be easy disguising my shits anymore but...'

'Well, he'll be hard pressed to find a woman who doesn't defecate,' Brooke points out in a hushed tone.

'True.'

'So, *you* must be feeling like your nose has been put out of joint,' Veronica practically shouts over the table toward Brooke, completely interrupting our conversation.

'What, me? No, not at all. Why would I?'

'Well, you'll be needing a new roommate, won't you? That is if you were actually planning to move in with your fiancé, Lizzie,' she quips, turning her attention to me. 'I don't know, these *feminists*,' she laughs bitchily.

Mother shoots her a look that says, 'Someone's forgotten their manners!'

I shoot Brian a look that says, 'Someone's been telling tales to Mummy!'

'Anyone for more champagne?' he says, rather than keep Duchess in check.

'Well, actually, I was rather hoping you guys would take me in as a lodger,' Brooke laughs, wiping the smirk straight from Veronica's face. 'I mean, I could have my own wing with the size of your place Brian and we feminists come as a package, you know! Right Lizzie?' she winks. 'Joke,' she adds when nobody except me laughs.

The first thing I do on waking next morning is to check the ring is still there and that this hasn't all been some sad, desperate dream arising from a deep-rooted fear of being left on the shelf. Eek! There it is, in all its glory! I turn my hand this way and that, watching it twinkle and feeling on top of the world. It's finally happened. I'm engaged! Me, Lizzie Bradshaw, the girl whom no guy ever liked back, engaged! And I haven't even had to use a single love spell! Who'd have thought it?

A mere fourteen hours post-marriage proposal, my descent from the top of the world begins as my phone starts vibrating with Mother's Facetime request. Ugh!

I slide to answer it, jumping in fright at the sight of her face at point blank range.

'Move it back, Mother!'

'What was that? *What*? Oh, *do* be quiet Desmond I'm trying to listen.'

'MOVE YOUR PHONE BACK!' I yell, exasperated. 'You've got it too bloody close to your face!'

'Oh! Is that better?' she asks as the phone zooms out, capturing Dad stood in his y-fronts putting on his tie.

'Brian's invited Daddy and I for dinner at his mansion tonight, dear. Wonderful, isn't it?' she says, beaming with delight.

No hello as usual, then!

'Yes,' I reply, wondering if I'm invited.

'Thankfully that Mother of his isn't coming. Dreadful woman, dreadful! She's right, though, although it pains me to say it. You really ought to be thinking of moving out of that apartment. What about tomorrow? Daddy and I could lend a ha...'

'NO!'

'Goodness, don't shout like that dear, you'll

blow the speaker on this thing!'

'It's all in-hand, Mother!'

'So, when's moving day?'

'Well, I haven't really...'

'Oh! Did I mention Daddy and I are going along to Fifth Avenue this morning? I wanted to have a mooch in the boutiques for wedding attire.'

'But Mother, we haven't even set a date ye...'

'It's never too early to start planning dear, I *am* the mother of the bride after all! And I will *not* have that awful woman outdoing me! Pfft! I can just see her now, waltzing in with some enormous, ridiculously odd hat!'

Funny! I can see *her* doing the same.

'Ah, so *that's* what this is in aid of!' I sigh, rolling my eyes.

'Not entirely, I'm going to pick up some wedding brochurrres whilst we're there so you and I can have a look through them at dinner tonight.'

'Well, I don't really need any wedding brochures, I've a wedding planning business, Mother.'

'Oh, that's nice, dear. Well, I'd best be awf, the knot in Daddy's tie looks like it needs the woman's touch. Looking forward to going through those brochurrres this evening, tally-bye!' she shrills, waving erratically before spinning upside down on my screen. 'Desmond, help! How do you turn this ruddy thing awf?!'

The mildest wave of melancholy hits as I stare vacantly into space. This is it. Goodbye single life forever. How did I pull this off? I mean I've come a long way, but I don't work out. Don't do Pilates. Don't eat chia seeds, almond butter, or avocados. Don't own a Pomeranian which I transport in a vast handbag across my arm. Don't consistently walk about with a Starbucks cup in my hand. Don't drape myself over sofas wearing a selection of loungewear apparel. Don't have the sought-after wasp waist/overly rounded bottom combo figure and I'm definitely not an influencer, rather I'm a prime example of what *not* to do. But look at me, I just took a massive leap ahead in the game. Somebody wants to marry me. I've made it!

I've spent my whole life thinking happiness is reserved for better people and yet here I am, a bride-to-be. *Me*! While someone as gorgeous as Brooke is alone and single – how is this even possible? It's as if our roles in life have been strangely reversed. She's the way better-looking sister I never had. *She* should be doing all of these things first, not me. Even though getting married has been the ultimate life-long wish, I'm really going to miss our shenanigans now that I'm to swap hangovers and TV dinners for posh slippers and early nights. Part of me wishes I *could* move her into her own wing of Brian's mansion.

On a go-slow and walking on air despite Brochuregate looming, I stroll into work where Brooke has been holding the fort all morning.

'Hey, how's tricks?'

'Busy! It's been non-stop enquiries all morning!' she puffs, sinking back into her office chair. 'Oh and Kylie Jenner called, she'd like to swap lives with you.'

'Well, she'd bloody regret it with Petunia Bradshaw as her new momager!' I sneer. 'Anyway, since it's the weekend I bought you a little treat to have with your coffee at lunch,' I announce, handing over a box from the bakery just as the phone rings.

'Ooh! Hope it's sugary as fuck!' she sings, grabbing it from me with one hand and answering the phone with the other. 'Hello, Two's Company,' she says in her put-on, professional voice. 'Uh-huh', she murmurs, opening the lid and pausing for a moment as she combines not listening to the caller with reading the words that have been iced onto the massive cookie lying before her: 'Be my maid of honour?'

'GAHH! *FUCK*, YEAH!' she screams in shock down the phone. Whoops.

∞∞∞

'Powder pink!' Mother squeals. 'It's timeless, elegant, suits all skin tones, goes with anything. You simply cannot go wrong, dear, you really can't.'

'Mother, do we have to do this now, we haven't even set a date y...'

'Yes well, powder pink was the Parker-Jones's choice for their Alice's colour theme, you know.'

Tempted as I am, I refrain from roaring, 'Alice? Who the fuck is Alice?!' since, as with most names Mother mentions, I haven't the foggiest who she is and, frankly, I couldn't give a fuck.

'Oh, how very original, *who*?' I ask, rolling my eyes.

'You know the Parker-Joneses, they own that garden centre in Chelsea, dear. They drive around in that enormous Range Rover.'

'Oh yes, I know just the place, being so green fingered and outdoorsy!' I scoff.

'So that's settled then, powwwder piiink,' she talk-scribbles into the genuine leather Filofax she's told me six times so far (and counting) that she specifically went out and bought this afternoon for planning ~~her~~ my wedding.

'No! I don't want powder bloody pin...' I almost manage in protest.

'Now, watch your language, dear. You can't go around speaking like that in church!'

'I'm not having it in a bloody chur...'

'Now, how many bridesmaids? Two, four?' she interrupts.

'Well...I don't kn...'

'Two is quite ample, I think. Better keep it to two. So, that's twwwo briiidesmaiiids,' she merrily jots down. 'Right, well that's the colour theme and bridesmaids covered, now, what about flower girls and page boys?'

'Well, I don't know Mother, why don't you decide on this one for me since you've not had much input' I huff, knocking back my Martini.

'Hmmm!' she sighs, clicking her tongue in deliberation. 'Well of course, they'd get the grannies talking, lots of oohs and ahhs and they always make for great photographs stood like little cherubs among all the lace and tulle, but if there's one thing I simply cannot stand, it's screaming, bastard children!' she trills, dropping the genuine leather Filofax in shock and covering her mouth with both hands in horror at her blasphemy. Finally! Something we both agree on!

'Good grief! Thank heavens Brian and your father are in the snooker room. It's this Don Perripong, I'm not used to drinking the super fancy stuff, it's really quite strong,' she remarks while I fill up her glass behind her back with a Grinch-like grin. 'Now, in terms of the guest list, I couldn't possibly make a start on that till

I'm back in London, dear. I shall be needing my other genuine leather Filofax for that, it has all my important contacts in. But if there's anyone you might like to invite, let me know and I'll pop them down dear. Would Brian like to bring a friend?'

What, to his own wedding? No! That would just be outlandish!

I close my eyes in exasperation, hoping the "Don Perripong" works its magic soon.

'Now, what next? Ahhhhhh, yes! Seating plan!' she booms, her voice getting louder and more excitable by the minute. 'Now, in keeping with tradition, and as mother of the bride, I thought I might sit on Brian's side,' she announces, her lips pulled into a snobby, magenta smirk.

'I think Duchess will have a thing or two to say about that,' I warn, imagining a full-on bitch fight at the top table with handbags and pearls flying about the place.

'Oh, I'm not bothered about what *she* thinks! It's tradition for the bride's family to organise everything and since she's merely the mother of the groom she'll have to fit in or … or jolly well frig off!' The genuine leather Filofax drops to the floor once again as Mother recoils in shock. 'Goodness! The language escaping my mouth this evening!' she exclaims. 'I don't know what on earth's the matter with me, I really don't!'

I do!

Fortunately, the butler arrives just in time to call us for dinner before Mother has a chance to dictate the date.

'So, you ladies source any quick-wins from your deep-dive into wedding planning? I guess with so many options these days, you've not even scratched the surface,' Brian asks as we sit down to eat.

Bless him, he really has no idea.

'Ohhh we're making grrreat progress!' Mother beams, knocking her cutlery straight to the floor with a reverberating, metallic clang as a consequence of all the sudden, wild hand gestures. 'I say! I say!' she shrills, clicking her fingers at the butler. 'Do you have any more of that Dong Peridom?'

I snigger behind my hand. 'Dong' isn't a word I would ever have imagined passing Mother's lips ... unless speaking in terms of bells, but why spoil it?

'I think you've had enough, Petunia,' Dad remarks, turning and mumbling something only partially audible about the price per bottle in her ear.

'No, no. It's great to see you cutting loose. Get it down you, Petunia,' Brian laughs.

'Ohhhhhh, don't you worry Brian, I will!' she

trills.

And she *does*, while Dad looks on in dread.

Later...

'Are you sure you guys don't want to crash here tonight? It's really no troub...' Brian says, frowning and trailing off as he observes me waving my arms about manically, shaking my head and making cutthroat gestures behind my parents' backs.

'Ohhhhhh yeeeeees, how wonderrrful!' Mother exclaims.

'No, no. We've got our hotel room for another two nights, remember? We can't let it go to waste,' Dad mutters disapprovingly into her ear like he's the father and she's his child.

'Yeees!' I chip in. 'What a terrible waste when homelessness is at an all-time high!'

'Yeeeeees, wellllll ... thank you for a bllloody suuuper evening Brian, it's been faaabulous!' Mother slurs, screwing one eye shut in an attempt to focus, lunging toward him with her arms outstretched and crashing into the enormous potted Kentia palm to his left. She sends it flying, prompting Brian, Dad and I to race toward it, saving it just in time while Mother brutally and haphazardly steadies herself on the butler.

'Oh, er, you're most welcome,' Brian pants, looking just as traumatised as the butler while catching his breath.

'Come on now, Petunia, we'd better get you to bed,' Dad insists, taking an incredibly rare stand.

In another all-time first, I don't hear a peep from Mother until the following evening. But I *do* receive a mortified text from Dad telling me she called room service to order a 'portion of Clint Eastwood' when they returned to the Four Seasons last night.

Chapter 16:

Three's a Crowd

Stationed at the huge lux dining table within the comfy confines of a sumptuous velvet chair, an enormous liqueur in one hand and one of Brian's posh fountain pens poised in the other, I do a little jig as I sign off my parents' Christmas card:

'Happy Christmas and best wishes for the new year. All our love from Lizzie & Brian x'

Look at that! No balderdash. No bullshit. Ha! To think that less than a couple of years ago, I did this as pure fantasy rather than necessity.

That said, buying cards and gifts for both sides of the family doesn't quite live up to the fantasy it was cracked up to be in my mind. In fact, it's been nothing but bloody stress. Christmas is now beyond commercialised. I mean, where do you start when confronting a sea of greetings cards within a rammed card shop where the choice is now so vast that there are Mother's Day cards from dogs to their "dog mum" as well as Christmas cards from the bloody dog. Talk about milking it! God forbid that anyone should be left out ever – human or not. All that's missing is "for you on my birthday," but give it bloody time.

Then there's gifts. It's hard enough remembering your arse from your elbow this time of year without needing to concern yourself with what neck size Uncle Frank is for a boxed shirt and tie set. Or what shoe size Aunt Moira is for that pair of dusky pink slippers. You spend hours pondering it all meticulously and when the big day comes, you don't even get a thank you. Ungrateful bastards.

With the cards written out in my best handwriting – getting progressively scruffier from card number four onwards – the gifts wrapped, presents distributed to Brian's side of the family, the "out of office" automatic reply set up on my email account and totes emosh goodbyes with Brooke all done, I'm ready!

∞∞∞

It's the 22nd December and Brian and I are onboard a flight out of New York to London Heathrow to celebrate Christmas with my parents. I must be a glutton for punishment accepting an invitation to spend the festive season alongside the most overbearing person on the planet but while I *adore* the US, there's nothing quite like a traditional British Christmas. And I suppose, despite her many faults, nobody does Christmas lunch with all the trimmings quite like Mother.

It's been around a year and a half since I was last on British soil and I'm excited to be heading back at this, the most wonderful time of the year – even with Mother's festive soiree tomorrow night, which I know full well is being thrown for the sole purpose of introducing Brian to all and sundry and showing off to Delia Davenport, the neighbours, and anyone else Mother considers competition. For the avoidance of doubt, Mother's festive soirée should in no way be confused with a Christmas party. Quintessentially British Christmas parties are where non-Christian people dressed in spangly clobber dance to the hits of the eighties, get extremely pissed and make arses of themselves in celebration of the birth of Christ. Mother's festive soirée is essentially a bunch of boorish bastards congregating around sausages on sticks, battling against one another to talk only about themselves. Throughout the years on these abysmal occasions, nobody acknowledges me beyond making fleeting remarks about me not getting any thinner and asking how the diet's going. It's as though I'm not a person at all, rather I am some strange sort of walking Stay Puft-style punchbag built to withstand endless scrutiny. If I should attempt to join in the conversation, I am met with a, 'Hmm, yeees, well, anyway' or similar, which is synonymous with, 'Go away tiresome juvenile, you are not wealthy or important, what-what-what.' A smug smile creeps up my face as I picture their faces at the unveiling of the all-new size 8 to 10, entrepreneurial me. Pompous bastards will be falling over themselves to talk to me now.

The flight duration makes for a lengthy period of reflection and taking stock, something I haven't really had much opportunity for up to now. I think back to the last flight I took to the US all those months ago, alone. I was a whole different person back then. Now, I'm flying back with my husband-to-be sat beside me in first-class where I am relieved to see there are no cheeky pre-schoolers, wailing infants or noisy, happy-clappy Earth Mums. To anyone watching, I have it all. And though my life has changed for the better beyond measure, I'd be lying if I said living with Brian has been out-and-out bliss. In many ways it has been, but, ultimately, it's no better or worse than most relationships. We would all do well to remember that wealth doesn't buy fairy tales, love is built *not* found and all that glitters, as they say, isn't gold. Like myself, Brian has his faults, including but not limited to:

Noticing when anything around the house has moved an inch.

Walking into the kitchen the second I go to snack on something unhealthy and giving me "that look".

Getting upset about make-up and fake tan on the bed sheets and bath towels.

Referring to his bloody mother as Duchess.

Wearing geeky socks.

Rage-inducing breathing/eating/mouth sounds.

His pompous aversion to me leaving evidence of my period about the place as though it's impolite to menstruate.

Those effing moccasin slippers!

Snoring like a morbidly obese, asthmatic hog and having the nerve to wear earplugs at night to shield himself from any noise which might compromise *his* forty winks!

The odd sound he makes when he reaches orgasm.

Doing a deep cough to disguise the splash of his number twos and thinking I've not guessed his lousy technique.

Simultaneously, Brian also happens to be one of the kindest people I've ever met. He makes me feel safe. He treats me like a princess and I would go as far as to say that I could trust him with my life.

Where sex is concerned:

Me: *I love Brian and I will not compare kissing and/or shagging with him to kissing and/or shagging with Dan Elliott. They are, after all, two very different people.*

Also, me: *I love Brian. If only he would kiss and shag more like Dan Elliott!*

Sex with Brian is cosy and safe, and our relationship is based on way more important things like trust and respect. I don't need for him to find undiscovered erogenous zones of my body in under sixty seconds, be able to go all night and leave me pulsating for hours after. Doh! Right, enough now. No more illicit thoughts of Dan Elliott – especially when my fiancé is sat beside me. As of this point on, I'm going to acquire an elastic band for my wrist and when I have such thoughts, I will ping it as hard as I can so as to train my brain not to think them. Although, for the greater good, my illicit thoughts of Dan Elliott really ought to be sealed in concrete and thrown into the depths of the ocean where they should stay forever more. No good, after all, can come from comparing what *was* pure sorcery with what *is* authentic love.

I turn to gaze lovingly at my future husband, sat sleeping beside me with his mouth hanging open through which he emits the odd, raspy boar-like snore and a series of periodic, unmanly whimpers in his slumber. Suddenly, I've gone from gazing lovingly at him to fantasising about smothering him with his complimentary first-class pillow. Extreme at this relatively early stage of our relationship, I know, but I've never been one for mouth sounds. Now I'm cursed with that irksome, heightened sense of awareness where everything's annoying. The sniffing! The fucking sniffing! Once you hear one sniff in a public setting, they seem to come at you in endless droves from all angles. Only unconsciousness can save me now.

∞∞∞

'WHAT?! WHAT'S HAPPENING?!' I yell as Brian attempts to gently wake me, causing the entire cabin to turn in panic and stare open-mouthed in our direction as though we're being hijacked.

'It's alright, it's okay, we're coming in to land,' he soothes, putting up his hands and giving the passengers and crew an apologetic nod.

Oh! I must've been out for the count, possibly a consequence of me not sleeping and staying up all night like an excited child. Sitting up, I pull a face at those still gawking at me and fasten my seatbelt, feeling an instant sense of home as the patchwork quilt-like familiar English greenery comes into view below an angry-looking sea of grey cloud. Minutes later we touch down onto British soil to a traditional, pointless round of applause, which I've never quite understood the reason for but would say is done more out of widespread relief not to be dead rather than in praise of the pilot.

I instantly spy Mother scouring the sea of passengers pouring in through arrivals for Brian and I like an excitable meerkat. She spots us and then the fawning and mad hugging starts. Eventually, she turns her attention to me, offering up one of her classic rigor mortis hugs by way of a motherly greeting.

'How was the flight?' she asks, not even letting me answer as she immediately launches into describing in great detail how she's made up the bed for us in the spare double room, miraculously managed to acquire a Christmas Eve Click and Collect grocery slot at Waitrose – though they were disappointingly all out of cranberries and one simply cannot have ready-made cranberry sauce – *and* that Delia Davenport has put her back out having slipped on a glace cherry at the country club Christmas dinner dance and therefore infuriatingly shan't be able to attend her festive soiree. And that's before we're even out the building! How the fuck am I to keep it together till New Year, I wonder?

'Great to see you again, darling,' says Dad, giving me a proper hug.

'Hi Dad! How's life?' I ask, knowing full well it must be verging on intolerable.

He says nothing, presses his lips firmly together and looks down at his feet – enough to tell me he's at the end of his rope.

The December air bites as we venture outside with me lagging behind as Mother, Dad and Brian stride off ahead, engaged in boring as hell conversation about delays, baggage fees and the latest on the airport's expansion plan.

I huffily drag my genuine – yes, genuine! – Louis Vuitton case behind me, deliberately slowing my walking speed in a child-like manner so as to make them feel extra bad for waltzing off ahead … should they happen to even notice my absence, that is.

I feel the first specks of rain, forcing me to walk faster, at which point I spy a guy getting out of a top-of-the-range sports car. Phwoar, *ding-dong*! I find myself having a stealthy perve as both his and Brian's backs are turned. Wait a minute, *that's* a familiar arse and I totally know that jawline. As he turns around, my heart instantly freezes in my chest and my throat seems to seize up. It's only Mr Wonderful!

Oh shit! What's *he* doing here? Now? At this exact moment?! It's as though, not satisfied to just leave it at that now that it's finally worked in my favour, fate now wishes to fuck with me!

I quicken my pace, cover my face with my hair and turn my head the other way. I'm like, a totally new person now, he'll never recognise m—

'Lizzie?!'

Oh, fuck! He *has*! Keep walking, keep walking.

'Hey! Lizzie?! Hold up!' he calls out, his footsteps sprinting over in my direction.

Knowing I'm busted, I stop walking and stand rooted to the spot in defeat for a few moments, before turning around to face him.

'Oh my god, it *is* you! I wasn't sure, I mean, you look so different,' he says, looking me up and down. 'But then I recognised that walk,' he laughs with that dashing grin of his.

I quickly avert my eyes. Observing that sexy smile again is as bad for me as looking directly at the sun; I dare not look for too long, terrified I'll be blinded by burning lust again.

'Um ... *what* walk?' I finally manage in response.

'Oh, I don't know, sort of stroppy, with overly-swinging arms,' he explains.

'*Oh*!' I frown, making a mental note to walk more supermodel-like in future.

'So, how are you? You good?' he asks.

'Yeah, yeah I'm good. You?'

'Yeah, all good! You just back from a holiday?'

'Er, no. I've been living in the States for a while.'

'Wow, the States? No, way!' he says in surprise. 'I'd always wondered where you'd gone. It was like you'd just vanished off the face of the earth.'

I force an awkward laugh, trying desperately not to meet his gaze. His voice seems to speak to my soul, invoking feelings I'd hoped were on the way to being dead and buried, instantly triggering "the Dan effect": a six-point chain reaction of the following:

1. Pulse (racing).

2. Breath (losing).

3. Stomach (butterflies going apeshit in).

4. Knees (trembling).

5. Legs (jellifying).

6. Resolve (weakening).

One look at those eyes would serve to finish me off!

'You look ... well,' he remarks.

'You hesitated just then!' I point out, with a chuckle.

'Well, I'm not used to seeing you this ... skinny ... *or* blonde.'

'Yeah, well, you knew *old* me, meet new, *im-*

proved me' I announce, doing a proud twirl.

He smiles half-heartedly. 'I preferred the old model.'

'Don't talk daft, I was a heifer!'

'Nah, you were all woman,' he says, getting me onto the ropes. 'Hey, we should meet up. Go for coffee or something, be great to catch up!'

'I can't Dan, I er...'

Before I can say another word, Brian jogs over. 'Hey! Who's this?' he asks cheerily, draping an arm around my shoulders.

I note the drop in Dan's smile as he hears the American accent and puts two and two together.

'Oh, er, Brian, this is Dan, an er, old friend.' (Somehow, it's never felt right mentioning Mr Wonderful.) 'Dan, this is Brian. My fiancé.'

Dan does well to hide his shock as he reaches out and shakes Brian's hand, but I see it. The disappointment in the face I know so well, the face I could – and did – sit and stare at for an eternity.

'Congratulations,' he smiles, meekly.

'So, Dan, you just flying out? Flying back in?' Brian asks, making friendly conversation.

'Er, no actually. I work here as a chauffeur. Those aren't *my* wheels over there, bloody wish they were, though!'

'You're not at Trip Hut anymore?' I ask in surprise.

'No, I got laid off after they had a bit of a downturn. So, then this job came up and I was kind of forced to snap it up,' he explains, almost apologetically. 'Still do my personal training too though'. Course he does. Oh, my life, the guns!

'Ah. Well, I'm sorry to hear that. It's a real shame when businesses have to throw their staff overboard to stay afloat,' says Brian, reaching out to shake his hand again. 'Listen, Dan. It was great meeting you.'

'You too and er, congrats again. You're a lucky guy!'

'Sure am,' he nods, giving me a loving look as he takes my case for me and turns heading back to the car with it.

'I ... won't be a minute,' I tell him, noticing Mother's head hovering above the roof of Dad's silver BMW saloon in the distance, the look on her face made up of equal parts horror and rage.

A rumble of thunder rings out in the rapidly blackening sky as I turn back toward Dan.

'I'm happy for you,' he tells me. 'You deserve to be happy.'

Oh, God. Please don't say that, makes it *so* much harder!

'I never understood why you just ended it like that,' he goes on to say, looking pained. 'I was so

... confused. It bugs me even now.'

'Dan, I'm engaged. There's no point going over old ground,' I tell him.

'I know, I know. And I'm happy that you're happy, really, I am. I'd just ... love to put it to bed once and for all, you know?'

Sighing deeply, I rack my brains for the sanest-sounding way to explain I'd done a love spell on him, got a tonne of bad karma from it and was subsequently compelled to flee the country to start a whole new life. In the end it all comes tumbling out as bluntly put as that.

'What? That's hilarious?!' he laughs, clutching his chest. 'You can't be serious?!'

'Hmmm, afraid, so. God, I feel so bloody stupid!' I cringe, covering my face with my hands. 'I guess ... I guess I liked you that much, I would've tried *anything* to...' I trail off, looking over in the direction of the others, who are all by now sat in the car waiting for me.

'Oh, come on! Don't tell me you really believe in all that!' he exclaims, still laughing, then stopping abruptly when the ensuing look on my face tells him I *do*.

'But Lizzie, that's crazy!'

'Thanks!' I huff.

'No, well, I mean, your Nan passing away, that wasn't bad karma, she had dementia. It was only a matter of time.'

'Yes but ... well, it's strange my entire life went down the pan from that point on!' I argue.

'It's called grief, Lizzie. Grief does that to people.'

'I lost my job.'

'Yeah, that tends to happen when employees go AWOL.'

I stand, rooted to the spot, gazing vacantly up at him.

'Don't you see what I'm trying to say?' he frowns, killing me softly with those eyes and that sexy furrowed brow.

I shrug in response.

He hangs his head a little, biting his lip. 'I liked you ... *loved* you the whole time,' he tells me, instantly delivering the final, knockout blow.

'You ... you d-did?' I stutter, in disbelief.

'Still do', he nods, going on to better explain. 'It was always the same types of women throwing themselves at me: vain, shallow. Just ... samey. I mean, everyone seems to look the same these days. No-one's unique anymore ... except *you*,' he tells me, his voice dipping. 'You were different. You didn't follow the crowd. You didn't pretend – I mean, the way you dressed, the nineties dance, the old films you watched. You were *you*. I guess

I found that so refreshing about you,' he tells me as I stand recalling the great lengths I went to trying to change for *him*. Needlessly, as I now know.

'You made me laugh,' he continues. 'You were always making an arse of yourself. That spider in your hair at work that time, I was literally under my desk crying! I couldn't look at you.'

'Oh! Nice.'

'But it was authentic. You were never a show-off or an attention seeker. I loved that. It took me ages to get the balls to ask you out on a date.'

'But you barely looked at me!' I argue.

'I couldn't.'

'What? *Why*?'

'Well, you always played it so cool! You never spoke to me.'

'Ditto!'

We both laugh ironically, realising our totally crossed wires. Ah shit.

'So, you're telling me I went to all that trouble to do a bloody spell on you and you liked me all along anyway?'

He nods, holding my gaze for a few moments just as the heavens begin to open and the rain starts to come down. We stand in it, numb, just staring at one another, neither of us quite knowing what to say.

Dad gives a toot-toot of the car horn, no doubt to Mother's orders.

'Lizzie...' Dan begins.

'Don't!' I order him, my voice breaking. 'Don't make this any harder than it is.'

Flinging my arms around him, we embrace for as long as I feel comfortable knowing Mother, Dad and my fiancé are mere metres away.

'It's great to see you again. I'm so glad I bumped into you,' he says as we pull apart.

'Me too,' I tell him, although in truth part of me wishes I hadn't. Ignorance can sometimes be bliss. 'I should go,' I blurt, my stomach caving in on itself as I turn and hurry off toward the car, leaving him standing in the rain.

'Thank heavens! I was about to come out and fetch you!' Mother barks as I bluster in out of the wet, closing the door firmly behind me with a clunk and feeling thoroughly relieved she hadn't. 'And what is *he* doing here?' she mutters through clenched teeth as Brian and Dad chat away in the front with their backs to us.

'He works here as a chauffeur,' I mumble back, trying to steady the wobble in my voice.

'Hmph! A chauffeur, by Jove! *He's* riding high, then. Told you he wasn't husband material' she scoffs under her breath.

Trouble is, not only *is* he husband material, I think he might be my soulmate. If that's not a fly in your Chardonnay when you're engaged to be married to someone else you love, with the date set, wedding preparations well underway and a whole new amazing life waiting on ice back in the US, I don't know what bloody is.

As I sink back in my seat, numb, the first anthemic bars of N Trance's "Set U Free" ring out on the car radio as if by fate, the lyrics ringing truer than ever. Up to now, it had been well over a year since I'd last played a nineties dance track. I'd moved on, not just in music taste but in life. Now, I feel an instant, overwhelming sadness as I find myself back in the old school faced with the ghost of my former self. The me who would beat myself up and put myself down for being too fat, too plain, too stupid, for never being good enough. Me who thought only sorcery could get the man I loved to love me back. The precious time I wasted and the painful struggles I endured trying to reinvent myself just to be enough, when I *had* been all along. I would laugh my arse off, were it not so sad.

As Dad reverses the car back, I turn and glance out of the rain-splattered window to observe Dan, still standing where I'd left him staring numbly in my direction. It's all I can do not to fling open the door, jump out and race back to him, leap into his arms and drink him up in the pouring rain like in the movies – I could *so* do that now without knocking him straight to the ground. But I can't. I've got to let him go all over again. This is all way too late in the day. The best example of the worst timing ever I knew. Life is such a bitch sometimes!

Bereft, I turn to look away again, the first of the tears that have long been threatening begin to spill silently down my cheeks. I dab at my eyes discreetly, the black hole in my chest expanding as the car sweeps further and further away from Mr Wonderful until he's gone … but definitely not forgotten.

About The Author

Gem Burman

Gem Burman is a British women's fiction author from Norwich, United Kingdom.

www.gemburman.com

Books In This Series

A Kind of Tragic
A three-part romantic comedy fiction series following the catastrophic life and daily struggles of plus-sized, potty-mouthed Lizzie Bradshaw and her brutally honest and hilarious experience of singledom, unrequited love and beyond.

A Kind Of Tragic Wedding

The date is set and the venue booked; everything in place for the nuptials of the future Mr & Mrs. Brian Garcia. But after a chance encounter with Dan Elliott (a.k.a Mr. Wonderful), what was all very simple and straightforward is now anything but!

Two love interests. Ninety-nine problems. One BIG decision ...

Lizzie Bradshaw is back!

A Kind Of Tragic Motherhood

They say that marriage and children are the biggest tests of any relationship, but for Lizzie Elliott, nee Bradshaw, this must only apply to other couples; after all, she and Dan are soulmates and this is all she's ever wanted. It's a dream come true!

No. The biggest test of a relationship is when Margot Robbie's body double arrives into your husband's daily life in the shape of the breathtaking Amber Ross. She's fun, she's fabulous, and she definitely doesn't eat yoghurts with a fork! But is she dazzling enough to take the shine out of Lizzie and Dan's marriage? With Dan growing ever more distant, it certainly seems that way. Something's off; something's changed. Is it all in Lizzie's head, or might it be that she doesn't truly know the one person she thought she knew inside-out?

With two under one's to care for, madder hair than ever, a flagging marriage to save, and no time to fart, this Calamity Jane is running on empty with a full swear jar!

Printed in Great Britain
by Amazon